D0957729

Praise for Christy Award finalist Susan May Warren and her novels

"Susie writes a delightful story…
A few hours of reading doesn't get better."
—Dee Henderson, #1 CBA bestselling author of the O'Malley series

"Susan Warren is definitely a writer to watch!"
—Deborah Raney, award-winning author of *A Vow to Cherish* and *Over the Waters*

"Warren's characters are well-developed, and she knows how to create a first rate contemporary romance."
—*Library Journal* on *Tying the Knot*

"Susan May Warren is an exciting...writer whose delightful stories weave the joy of romantic devotion together with the truth of God's love."
—Catherine Palmer, bestselling author of *Leaves of Hope*

"Susan's characters deliver love and laughter and a solid story with every book...a great read!"
—Lori Copeland, bestselling author of the Brides of the West series on *The Perfect Match*

"...authentic detail...plunked me into Russian life. The result was a dynamic read!"
—Colleen Coble, bestselling author of *Dangerous Depths* on *Nadia*

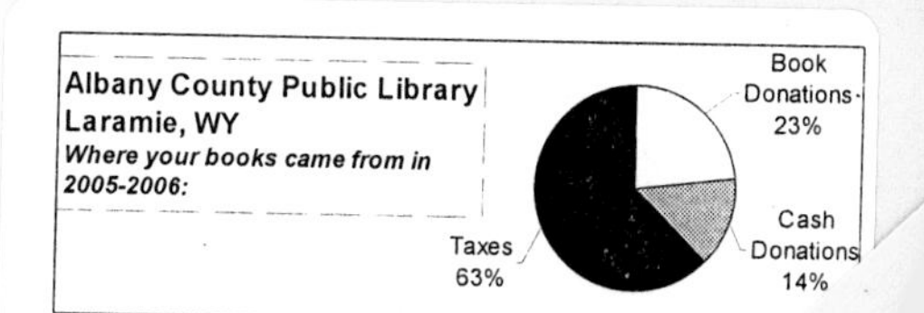

"...a nail-biting, fast-paced chase through the wilds of Russia. A deft combination of action and romance provides superb balance. Spectacular descriptions place the reader in the center of the intriguing setting."
—*Romantic Times BOOKclub* on *In Sheep's Clothing*

"*In Sheep's Clothing* is an excellent novel that will keep you guessing until the very end."
—*FaithfulReader.com*

SUSAN MAY WARREN

SANDS OF TIME

WITHDRAWN

Albany County
Public Library
Laramie, Wyoming

Steeple
Hill®

Published by Steeple Hill Books™

If you purchased this book without a cover you should be aware that this book is stolen property. It was reported as "unsold and destroyed" to the publisher, and neither the author nor the publisher has received any payment for this "stripped book."

For Your glory, Lord

STEEPLE HILL BOOKS

ISBN-13: 978-0-373-78568-1
ISBN-10: 0-373-78568-2

SANDS OF TIME

Copyright © 2006 by Susan M. Warren

All rights reserved. Except for use in any review, the reproduction or utilization of this work in whole or in part in any form by any electronic, mechanical or other means, now known or hereafter invented, including xerography, photocopying and recording, or in any information storage or retrieval system, is forbidden without the written permission of the editorial office, Steeple Hill Books, 233 Broadway, New York, NY 10279 U.S.A.

This book is a work of fiction. The names, characters, incidents and places are the products of the author's imagination, and are not to be construed as real. While the author was inspired in part by actual events, none of the characters in the book is based on an actual person. Any resemblance to persons living or dead is entirely coincidental and unintentional.

This edition published by arrangement with Steeple Hill Books.

® and TM are trademarks of Steeple Hill Books, used under license. Trademarks indicated with ® are registered in the United States Patent and Trademark Office, the Canadian Trade Marks Office and in other countries.

www.SteepleHill.com

Printed in U.S.A.

Acknowledgments

"Don't go out for the next few days." The e-mail from the U.S. Consulate sent a chill through me. At the time, America had dropped bombs on Yugoslavia, and tensions in Russia toward Americans were high. Demonstrations in capital cities threatened consulates and embassies, and Americans lay low. Not only that, we were advised to pack bags in the event we had to hightail it out of the country.

I remember thinking…what if I lived not in a big city, but out in one of the tiny villages in remote Siberia? What if I didn't get e-mail and didn't know what was happening in the world? Worse, what if we *were* ordered out of the country…and didn't know it? Would we be arrested? There and then the idea for *Sands of Time* was born. Fast-forward five years. My husband and I were wrestling with the hard decision to return to the States. Andrew loved what we did as missionaries. But our children needed some time in America, and I was exhausted and burned out. More than that, God was closing the door to ministry in Russia. Andrew felt as if God was asking him to make the ultimate surrender—his life goals for the good of others. But he'd trained and worked with excellent Russian brothers who could fill in the gap created by his leaving. And, after he left, he realized that God would continue the work He'd started with Andrew.

I respect my husband for the sacrifice he made. And in many ways, Sarai and Roman embody Andrew's struggle. We both learned that we are not indispensable. More than that, we learned that surrender opens new doors to God's provision and God's blessings.

My deepest gratitude goes to Krista and Joan and Steeple Hill for believing in *Sands of Time,* and allowing me to write about Russia and my mixed bag of heroes and heroines. And thank you to Andrew, who every day teaches me about sacrificial love, and keeping an eternal perspective. I do need a hero.

Prologue

"*You always have to be a hero, don't you?*" It seemed unfair that, at the most inopportune of moments, Sarai Curtiss's accusations could split Roman's mind like lightning, cutting right to the fears that lurked in the darkest corners of his heart. And his raw and bleeding bare feet churning up the pavement drilled that question into his soul.

No, he didn't have to be a hero—just the guy who got it right, who went the distance, especially when it had to do with issues like world peace and international freedom. And nabbing a six-foot-two, sweaty Russian smuggler named Gregori Smirnov.

At least, Roman *hoped* the guy he was chasing was Gregori. The man, dressed in typical Russian-on-holiday attire—a striped dress shirt, cutoff Bermudas, dark socks and tennis shoes and carrying a backpack—had taken one look at Roman, innocently slurping the ear off a Mickey Mouse ice cream stick, and bolted through the crowd.

Now, wasn't that interesting?

Roman had no choice but to ditch the ice cream and his flip-flops, take off in hot pursuit and pray he wasn't going to take down a day trader from Jersey.

Still, it wasn't every day he, a Russian FSB captain who hunted mafia smugglers for a living spotted what looked like one of Russia's most wanted strolling out of the Reflections of China exhibit at Disney's Epcot Center. He wasn't about to lose the little rat in the beer halls of Germany, the pagodas of Japan or even the pines of Canada.

Except Roman had a sick feeling in his gut that Slimeball Smirnov was heading for the American exhibit.

Deep inside, Russians possessed a keen sense of irony.

Roman dodged a family of four pushing a rented double stroller and barely missed being speared by a replica of the Eiffel Tower. Shocked play-by-plays littered his wake as he zagged through the crowd, leaped a planter, and nearly took out a slushy stand. *"Perestan Smirnov! Stop!"*

Gregori didn't even slow.

Roman shot a look behind him. Yes, *thank you,* his pal David was on his tail. Except the vacationing Delta Force captain didn't look happy. In fact, if Roman didn't know better, he would have thought David might be ticked at him.

He'd explain his actions later.

Five months ago, Roman had gone fist-to-fist with Smirnov on his home turf, Khabarovsk, Far East Russia.

And, after Roman had been dragged through the icy

Amur river, and had wrestled the pirate on the bottom of a fishing skiff, Smirnov had jumped ship, leaving behind his baggage—a silver canister. A *heavy* silver canister. Twenty kilos, without a doubt. As Roman screwed off the lid, internal warnings had buzzed. Warnings that seeded his nightmares—nightmares fertilized by Roman's day job hunting the terrorists who made a living parceling out Russia's only remaining commodities, namely weapons, for cold Western cash—aka *Bucksov*.

For a second, as Roman stared inside the container, time had stopped. Saliva pooled in his throat, and his hands felt clammy.

Paste. Or what looked like it. Odorless. Silvery white.

Probably radioactive, even in minimal doses.

Twenty-five kilos of Highly Enriched Uranium (HEU). The fuel for a nuclear bomb. Another Russian commodity for sale.

He'd put the lid back on the canister, feeling painfully light-headed.

Thankfully, all his tests for infection had come back negative…so far.

Since then, Roman had dedicated his life to not only finding Smirnov, but unearthing his source. Roman had a sick feeling he'd find answers buried deep inside the former Soviet Union, namely at one of the untended, decommissioned reactors. But the source wasn't the biggest problem.

It was the supplier. And how did said supplier get his

mitts on the nearly eight hundred kilos of still lethal *HEU* stockpiled in the former Soviet Union?

However, for the past week, Roman had left his questions happily, blissfully, behind as he vacationed in Orlando with his Moscow University pal, American David Curtiss. They both knew their friendship wasn't easily stomached by the powers that be, and they'd had to submit to more than thorough scrutiny. Still, to Roman it was worth the at-a-distance surveillance and guarded conversations to hang out with a guy who still felt like a brother at arms. The fact that David shared, no *mentored,* Roman's Christian walk, made the vacation more than relaxing.

Roman might even call it rejuvenating. A guy who spent most of his time tracking mafia barons and weapons pirates needed a dose of eternal perspective to keep him on task. Thus, it seemed divinely appointed that Roman might spot his nemesis from across the ocean—Smirnov— right under his nose. Too bad Roman was dressed in cargo shorts and a muscle shirt. With no weapon save the neon necklace he'd purchased for the laser light show that evening.

Thankfully, Disney had some of the best security in the world.

As Roman dodged another yuppie couple and leaped over the leash tethering their children to their wrists, he could hear said security gathering momentum behind him. He'd consider them backup. As long as they remembered he was one of the good guys.

Don't lose Smirnov.

He saw the guy whiz into the American exhibit, a replica of an old town courthouse.

Tochna! How he hated when he was right. Kind of.

Roman sped into the courtyard, nearly taking out a woman with a tray of milk shakes and hot dogs, and flew into the building.

Cool air. It raised gooseflesh on his skin as he stared in horror at the packed lines leading to the food counter. The smell of French fries and the buzz of excited children echoed off the white tile. Roman's panic filled his chest as he scanned the lines.

No Smirnov. Roman beelined to the far door.

Smirnov could be bellying up for a double cheeseburger, O-rings and a chocolate shake, and Roman wouldn't have a hope of spotting him.

Roman scrambled through the crowd and out into the foyer, gripped his knees and hauled in searing breaths.

He saw David enter the building. His dark gaze caught Roman's and he stalked his direction. His expression didn't bode well for the rest of their vacation. Or Roman's future tourist visa applications. He mentally braced himself as he stood and scanned the tourists. Smirnov had to be in that crowd.

Or…Roman saw the end of a tour line disappear into a movie theater. He whirled and scooted into the darkened room.

A 360-degree domed screen, trapped air and a blanket of darkness descended over him. The crowd was hushed, many lined up against walls, most clumped in the middle.

Roman walked through them, glancing up at faces, then staring at shoes, socks.

A family of six sat on the floor right in front of him. He nearly tripped over them, mumbled his apologies, stood and turned slowly as the screen lit up.

"I'm sorry, sir, but you can't—"

Spotting a far door closing, Roman heard the click and the soft whoosh of sprung-loaded hinges. He sprinted toward it, ignoring the attendant, and caught Smirnov racing along the back hallway.

"Perestan!"

Smirnov glanced over his shoulder. Smirked.

It was the smirk that Roman remembered later as he tackled the guy into the World Showcase Lagoon.

Kicking to the surface, Smirnov landed a blow to his adversary's jaw that made Roman's head spin. Two-hundred-and-fifty pounds of "wanna-get-away," Smirnov put up a fight that left Roman just a little glad that David hadn't asked questions and simply dove in after them.

Smirnov roared as David and Roman hauled him ashore. Roman threw him on the deck, kneed him in the back and twisted his hand back in a submission hold.

Breathing hard, David sat down next to him. "I'm assuming you have a really good reason for tackling this tourist. One that isn't going to land us both in lockup for the duration of your vacation. Or worse, deport you in your shorts and bare feet."

Roman tightened his hold on Smirnov and patted him down. "Trust me."

He unearthed a soggy Epcot ticket, a disposable camera and a now out-of-commission cell phone.

"What are you looking for?" David asked as he climbed to his feet and wrung out his T-shirt. "Did he take your five-day pass?" He looked down at Roman and grinned.

And just like that, Smirnov's smirk filled Roman's mind. *The backpack.*

A shiver of fear crept down Roman's body. He leaned close to Smirnov, who curled his lip in disgust.

"Where is it?" Roman asked in Russian.

David's smile vanished. He went very still.

Smirnov laughed.

"Where is it, Smirnov?" Roman asked again, this time adding some oomph to his question by digging Smirnov's jaw into the pavement. David moved closer. Roman wasn't sure if that was for his own protection—or Smirnov's.

Back off, David. Roman might not be wearing his black-and-gold FSB Cobra patch, but he was in charge of this interrogation.

Roman tightened his grip on Smirnov's hand and was rewarded with a pain-filled grunt. "You'd better hope that backpack only has souvenirs and a bottle of juice, pal, or I swear, I'll turn you over to the Americans. And I'm telling you, they're taking this war on terror thing seriously."

David stared at him. "What's in the bag, Roma?"

In his mind's eye, right behind the reality of happy families watching the Tapestry of Dreams nightly parade, Roman heard screams, saw charred bodies and fire spitting out the remains of the Universe of Energy building and sparking the fireworks now floating in the center of the Lagoon. He could see the headlines—Epcot Bombed, Hundreds Killed—and the resulting investigation that led right back to the shores of Khabarovsk and a botched arrest, one with his name attached.

For a moment, he felt the spur of bittersweet thankfulness that Sarai Curtiss was safely tucked away on the other side of the planet, in a village on the backside of Russia.

Even if he'd never see her again.

He shook away the thought, frustrated that she so easily slid into his brain. Just because he was wet, angry and facing the brutal realities of terrorist new millennium tactics didn't mean he had to surrender to the realm of what-ifs.

Sarai wasn't going to be more than a blip on his radar. Ever. Again.

Then again, he'd clung to that blip like a sailor might a light across a black sea.

Because, while he didn't always have to be the world's hero, he longed to be Sarai's—a woman who had once changed his world with her smile. And while the reasons he dove headfirst into trouble sometimes seemed fuzzy, he knew he had his eyes fixed on one hope—that someday God would intersect their paths. And this time, Roman wouldn't let her walk away. Not, at least, until he knew why she wanted him out of her world.

Roman resisted the urge to wipe the smirk off Smirnov's face with his knuckles and swallowed against a wall of frustration. "Cuff him," he said to the round of security guards now huffing their way toward the spectacle. "If you do an Interpol search, you'll find a warrant already posted for his arrest."

Roman let the Disney guards take Smirnov and turned to David. "Who do we need to call to evacuate Epcot Center?"

For a sunny day, and despite the tan David had cultivated standing in the Tower of Terror line, he turned a fine shade of chalky white.

Chapter One

By Sarai Curtiss's best analysis, Sasha Bednov had less than twenty-four hours to live. Just long enough for his mother to watch him slip into a coma, for his governor-candidate father to win the election and for Sarai to hear the door of opportunity close with a soft and definitive click.

So much for trying to ease suffering and save lives in the vast wasteland of Siberia, Russia.

She'd trade everything she'd worked for over the past two years for the right medicines to save this thirteen-year-old boy's life. Medicines she would also like to have had to save the countless others she'd tried to treat.

She took his limp hand and pressed it against her forehead, frustration pushing to the surface, burning tears into her eyes. She closed them, fighting a whimper. Sasha lay in the bed, his pallor gray, his shallow breathing giving off a sickly sweet odor. Maybe if she'd gotten here earlier. Then again, an earlier diagnosis would have meant intervention. Drugs, dialysis, maybe a transplant.

Not a chance of any of that in a country that still couldn't manage indoor plumbing for seventy percent of its inhabitants.

How did an otherwise healthy teen die of acute renal failure?

She heard conversation outside Sasha's bedroom door, where bodyguards and a maid murmured platitudes to his mother. Sarai set down his hand, ran hers over his smooth skin. Maybe, if she was in Moscow at the International Clinic…definitely if they were back home, at Johns Hopkins. Sasha would be heading home in a week, pink cheeks, a smile in those blue eyes.

Sometimes, despite her years invested in the backside of Russia, she hated the motherland. Loved the people. Hated the lack of resources.

Loved the friendships.

Hated her own limitations.

All she prayed for was that God would use her medical expertise to minister to the lost in Smolsk, and to be His tool, His girl. Instead she got heartache and failure. It made a girl wonder what she might be doing wrong.

She rose, hearing the muffled sobs from the next room. She stood above Sasha's bed, her throat thick. Genye was out there, Bible in his hand, hopefully speaking words of comfort to Julia Bednova. But what comfort, really, could he offer an atheist who had to say goodbye to her only son? Her only *child.*

Pain centered in Sarai's chest and she fought the grip of despair. *God, please...intervene.*

She opened the door, stepped out into the tiny hall. Even for a palatial Russian politician's flat, the penthouse apartment felt cramped. Sterile. Fake plants hung from the gold wallpapered walls, framing a beveled mirror. Under it, a mahogany-veneered side table held a Kazakhstani vase. On the black velvet settee in the next room, Julia sat hunched over, her head in her soft, manicured hands, looking every inch the trophy wife in her size four turquoise suit, her alligator stilettos. But her broken expression and the trails of mascara down her sculpted face as she looked up told Sarai the truth.

Grief would wedge through the hairline cracks in her composure and furrow scars that would mark Julia for eternity.

She understood scars. Sarai had never recovered from her own broken heart. Not really. In her darkest, most private moments, the day she walked away from Roman Novik still felt as raw, as searingly painful as it had thirteen years ago.

And *she* had a Savior who gave her life purpose beyond that moment. Julia had—what? A powerful husband, a bodyguard, a chauffeur, a glamorous apartment and enough fur coats to clothe every child in orphanage twenty-one back in Sarai's adopted village of Smolsk.

"*Nu,* how...is he?" Julia rose, extended her hand and Sarai caught it. Julia's long fingernails pressed into Sarai's palm and Sarai opted to pull the woman into a hug. She felt

Julia's bones dig into her as the woman trembled. Sarai hung on a bit longer than Julia might have expected for a medical doctor.

Over Julia's shoulder, Sarai glanced at Genye. Beside him, his wife and fellow M.D., Anya, held the telephone receiver, calling for an ambulance. Sarai shook her head. It wouldn't do any good. Russians brought their sick to the hospital to die. They would find no hope in the barren, roach-infested, concrete-chipped halls of Balnitza eighty-three.

Sarai helped Julia to the settee and gave Anya a *help-me* glance, not wanting to make matters worse by delivering the news badly, in distorted Russian.

Anya crouched next to Julia and slowly, deliberately, gently told the woman that her son would die.

An hour later, Julia's wail still echoed off the sides of Sarai's heart. A wail that sounded painfully familiar, painfully close.

Painfully prophetic.

She'd heard that wail one too many times in her secreted, most frail places. The sound of being alone in her darkest hour.

Sarai prescribed a sedative, and one of Julia's bodyguards administered it along with a shot of vodka. Sarai tried to step in, to ease the shot glass from Julia's grip.

The woman glared at her.

They took the stairs down as they left, Sarai still elevator-shy after being stuck in a box the size of a telephone booth for two-plus hours the previous January. Genye seemed more subdued than usual. Anya reached for Sarai's hand.

Sarai had piled way too much hope into this meeting, and her Russian assistants knew it. She recalled the way her heart raced, her mind plowing ahead to opportunities and permissions this divine appointment might yield. Yes, she could admit she'd started to think like a Russian over the past two years. Friendships. Contacts. A favor here, another returned.

Helping the son of the governor-elect just might have given her desperately needed permissions for medicines and equipment for The Savior's Hands Medical Clinic. Maybe even funding.

Shame roiled through her. Since when had her help come with strings?

Never. Not now. Not in the future. Still, after a decade serving as a medical missionary around the world, it might put some significance to her 24/7, 365-days-per-year sacrifice to see lives changed.

Maybe God had simply forgotten the petite blonde trying to save lives in the middle of nowhere. It sure felt like it.

They emerged into the foyer of the apartment building, signed out with the *storge*, then exited to the street. The security door locked behind them.

A popping sound and an explosion made Sarai jump. "What was that?"

"*Neznaiou!* Get down!" Genye put his arm around Anya, and they crouched behind a shiny new Lada. Sarai ducked behind a black Mercedes and peeked over the hood. Overhead, cirrus clouds fractured an otherwise blue sky. In the distance, a plume of black rose beyond the skyline of nine-story buildings that ringed downtown Irkutsk. Smoke tinged the air and Sarai heard sirens wailing, as if in mournful response to the sudden chaos.

Crackling, like the sound of fireworks, raised the fine hairs on Sarai's arms.

"That's gunfire," Genye said.

Sarai glanced over at him, saw history streak across his aged face. Before becoming a man of God, Genye had done serious time as a Spetsnaz commando—special forces—soldier in Afghanistan. If he said gunfire, she'd believe him. "What do we do?"

"Stay here." He rose, ran to the door of the apartment building. Pounded. "Let us in!"

Sarai watched as the *storge* shook his head. Oh, swell. Let the nice doctor and her friends perish on the street.

As if in response to her thoughts, a rumble, and the sound of metal grinding against itself rattled the air. She watched, paralyzed, as a T-90S tank rolled down the street. Thank you, Genye, for that military armament lesson last May Day parade.

Because, really she didn't need to know about the firepower, the thermal imagers and the Explosive Reactive Armor painted in camouflage to know that something was very, very wrong.

A tank.

Right here, in the relatively quiet capital city of Irkutia

Province, central Russia, population six hundred thousand. A nice city. A city where one might find Pepsi, or even Mountain Dew. A city that had working telephones, the Internet and even a decent pizza joint. And, on a good day, hot water and electricity.

This did not seem to be a good day. This day contained a tank. She stared at it, and the soldiers dressed in jungle green camouflage following behind it, armed with Kalashnikovs.

What?

She rose, and a shot whizzed over her head, chipping concrete off the building behind her.

"Get down, Sarai!" Anya ran over, and Sarai's knees burned as Anya pushed her into the sidewalk.

"What's going on?"

"I don't know." Genye pulled out his keys. "But we must get out of here, back to the village. Come on."

He crouched, running over to their Nissan Largo van across the street. Keeping low, he unlocked the door, pulled open the sliding passenger door. "Poshli!"

Anya took off to his command to "move it," obviously completely trusting her soldier-turned-pastor husband. Sarai froze.

"Sarai—run!" Genye yelled. He pushed his wife in, turned and made to dash toward Sarai.

An explosion at the end of the street knocked Genye to the ground, smashing his face in the gravel. Sarai ducked. "Genye!"

Dirt rained down on the cars, a puff of residue blanketed

the road. Gunfire erupted, sounding closer. Screams reverberated as background noise against the grumble of tanks and marching feet.

Sarai buried her head under her arms as her blood coursed hot through her. It was the Moscow coup all over again, complete with tanks and Molotov cocktails and Roman Novik lying in the street, bloodied.

Roman!

Not again. She wasn't going to lose him again.

She found her knees, gathered her feet beneath her. "Roman!"

A hand fisted her hair, yanked her onto her backside. The flash of a knife, then dark eyes found hers. "American, go home," a man growled in English.

No, it wasn't the Moscow coup. Because, this time, Roman wasn't there to save her.

Roman Novik stood in the casino bathroom in downtown Khabarovsk, Russia, staring at the prone and soused form of what might be an American—judging from his slightly worn Morrell hikers. One thought flashed, like gunfire, through his mind.

Only by the grace of God had he not ended up just like this rummy. A pile of disgrace lying in his own filth.

Like father, like son.

Roman flinched out of the thought, stepped over the form and headed toward the window. Thankfully, someone had cracked it, like fresh air from the street outside might dent, even slightly, the smell of urine embedding the casino bathroom.

What a way to die. A knife to the carotid artery for a mere hundred or so dollars, according to the dealers who'd been counting the victim's take at the tables.

Obviously, they hadn't been the only ones counting. Stupid American, flashing his cash around. Probably thought that he might be immune to danger.

Or, maybe too drunk to realize that he wasn't invisible in a room owned by the Russian mafia. Especially at the Klondike hotel in Khabarovsk.

Vicktor Shubnikov, the FSB investigator assigned to foreign crimes, squatted beside the victim. "This isn't pretty."

Roman turned, cracked a one-sided smile at his best friend. "I'm glad I don't have your job."

Vicktor glanced up at him. He wore a black leather jacket turned up at the collar, over a pair of wool suit pants and dress shoes—Mr. Fashion at a crime scene. With dark hair, dark blue eyes, a rare smile and enough menace on the hockey rink to make Roman's blood freeze when the man zeroed in for a check, Vicktor took his job pretty seriously. Something that nearly got him killed more times than Roman wanted to count.

They'd been playing a cutthroat one-on-one game of slapstick down at Dynamo stadium when the call came in to Vicktor, courtesy of his old boss at Militia HQ, Investigator Arkady Sternin. Roman had lost three-one, but scoping out the scene with Vicktor seemed unfair penance. Especially with Arkady standing at the door, smoking and giving Roman a look that would make a lesser man cringe.

Just because Roman had broken a few laws six months ago saving Vicktor. Or maybe it was because Roman had pulled the strings that switched Vicktor's allegiance from local cop to federal investigator.

Whatever. That move had granted the FSB the coup of landing one of Russia's rogue KGB spies, had freed Vicktor of a thousand personal demons and introduced him to a woman who was slowly changing his life. Roman would accept the venomous glare from Arkady as collateral damage.

Roman crouched opposite Vicktor, beside the body. "Americans just don't know when to keep their mouths shut."

Vicktor shot him a look, raising an eyebrow. "And this from the man who emptied Epcot on a hunch?"

Roman crossed his arms over his chest. "It was more than a hunch. Try instinct and history. I thought there was a bomb. What if I'd been right?"

"But you weren't." Arkady leaned his bulk against the door frame. "You made us look like a bunch of idiots." He shoved a bond cigarette between his lips and lit it. The smoke bobbed as he spoke. "Trying to be hero, as usual."

Roman took a deep breath. "Yeah, well, after the attack on America, I'll take my chances on being wrong." He knew his eyes had grown shiny, and he forced himself to take a breath. "Or would you rather I just sat on my hands? Hey, I know, I'll trade jobs with you. Track down purse snatchers and hardened jaywalkers."

Arkady pursed his lips, his eyes scraping over Roman. "You wouldn't take my job if they gave you an office in the Kremlin." He turned from the doorway, back into the hall. "Not enough glory."

Roman felt his body move before his brain engaged. Vicktor sprang to his feet and stopped him with a hand to his chest. "Don't. Arkady's just tense because his daughter announced her engagement to the competition. She's been recruited by the FSB and he's not pleased."

Roman barely let that information register. Instead, Arkady's words burned into his brain. Glory.

He'd settle for respect.

Even self-respect. Yes, Roman *had* had reason to believe Smirnov had terror in his touring agenda. But sometimes he just wanted to bang his head against the wall. One more stupid decision and he just might be relegated to opening doors for Arkady and bagging dead bodies at crime scenes.

What are you trying to prove? Roman flinched as the voice swept into his brain.

"You okay?" Vicktor gave him a one-eyed frown.

"*Da.*" Roman stepped away from Vicktor with an uncharacteristic sigh. After a decade, he thought he'd be free of Sarai's indictment. Or the effect of her memory on his pulse.

"No witnesses, although I'll bet if we apply pressure to the hotel staff and the casino guests, we might find a few locals who aren't on the payroll." Vicktor stood and glanced at Roman. "I'm going upstairs to check out his hotel room."

Vicktor snapped on a pair of rubber gloves when they reached the third floor. "I called the forensic team. Utuzh should be here soon." He used the maid's key to enter the room.

Roman didn't comment. Vladimir Utuzh, the city medical examiner, had a way of making a man check his pulse and be grateful he still had one. The size of a small grizzly, Utuzh also looked and smelled like one, and Roman secretly thanked God for putting him on the side of tracking down the living instead of examining the dead.

The latest turn of events, however, namely, the arrest and so-called suicide of super-smuggler Gregori Smirnov, had Roman rethinking his career—a career that, until three months ago, seemed fast-tracked to glory. Instead, he'd made a laughingstock of his country in front of the world by clearing out Disney World's Epcot Center for a soggy sandwich and a warm soda.

He'd be lucky if his pal David ever talked to him again, especially since Roman had been shipped out of the country faster than they could say "false alarm." Moscow didn't think it was funny, either, despite Roman's reminder that they had nabbed Smirnov.

It only made things worse that, while locked up in Lubyanka prison in Moscow, the smuggler had conveniently hanged himself.

Like Roman believed *that*... He still wanted to hit something, like a deadweight, or maybe a puck, really, *really* hard every time he thought of it.

They'd gotten nothing out of Smirnov and deep in his gut Roman knew Smirnov's supplier was still in business, still smuggling nuclear fuel out of the country. And, until

Roman tracked him down, he saw behind every suspect the bleeding eyes and decaying flesh of radiation poisoning, courtesy of the International Atomic Energy Agency—IAEA—training video he and the other mafia-fighting COBRAs had been forced to watch last spring.

Those were visuals Roman didn't need, especially late at night as he lay alone in his flat, perspiration beading on his temples.

Thankfully, he hadn't been exposed to the uranium last spring. He heard those words, clung to them, watching for nausea, or open sores. Highly enriched uranium wasn't toxic unless it was ingested.

Or, spent, as in used in a nuclear reactor. Which would classify it as nuclear waste, and make it much less marketable. Unfortunately, the HEU Smirnov had been transporting, which Roman confiscated after Smirnov conveniently left it like a gift, or a bomb, in the boat, hadn't yet been used. Which meant that it had come from a weapon.

Or a decommissioned nuclear reactor.

Tracking down trace amounts of HEU from the hundred or so reactors scattered about Russia felt a little like looking for someone during the reign of Stalin who wasn't afraid of the KGB.

Yeah, right.

"He smelled like he downed a couple pints of vodka," Vicktor said as he searched the dead man's suitcase for identification.

"*Nyet.* Too sweet." Roman didn't meet Vicktor's gaze as he surveyed the hotel room, taking in the three empty pints of vodka in the garbage can, a down parka tossed on the single bed and a metal briefcase tucked under a straight-back chair. He knew, painfully well, just how three pints of vodka might smell on a man. Exactly what the term, "dead-weight" meant. Roman shoved the memory back into his past. "He hadn't been here long enough to drink that much, or even get comfortable. Probably went right down to the tables." Roman nodded to a pair of slippers tucked under the vanity by the door. While Russian hotels didn't have the plush carpets, cable televisions and king-size beds indicative of Western culture, hotels often provided a pair of complimentary slippers. This guy hadn't even taken them out of the wrapper.

"What do you suppose he was doing here?" Roman asked as he reached for a fanny pack laying on the night table. Vicktor grabbed his wrist.

"Gloves, Roma."

Roman took one, snapped it on his right hand, using the other to hold the pack while he zipped it open: passport, a used train ticket, a boarding pass, an airplane ticket, breath mints and a taster of vodka, the kind they handed out in Aeroflot's first class on the Trans-Siberian line, or from hotel room bars. Roman read the label and didn't recognize the brand. He put it back, fished through the pack and found a Nokia cell phone, iPod and a pocket PC. He picked up the passport and read the name.

"Barry Riddle. Born in Chicago, Illinois."

"Now residing in Fargo, North Dakota." Vicktor held up his driver's license. "What's he doing in Far East Russia?"

Roman pulled out the visa. "Tourist class. With a stamp to Buryatia, Chelyabinsk, Irkutsk and Moscow. Not in that order." He pulled out the boarding pass. "Irkutsk, dated six days ago, and it looks like, from his plane ticket, he's on his way to Sakhalin Island via Vladivostok."

Vicktor opened his cell phone and dialed. "So, is he here on business, or is he a formerly happy tourist, taking the Trans-Siberian train to Vladivostok?"

Roman picked up the victim's cell phone. No signal, power off. He tried to click it on, but it died. "This thing's drained."

"Hand me his passport." Vicktor reached out for the identification as he spoke into the phone. "Yanna, it's me. I need information for Barry Riddle, Fargo, North Dakota." He read off the social security number and outlined the victim's travel information. "Thanks. Yeah, I got back Thursday." He paused. "Sure, see you tonight." He snapped the phone shut. "I think she's still mad at me for not going to her volleyball finals. Wants me to meet her for dinner."

Roman looked up from playing with the iPod. The man had an interesting selection of music—hip-hop to Styx. Roman still had a Styx album tucked away in a box somewhere, postmarked from Irkutsk after his father passed. The fact Barry Riddle knew the same songs felt creepy. "Yanna and her team worked hard to get into the finals, and we're her only family. She saw you missing it for a trip to the States as a personal snub. You owe her dinner, and probably first shot at your new American videos."

"I might remind you that not only hadn't I seen Gracie

in nearly six months, nowadays getting a two-week tourist visa is almost as rare as winning the green card lottery. I had to use it when I got it. Besides, I missed Gracie."

Roman hid the smile. He'd been the one who suggested that Vicktor needed the love of a good woman—and Gracie was off the charts. Who would have thought Vicktor would break his own rules and fall for a woman under his protection? Then again, Gracie had done some protecting of her own—protecting Vicktor from a life of bitterness. Roman had to admit he enjoyed seeing his steel-hearted pal turn to *kasha* over a lady. "How is that going, by the way?" Roman put the iPod back into the pouch, picked up the PC.

"What, Gracie, or the green card?"

Roman's breath sucked out of him. "You're applying for a green card?" Okay, that wasn't fair. Yes, he'd been glad when his buddy found the woman of his dreams, and because of it became a Christian. But move to America?

Vicktor smirked. "Don't panic, Redman. I'm not moving. Yet. Besides, I'm thinking my status as an FSB agent just might raise a few flags. But I want to know my optioins about our future country of residence."

Roman gave him a sad smile. Okay, so maybe he shouldn't jump to conclusions, nor rib his pal about his long-distance romance. It couldn't be easy to fall for a woman who lived a billion miles across the ocean and had a stubborn streak to make even a Russian scream. Besides, even if Vicktor left, it wasn't as if he wouldn't see him again.

Who was he kidding? Just like he saw his best friend,

David Curtiss? Or even the woman who he thought he couldn't live without, Sarai Curtiss?

Vicktor would walk out of his life, and it would just be Roman and his take-no-prisoners career, trying to find a place of peace inside the chaos of his life.

Roman's chest tightened.

"What's in the case?" Vicktor strode over to the metal briefcase, picked it up, put it on the chair. "Looks like a computer case. And it's unlocked." He started to open it.

Roman touched his arm. "Why would a guy who has a pocket PC in his fanny pack have a computer case?"

Vicktor glanced at him, set the case down. Stared at it.

Roman's stomach coiled, and he felt strangely light-headed. Probably too many wide-eyed nightmares playing in his head. Scenarios he prayed would never see the light of day. "Just...be careful."

Vicktor blew out a long breath, crouched and slowly opened the case.

Roman felt his breath reel out in a long, slow hiss.

Inside, cushioned in eggshell foam, lay a long cylindrical container.

Vicktor reached for it.

Roman clamped him on the shoulder. "Don't touch it."

Vicktor frowned at him. "What, do you think it'll blow up?"

"I'm not kidding, Stripes. Close it. Now." Despite his use of his friend's nickname, Roman heard the edge in his voice even as he stepped outside the room, nausea rolling over him.

So much for his feeble hope that Smirnov's radioactive cargo had been a one-time fluke.

"What do we do with it?" Vicktor asked in a whisper as he joined him in the hall.

Roman swallowed, words not forming. Run? Wish that he might turn back the sands of time and rethink his life's choices? Starting with the day he let Sarai Curtiss walk out of his life. He'd return to a time when life seemed simpler, filled with promise, when he had a good reason to face the chaos.

"I dunno."

As if reacting to the desperation of their moment, Roman's cell phone trilled. Once. Twice.

Roman stared at the metal case as he pulled the cell phone out of his pocket.

"*Slyshaio.*"

The connection crackled and the sound made Roman lean into the phone, his attention now at least half-arrested. "Hello?"

"Roman?"

"David?"

Vicktor shot him a frown. Roman could count on one hand the number of times David had used Roman's cell phone to contact him. And, even if the call was scrambled, and probably came through a couple dozen satellites, every time it had one simple subject.

"*Shto Snachet?*" Roman asked, bracing himself for David's answer to his casual, "What's up?" question.

"It's Sarai. I need you, Roma. She's in trouble."

Chapter Two

"Where did you learn to fight like that, Sarai?" Genye gripped the steering wheel with whitened fists as he maneuvered around traffic. They were nearing the edge of town, and true to his Russian—and probably soldier—heritage, he was employing any means possible to put distance between them and the guy he and Sarai had left, crumpled, outside Julia's apartment.

Which meant driving on sidewalks, the wrong side of the road and, right now, down the center line.

Good thing she had a seat belt. Still, Sarai flinched as they nearly peeled paint off a rusty Toyota sedan. Anya sat with one hand braced on the roof, the other on the dash as they whizzed into the oncoming traffic lane to pass a Kamaz truck full of soldiers. Sarai ducked her head, feeling instinctively like she might be some sort red, neon light. The thug's words still sizzled in her brain. *American, go home.*

Sadly, she *was* home. Rather, she had considered this home for the past two years. For the first time she felt like she might be making a difference. And some hooligan's sneer wasn't going to drive her from the people she'd come to love like family.

Maybe even more than family. Because, unlike *her* family, the Russians in Smolsk paid attention when she walked into a room. Thought she was capable. Smart. Special. Not that her brother David didn't, but still, she'd always be Sarey Beary to him, and frankly, she'd been trying to shed that image pretty much since the third grade.

For a Delta Force captain, he didn't catch on real quick.

As for her parents, well, she couldn't hope to compete for significance against a couple who had pioneered missions in the rural Philippines. That was all about to change, however. The Savior's Hands Medical Clinic would change the landscape of medicine and missions in Siberia. A beacon of light and hope.

"My brother is a special ops soldier in America," she said to Genye. "He likes to teach me stuff when we get together for Christmas."

Genye glanced in the rearview mirror. Sarai tried not to flinch at the dribble of now dried blood at the corner of his mouth—her assailant's reply to Genye's not-so-gentle hello.

Then again, she'd already rung the thug's bell with her medical bag and followed with a knee to his midsection that at least released the hold on her hair. She was silently taking back all those times she rolled her eyes at David's passion to teach her self-defense.

But she wouldn't have escaped without Genye's takedown. They'd disarmed the kid—and it *was* a kid, no older than twenty, with skinny arms and zeal for brains—and left him on the sidewalk scraping up his pride while they piled into Genye's vehicle.

Another explosion had rocked the van onto its front wheels as they floored it out of the complex and northwest, toward Smolsk.

"Turn on the radio," Sarai said, and reached forward between the bucket seats to do it herself.

The station was already tuned to Irkutsk, and the rushed, staticky Russian was almost too fast for her to catch. Something about the election. And the governor having been kidnapped?

"I can't catch it, Genye. What are they staying?"

Genye pulled the van into the right lane, put it into fifth gear. Sarai had to admit, having Genye at the helm pumped calm into her veins. The fifty-something former-soldier, former-pilot, now-pastor had courage, as well as savvy behind his gentle brown eyes, and more than once he'd stepped between her and trouble from the locals. Not that trouble brewed thick in their tiny village. Smolsk had a total population of three thousand, including the outlying hunters and farmers. Still, the gangs had their own toehold, and like to play their version of mafia extortion. The cute, freckled American with an optimistic smile seemed to be their favorite target.

Too bad for them that, long ago, she'd made friends with the local militia, mostly by treating their chief for a long-time gastric disorder. Something that netted her a standing smile and unquestioned protection. And one shouldn't put too much trust in freckles. Behind those sun kisses was a woman who might be tiny, but who paid attention when David tried to teach her tae kwon do, as evidenced by her on-her-feet thinking outside the Bednov's apartment.

And Genye was always there backing her up, and watching her "six," as David would say.

Not that she especially needed a hero, however. Sarai had learned over the past three years how to maneuver through Russia on her own. She even had a Russian driver's license. She learned long ago that any sort of help she might need came with strings…and concerns attached.

Probably why she avoided heroes—real ones, with hazel-green eyes and sandy brown hair and enough muscles stacked in his arms to make a girl want to hang on forever.

Oops. There she went again, dreaming of Roman Novik. She should have thought of those arms before she slammed the door on Roman's beautiful smile and gone chasing after her noble ambitions. Or had she been simply running from her darkest fears?

Whatever.

The Irkutsk skyline flickered with flames against the encroaching night. The air smelled of burning oil, and she could still hear the occasional pop of gunfire.

Genye reached over, turned down the chatter on the radio. "Governor Kazlov is dead. Or at least, that's what they're saying. He's disappeared. In the meantime, Governor-elect Bednov has taken control."

"It's a coup!" Sarai sat back in the seat, feeling a tremor work its way through her. "I can't believe it." It was Moscow, August 1991 all over again. The rumble of tanks into Red Square. She felt the old panic rise from the hidden places and claw at her calm.

"The *Underground Pravda* has rumored that Bednov's been assembling his own army for some time. I can't believe they elected him," Genye continued.

Anya spoke, her voice tight. "I can't believe you've been reading that rag, again."

"It's the only truly free press, even in today's Russia." Genye swerved around an open manhole.

Anya yelped. "Evgeny Pomochnov! Slow down."

Genye glanced at his wife, but Sarai saw no movement to heed her command. A small smile touched Sarai's lips. These two might be her right and left hands, but the power struggle between them made for lively discussions around a *perog* and a carafe of hot chai, and she often wondered who, exactly, was in charge.

"Besides, Bednov is a good man," Anya continued after a moment. Sarai heard the clenched jaw stance in Anya's words. "It's the conservatives with the armies—old hardliners who think we'd be better off turning around and heading back into the age of Stalin. They're behind this."

"No. Listen to me, Anya. Bednov is a former Communist. Don't believe a word he says. The *UP* says he's going to tighten borders, kick out the foreign investors, clamp down on smuggling and black market crime, and destroy the mafia."

"There's no black market anymore, Genye. We live in a free economy. But as for mafia, well it might be nice to feel safe again. Besides, we elected him—why would he stage a coup? Don't be ridiculous."

"Don't be naive." Genye's hands whitened on the wheel.

Sarai felt her heart thump against her chest, their conversation drilling into her. Maybe they'd all been naive to think that Russia might be free, a true democracy. Anya wanted to see a safe Russia. *Safe* used to mean anyone who was arrested got sent north, to the gulags of Yakutia, without so much as a trial. Safe, as in suspected murderers were executed days after their arrest, and petty thieves beaten in their cells as they awaited release. *Safe* in pre-free Russia meant fear. And persecution.

And no foreigners. If they wanted "safe" she might as well bid farewell to The Savior's Hands Medical Clinic, and all the hopes she had of saving lives like Sasha's. But, if she left, who would be there to administer vaccinations, petition the government for insulin, dress and stitch the wounds? Who would do the emergency appendectomies, set the broken bones, give first aid?

They needed her. And she'd stay because, well, that was what she'd been training for. To see people healed and suffering eased.

There were times, however, when she thought that she might be making a deeper etching in the world if she'd joined the army, became a special forces soldier and hunted down terrorists for a living, like her big brother.

She heard about David's exploits often enough to recite them in her sleep.

Except…that last one hadn't gone too well. She still chuckled, thinking of him emptying out the Epcot Center, based on Roman's panic. Although, to be honest, she did feel a twinge of pain for the dynamic duo at the thought of finding their criminal's slimy gyro sandwich in the dregs of his dropped backpack.

Still, Roman's intentions had been noble. She could never fault him for that. Like the time he'd followed her for a week around Moscow while she handed out Bibles for the International Bible League. She'd known he was shadowing her. Still, it had been…sweet. And, at the time, she'd thought he'd wanted to hand out Bibles with her.

No, he wasn't nearly as interested in sowing the seeds of faith as he was sowing the seeds of romance.

She'd been so, *so* foolish.

Genye and Anya were arguing in the front seat in fast Russian. She tried to keep up, but her brain felt like stewed prunes. She leaned back on the seat, letting her head bounce, closed her eyes.

Yes, leaving Roman had cut deep wounds in her heart.

But, a village deep inside Siberia seemed exactly the place to finally let them scar over, deaden the nerve endings and forget the memory of his hands in her hair, pulling her face close, kissing her in a way that still made her stomach warm.

Oh, brother.

Anya and Genye's argument ceased as Genye turned up the radio. Eyes closed, Sarai listened. Now out of the range of the city, the nerve-crackling gunfire and the smell of flames, she dissected the words.

"Governor Bednov will be sworn in later tomorrow, after the funeral of his only son, Sasha."

Tears flooded Sarai's eyes and she let them burn a trail down her cheeks.

So much for saving lives.

"You're not going to Irkutsk, Captain Novik, so drive that thought from your brain."

Major Evgeny Malenkov stood from behind his desk at FSB headquarters, putting his six-foot-two, hundred-plus kilo bulk behind his words. Roman tried a deep, calming breath. Okay, this didn't have to get ugly. Nor did Malenkov have to know about David's request.

"The victim had a visa from Irkutsk—"

"Along with stamps from Moscow, Chelyabinsk and Buryatia. This is why we have departments in other regions. You're not the only one with a yen to nail down Smirnov's supplier. E-mail them the information. They'll do the legwork."

Sure they would. Sometime in the next millennium. Sorry, but this felt too personal to hand it off to some *blini*-eating comrade five time zones away.

"Sir, Irkutsk has three known decommissioned reactors. I just want to sniff around—"

"Not with Irkutsk in flames." Malenkov gestured past Roman, through his open door to the office area where Channel 13 played gruesome pictures of the chaos in Irkutsk. Roman felt oddly nauseated as the reporter listed off the casualties. Seven. And a missing Governor Kazlov.

Please don't let one of those casualties be Sarai.

"Novik, you've torn so many holes in our reputation out here, Moscow has me filing reports every time anyone even breathes. Which means that if you so much as sneeze wrong, I'm up to my armpits in whys. It'll take me a year to unravel the snafu you made in America, and it's been suggested you might do some sitting time in Bekin. And I don't mean as a prison guard." He shook his head. "If you show up on the wrong radar, I'm going to be cleaning toilets with my toothbrush. So, not only are you *not* going to Irkutsk, I want you in this office, every morning, with a smile on your clean-shaven face." He leaned forward on his desk, years of experience in the KGB in his say-so expression. "And don't think I won't know if you jump the next plane for Irkutsk—I'm not that stupid."

Roman coiled his response into a small, tight voice. "And, just what am I going to do from here? I thought we were about nabbing these guys. And don't tell me Moscow wouldn't smile at that."

"Last time I looked, we had most of the gadgets they do back in America—a telephone, a fax machine, even e-mail. Amazing, no?" Malenkov sat, picked up the telephone. "Dig up everything you can find on where this guy has been, and why. Then, when you come back to me with substantial leads, in *written* form, I might consider a trip to Irkutsk, *with a babysitter.*"

He turned his attention to the victim at the other end of the telephone, dismissing Roman with a nod. Roman rose, frustration biting at the back of his neck. Probably, David was just jumping to conclusions about Sarai.

Right?

I can't get her on her satellite phone. And it's only going to get tighter over there. Roman, I'm asking you as a friend…

Roman strode out of the office, leaned against the wall, arms akimbo, watching the fires crackle behind the news reporter on screen. "Governor-elect Bednov, while still mourning the death of his son, Sasha, has initiated martial law procedures for the region…"

Martial law? And, more importantly, how did David Curtiss know about it before the FSB did?

Roman didn't want an answer to that question. Not really. He was just happy that David was speaking to him.

Sorta.

Staring at the images on the screen, Roman felt his chest tighten. *Please, God, don't let Sarai be in the middle of that mess.*

"He's in the morgue," a voice said behind him. Roman turned to see Vicktor striding up. "Utuzh has scheduled him for a mandatory autopsy in the morning. He has no next of kin, and his emergency contact was listed at Alexander Oil. They're sending a man over later to ID him." Vicktor had his hands shoved into his leather jacket, and fatigue weighed on his face.

"Who?" Roman asked, trying to get a fix on something other than the image of Sarai in one of those burning buildings. Last he heard, she was in the Irkutsk region, but he thought she was serving in some remote village. There was no good reason she'd be in the city. None.

Except, of course, for her propensity to not listen to good advice and charge ahead into the danger spots in the world. They—her family, her friends—had all breathed a sigh of relief when she'd accepted the assignment in Siberia.

As if freezing to death might be a better alternative to being shot in Somalia. Or kidnapped in Chechnya. Or tracked by the MSS in Beijing.

Yeah, loving Sarai was a real picnic.

It might be easier if she loved him back, just a little. But she'd dumped *him*. A smart man might remember that. Still, he couldn't help feel that somehow he'd let her down. That he might have been more.

Should have been more. Better. Stronger. Wiser.

The story of his life. A legacy the Novik family just couldn't seem to shake.

He watched the screen, vaguely aware that Vicktor had answered him with a sorry shake of his head, then dialed Yanna's number. The short hand clicked toward eleven on the station clock. Roman should head home, see if David had sent him an e-mail. The guy worried too much about his kid sister. As if she was going to get gunned down by terrorists way out there in the middle of nowhere. David should know her better than that—he spent enough time making sure she knew how to survive.

Besides, Roman was the last person Sarai would run to should she need help. She'd proved that in Moscow.

As if on cue, memories put him right back in the middle of the road, with gunshots, screams and explosions shattering windows overhead. A nearby Molotov cocktail had taken him down, and a piece of glass nearly shaved off part of his head, missing his jugular by about eight inches.

Roman, what if you were killed? Sarai had asked, with enough worry to tug at his heart. Her jade green eyes in his, concerned, even glossy with unshed tears, still had the power to sweep the words from his brain. He sat there, letting her hold a cloth to his wound and just…enjoyed it. Enjoyed the worry on her beautiful face and the fact that being around her made all the noise outside—and inside—his brain subside to a warm hum. Sarai embodied calm and focus, the eye inside the storm. Somehow, she made him slow down enough to take a deep, sweet breath. At that moment, all he could think of was the way her hand cupped his face, and how he wanted to put something on the angry scrape on her chin.

Her next words had snapped him out of happy moment, right into hurt.

"What are you trying to prove? You're going to get yourself killed, and you won't even know why. I don't need a hero. I just want a man who loves God!"

Whoa. Ouch. But still, maybe that was just fear talking. Days later, however when she wouldn't return his telephone calls, her words began to throb. And the thirteen year silence since then gave the message resonance. Got it. No hero. Why, he wasn't sure. Obviously, however, he was the only one receiving Sarai's very clear message because every time trouble so much as whimpered on this side of the ocean, David dialed Roman's cell.

Then again, that might have more to do with David's trust in Roman than Sarai's need for a knight. Thankfully, up to now, Roman had been able to do hero-duty from a distance, through favors, or friends.

Because, while he had no idea what Sarai did want, he had a crystal-clear picture of what she didn't.

Him. Especially now that he was a full-fledged FSB Cobra captain—throwing his life away for glory, as she had so often accused.

Right. There were parades in his honor every day.

He turned away from the news. He might just arrest himself if he didn't get a shower, and soon.

One of the hot shots on his Cobra squad cranked up the volume.

"In an effort to subdue the violence, and pinpoint the source of the coup, Governor-elect Bednov has issued orders that all persons holding a foreign visa leave the Irkutsk province within three days. Any remaining foreigners will be arrested and held as international terrorists."

Roman stopped, glanced at Vicktor, feeling sick. Vicktor caught his eye, shook his head.

Maybe he should turn off his cell phone.

Sure, and then maybe his heart.

Chapter Three

"What kind of idiot are you?"

Governor Alexander Bednov heard the sharp edge of his words and saw them cut through his wife's grief to reveal fear.

She *should* be afraid. Especially today. "Where did you find this American doctor, and what did you tell her?"

"Nothing, I told her nothing. Just that…he…Sasha was so sick." She held her trembling hands in front of her, as if in surrender.

Shaking, he advanced toward her, fighting his fraying edges. This day hadn't been easy for either of them. He had anarchy reigning in the streets, and she'd lost her son.

He never liked Sasha much, anyway. But he'd hid it well, with gifts and vacations and lots of electronics from America, courtesy of his overseas affiliations.

Affiliations that he'd gladly cut off at the neck.

For Julia's sake, he'd gulp a breath, offer her comfort while he quietly sorted through chaos and initiated some damage control. "Where is this doctor from?"

"I don't know. I think a village in the north. I got her name from Katya."

The maid. Of course. The woman from the Evenk people of Khanda seemed set on sticking her chin into their lives. Second thing he did after ridding Irkutia province of foreigners would be to herd the indigenous plague into a pen and lock the gate.

He rose, went to the door and summoned a bodyguard. "Find Katya. I want to talk to her. Now."

Julia sat on the bed, quietly sobbing.

She looked and smelled brutal. Probably had emptied the liquor cabinet by herself over the last three hours.

He knelt before her, pulled her into his arms. "*Maya Doragaya,* don't cry. I'm sorry. I know you were only thinking of Sasha."

At his endearment, Julia held on to him, shaking. In the next room, he could hear the sounds of the medical technicians he'd hired to prepare Sasha for burial. Murmurs and low tones. He'd paid them well enough to keep their silence. Besides, this day, the entire region sympathized with his grief.

"Alexei, please, I want an autopsy." Julia leaned away from him and pleaded with him with her bloodshot eyes. "Please. I have to know if…if…well, *why* he died."

Alexei ran his hand over her long hair. He loved her hair most of all, the way it slid through his fingers. And her sleek, thin neck. She might not have Natasha's political savvy, but Julia pleased him in ways his first wife couldn't begin to imagine.

Still, he had a pretty good idea of what killed the son he never wanted. And keeping that to himself rated only second to cleansing Irkutia—and then the Motherland—from the influence of foreign poison. With the right leader, and plenty of cash, they could again be a world power.

The *only* world power.

"*Nyet*, Julia," he said, pressing a kiss to her head. "Sasha is gone. It won't help to let someone cut him open." He let the words be brutal and, as he hoped, she flinched.

"But we do need to find that doctor. And you'd better hope that she knows nothing, or she'll be the first foreigner to get a firsthand glimpse of a Siberian gulag."

"I say you sit tight and see if she turns up." Yanna sat on Vicktor's black leather sofa, legs pulled up to her chest, watching the news.

"And what if she is in Irkutsk, trapped, or hurt?" Roman looked up from his pile of clothes, pretty sure he'd lost most of his mind over the past hour. As news in Irkutsk progressed from bad to stomach clenching, his instincts had made up his mind for him. Just like they had in Moscow.

This excursion into the past was really going to hurt. Or maybe not? In his wildest imagination, Sarai actually gave him an ecstatic smile and dove into his arms.

Right after she told him how she'd been hoping he'd show up. Apparently he needed a good kick in the head.

Still, David had asked. Twice.

Vicktor sat at his laptop, IMing with the guy in their private chat room David had set up for their covert communications. They had no doubt it was probably under surveillance, but at least the people reading their mail knew neither side was passing information. Just…encouragement.

Mostly, David, user-name Preach, was the guy with wisdom. And when it didn't involve his independent sister, David's wisdom was worth pure gold.

This time, Roman had to wonder if said wisdom was going to cost him any last chance he had with Sarai. She wasn't especially known for her tuck-tail-and-leave tendencies. To the best of his recollection, her brother had to send in some of his Delta buddies to get her out of Somalia the last time. According to David, she hadn't been especially impressed—or convinced she needed saving.

Which left him at a stalemate. If she wasn't in trouble, well, she wasn't moving. And if she was…

He didn't want to go there.

Now that Govenor Bednov had issued the seventy-two-hour window, Roman heard the doom clock ticking.

Maybe, she could, for once, just *trust* him?

"Listen, Bednov's not kidding, Yanna. I know him, and let's just say he's used to getting his way. He was a hard-line Communist for years, and he hasn't changed philosophies, if you know what I mean. If they lock up Sarai—or anyone for that matter—he'll bury the case in paperwork for the next century. If we're lucky, Sarai will just wind up in woman's prison and not a political gulag." He felt sick at that thought and threw an extra pair of wool socks and a black sweater into his duffel. Political gulag wasn't the white-collar crime prison of the West. Russia reserved them for the criminals they seriously wanted to torture.

"And how are you going to find her?" Yanna asked. "Irkutsk is a mess."

"I'll start at her village. If she's not there, maybe someone will know where to look." Roman threw in a pair of gloves, and his 9 mm Grach service pistol. He caught Yanna's wide-eyed look and shrugged. "Not sure exactly what I might meet out there."

"Just don't use it on Sarai."

"Excuse me?" He grabbed the map Vicktor had downloaded from FSB HQ files of Irkutia. He might be able to navigate his hometown of Irkutsk in his sleep, but the western territory was still uncharted—mostly because for the past seventy years it had been closed to the Russian public, inhabited mostly by indigenous people or sectioned off for nuclear research. And now much of it had turned into oil fields. Smolsk was located on the south side of one of the largest fields in all of Siberia.

"I just mean when she puts up a fight, I hope you don't have to, ah, resort to extreme means," Yanna said. She unclipped her long mink brown hair from its inverted ponytail and shook it out.

He cringed at the mental image of having to arrest Sarai, for her own good, and toss her out of Irkutia. Not only that, but an arrest on her record might insure that she never set foot in Irkutia—or even Russia—again.

He pulled on his black parka. "Don't worry. I'm going to sweet-talk her to her senses. I won't be taking anyone into custody on this trip."

Yanna smirked and even Vicktor turned in his chair. "You're in over your head, Redman. You're going to need a better game plan than that. I recall that last time you tried to sweet-talk her out of something, it ended with you bleeding in Red Square."

"That was a long time ago. I'm older and wiser."

Yanna laughed, and for some reason it didn't sound supportive.

Roman glared at her. "Sarai is a smart woman. She'll see reason."

Vicktor shook his head. Smirked. "Oh, by the way, if you see any international terrorists, how about giving us a call before you, say, evacuate half of Siberia?"

Roman gave him a dark look.

Yanna rose from the sofa, walked to the entry and began to pull on her boots. "I'll give you a ride to the airport." She grabbed her bag, unzipped it. "But I wanted to give you this." She held out what looked like a small pocket PC.

"What is it?" Roman took it, opened it.

"It's a sat phone. My design. It's got a GPS and is linked to a program on my computer. If you get into trouble, and you can't get a good signal, you can type out a text message, or even tap out Morse code on the keys and we'll be able to find you."

"No hiding from you guys, huh?" Roman pocketed the phone, turned to Vicktor. "You'll cover for me with Comrade Major Malenkov?"

"He didn't okay your travel plans?" Vicktor raised one dark eyebrow. "How did you get that travel pass?"

Roman didn't answer as he laced up his boots. He had traded in some favors to get an FSB pass from the Irkutsk office. Favors that he would have just as soon kept unredeemed and in the past. "I told them I was investigating a murder, which is the truth."

Vicktor cringed. "Roma, if he finds out you're AWOL…"

"Just— If Utuzh finds anything of interest during the autopsy of our American *smerchik*, page me."

Vicktor didn't smile. He stood up, crossed his arms over his chest. "I've got a bad feeling about this. Maybe I should be going. *I'm* not on probation—"

"No." Even Roman could tell he sounded a bit defensive. Or maybe possessive? He grabbed his wool hat off Vicktor's bench. Vicktor's Great Dane, Alfred, raised his head, gave him a disdainful sniff. "Listen, this won't be hard. Twenty-four hours, I'll be back here and Malenkov won't even know I've gone. I'll get into Irkutia, track down Sarai, convince her that she needs to leave and then we'll all come back to Khabarovsk—"

"And live happily ever after." Yanna shoved on her gloves. "You're such a dreamer, Roman."

Yeah, anyone with a wide-angle perspective on this trip could see that.

Vicktor opened the door for them. "Just be careful. And

come back. Because if you don't get her out under the three-day window, she's not going to be the only one in trouble." He ran a hand behind his neck, rubbed a stiff muscle. "I don't want to see your name on some interagency bureau report as AWOL, or worse—aiding and abetting a fugitive, Roman."

The words resonated through Roman, lingering long after he rode to the airport in silence with Yanna, and climbed aboard the 1962 AN2 cargo plane to Irkutsk.

By the time Roman landed at the Irkutia airport, he felt like an iceberg. He requisitioned a hardtop jeep, tried not to think about the smell of smoke layering the air and drove northwest, to Smolsk.

Despite the numbing cold pressing in on his toes and hands, he couldn't deny the smolder that had begun to burn in the middle of his chest. Sarai, just ahead on the horizon.

Intersecting his path.

Just like she had thirteen years ago.

Without closing his eyes, he could put himself right back to that fateful day at the Moscow circus, when he'd had nearly everything he'd ever hoped for. The circus, and the surreal world it created, should be some sort of metaphor for his relationship with Sarai.

What a summer. Although he'd known her for two months, and spent nearly every waking hour vying for her attention, she still took his breath away every time she looked his direction. She hadn't the foggiest idea that her smile made his heartbeat hiccup, or that her laughter felt like a balm on his raw and bruised heart. She believed in him. Respected him. After his last visit home, Roman needed that like he needed water.

"Look at those dogs, Roman!" Sarai spilled a few popcorn kernels into her mouth, her gaze fixed on the poodles that now walked on their front paws through rings. He barely glanced at them, happy instead to trace her face, her freckles that looked like spilled sunshine over her nose, her beautiful green eyes the hue of pale jade and her silky dark blond hair that never wanted to stay in her braid. She had a simplicity about her, no games, no hidden agenda. When she'd walked into his life, suddenly everything made sense.

Roman didn't care that she was the little sister of his best friend. Or that she was American, and that despite Perestroika and Glasnost, American-Russian relations still felt strained. Her visa deadline felt like a noose around his neck. Three weeks and she'd head back to Boston to medical school unless he did something.

Like ask her to marry him?

He'd wrestled that question, weighing it against her dreams and his skills. He wanted to be a soldier. One who kept Russia heading in the direction of freedom.

She hoped to be a doctor, and the way she'd patched him up a few times this summer, he knew she had the touch. She'd certainly healed him, in more ways than she could imagine.

Most of all, she made him realize that there could be room for someone in his life. He could admit that he needed that smile to come home to. He *had* to marry her. They could make it work, somehow. They had to—he wasn't sure if he could go on breathing if they didn't.

Sarai put down her popcorn, clapping as the dogs ran out of the center ring. The room darkened and Roman put his arm around her. She settled perfectly into his embrace.

"What are they saying?" she asked as the announcer came on.

"They're introducing the high-wire walker." He pointed to a spotlighted man on a wire high above their heads.

Sarai sucked in her breath. "You'd never get me up there. My hands are slick just thinking about it."

Roman took her hand and she giggled.

"What if I was up there, carrying you across?" Why did he say stupid things like that? He wanted to yank his words back. They only betrayed how desperate he felt to fill in the tiniest gaps in her life. She so didn't need him, yet he couldn't get by a day without her.

She glanced at him with sweetness in her eyes. "I love you."

He smiled back. *Marry me.* The words were right there, but he couldn't push them out, too paralyzed by her possible no. Instead, he cupped her face in his hand and kissed her.

She smiled as she leaned back, and her gaze traced his face. "Yeah, Roman, I'd let you carry me. Because I trust you."

No, she'd trusted the man she wanted him to be. Yes, he was the bodyguard who followed her around Moscow, making sure she was safe. But when she'd gotten a taste of reality and a glimpse of what that really meant, she'd fled.

Thirteen years later, she could still turn his life in a circus. A real three-ring mess.

The wind buffeted his Jeep, pushing it now and again toward the ditch. His headlights carved out the darkness, revealing fields of chaff dusted with snow, and drifts outlining the road.

Please, Sarai, be in Smolsk. And please be in a good mood.

He was snared in that thought, pushing scenarios around when he caught the glint of light, then movement as something darted out into his peripheral. Roman crunched the brakes. He felt them lock.

Panic gripped his brain as he slid toward the figure standing frozen in the middle of the road.

A coup? What, did she have some sort of red-and-white target written on her head? Or worse, maybe her presence just inspired anarchy. Because, according to Sarai's count, this was the third time she'd had the pleasure of being in a country under martial law.

It was starting to get old.

As she drove into Smolsk, she saw that the villagers had absorbed the information with the standard Russian unflappability. Oh. Another revolution? But will I get my daily portion of bread?

She probably needed a slap. But, she had to agree, when life crumbled, people across the world wanted the same basics. Life. Food. Family. And, sometimes, love.

Maybe the last one wasn't a basic.

Sarai climbed out of Genye's van and waved as he drove

away. The clinic seemed forlorn tonight—two stories of gray concrete, dark, expressionless windows gazing out into the weedy snowdrifted yard. Inside, fresh paint, the smell of antiseptic, and the comforts of running water, heat and electricity welcomed her like a long lost friend. Sarai let herself enjoy a moment of congratulations. Maybe, a year from now when kids like Sasha fell ill, their parents would bring them to The Savior's Hands, and she'd find a cure instead of finding a way to ease their pain as they died.

And then the people of Smolsk, and beyond, might see that Jesus cared about them. She wasn't a fool to think that by her helping save lives, Russians would drop to their knees in repentance. But if she could earn their trust with their physical wounds, they might listen to her words of truth for their spiritual ones.

It seemed like a good plan, and one that she'd invested two years creating. She felt like a smuggler or some sort of spy half the time, meeting with shipping agents, negotiating red tape and tracking down the powers that be for yet another stamp of approval.

But, well, the clinic would officially open its doors on Thanksgiving Day, less than three weeks away. While it wasn't a Russian holiday, it seemed especially poignant to Sarai. A day of gratitude—for her, and for the community—for God's provision in this barren land.

Sarai unlocked the door to the clinic, closed it behind her and walked in the darkness toward her office. She'd long ago added a cot to the room—a necessity for her late hours and fitful sleeping habits. She couldn't remember the last time she'd slept through the night.

No, that wasn't true. She'd slept pretty well the summer she spent in Moscow so long ago. She thought it was jet lag catching up to her. Or maybe residual exhaustion from her last year in college. For the first time in her life, she didn't have a goal pressing against her to keep her stumbling ahead. Just three clear months of hanging out with her brother before starting medical school. Still, despite the hours the sun reigned in the sky over Moscow lighting the nights, and the fact that she spent most of her waking hours with David's best friend, Roman, she'd never felt so rested.

Probably that was because she never felt like she really caught her breath when she was with Roman. She always felt a gasp coming on that Mr. Charm looked her way, and more. So, at night she fell into an exhausted…and peaceful slumber.

Or, maybe it was because, despite being exhilarating, Roman, with his surety about life, his control of every situation and especially the way he filled out his muscle shirt, always made her feel safe. Even when she wasn't with him, she knew he held her in his thoughts. She read it in his eyes.

Sometimes she wondered if that was what she missed the most.

Sarai flicked on the light to her office, let her bag drop and beelined to the cot. Fatigue already weighted her body, her eyes, and she didn't bother to change clothes, just curled up on the cot, toed off her shoes and pulled up the blanket.

Ah. Yes. Sleep.

Only, just like every night, Roman filled her mind, and she gave herself a moment to smile into the memory before she blinked him away. Roman, looking tousled and dangerously handsome when she interrupted his game of street hockey.

"Roman, meet my sister!" David had called.

And, despite the sweat that spiked his tawny brown hair, dripped down his face, past his reddish blond whiskers and into his hockey jersey, she couldn't help but decide she'd seen all the scenery necessary on this little vacation.

In fact, Russia just might be the most beautiful place she'd ever been, including Japan, Germany and Paris. She smiled, feeling young and free and decided that maybe she'd loosen up on a few rules this summer.

Perhaps she should have kept the one about not falling in love.

Sarai leaned up, slammed her fist into her pillow and drove Roman from her mind. He'd certainly forgotten her. So why did she hang on to him like a souvenir?

She should be glad he hadn't been killed over the years. And that David still dropped tidbits of information about Roman now and then. She never told him she lapped them up like a ravenous wolf.

She secretly prayed that Roman would abandon his world-saving career and join her sowing seeds for the Kingdom in Siberia. All she wanted was a guy who loved God like she did. Was that so much to ask?

Apparently, yes. Because here she was, thirty-five years

old, single and shivering under a wool blanket in the middle of nowhere Siberia. Alone. Forgotten.

She felt Julia's wail again, deep inside the corridors of her heart.

The wind picked up and rattled the windowpanes. Hunger drilled at her but she didn't have muscle to rise and heat so much as a pot of Ramen noodles. She drifted off, letting the embrace of fatigue draw her inside oblivion. At some point within REM she sensed a chill creep in, hover over her ears, linger at the foot of her bed. Heard a dog bark, once, twice.

A door slammed. It echoed through the clinic like a gunshot.

Sarai jerked. Opened her eyes. She heard feet shuffling on the concrete floor. Stiffening, she held her breath. On occasion the clinic had been vandalized and precious medicines stolen.

More footsteps. Her heartbeat thudded in her ears. Had she locked the office? She sat up, tried to listen past the rush of blood. Then a hand on her door rattled the knob.

Her mouth dried. Okay, think. *Think!* A weapon maybe? Or hide? Options rushed through her as the intruder knocked.

Knocked?

"Hello? Dr. Sarai Curtiss, are you in there?"

Accented academic English, and as she sat in silence, holding her breath, recognition clicked into place. No, it couldn't be. But the voice resonated just under her skin, a rumble of pleasure, and the slightest thrill of fear. Oh. *No.*

"Hello, Sarai?"

Oh. *Yes*. "Roman?"

Down girl. Down, down. Don't get your hopes up. She was simply dreaming. And, at the moment, liking it. So much, in fact, she rose, walked over to the door, unlocked it.

And nearly screamed.

It was Roman Novik all right. All six-foot gorgeous of him, with short tousled brown hair, red-tinted whiskers, dressed in head-to-toe muscles and danger black and plenty of blood dripping from a head wound on his forehead.

Things hadn't changed much in thirteen years.

He gave her a sheepish smile, and those knock-her-to-her-knees incredibly hazel eyes turned her brain to knots.

Nothing had changed, indeed.

Chapter Four

"I must be dreaming, because I can't believe it's you." Sarai stood in the door, outlined by darkness, dressed in a rumpled sweatshirt, a pair of jeans, her blond hair escaping from her braid, those green eyes blinking at him as if she might be trying to wake up.

Perhaps it would be better if she just kept dreaming. Especially if he could just join her with his own version of altered reality...right in the middle of the what-could-have-beens.

Waking up meant things were going to turn ugly.

Or maybe not. That startled look could mean she'd been...missing him? Even expecting him? That maybe she might trust him, just a little, and believe him when he told her she had to leave?

Except *she didn't need a hero.* She'd made that plain thirteen years ago. And, by the look of her—hands on her hips, jaw tight, eyes hard—things hadn't exactly relaxed in that area.

Still, *Sarai Curtiss.*

It simply wasn't fair that he could wake her from a sound sleep in the middle of the night and she could still take his breath away, turn words to paste in his mouth. Meanwhile, he looked like roadkill, which he'd almost become trying to avoid the deer. He'd barely coaxed his mangled jeep to the clinic door.

He inspired truckloads of confidence. He should probably be grateful she didn't slam the door in his face.

Epcot fiasco or not, David owed him big. Especially if—no *when* at this rate—his boss discovered just what kind of midnight field trip Roman had taken. He'd hoped to be back in the office by, well, noon at least.

Sarai wasn't the only one dreaming at the moment.

Roman braced his hand against the doorjamb and tried to compose himself. *"Privyet."*

"Don't you 'Hi' me!" she snapped. "I can't believe you show up here bleeding."

Uh-oh. Fully awake now, and getting right to the point. Never mind a "Hey, how are you, Roman?" Or, "How did you find me?" Or even—in his wildest dreams—"Glad to see you!" Just…not good enough, as usual. He should have guessed.

"I'm fine thanks, how are you?" He took a breath and slid the smile off his face. So much for trying to charm her.

She looked mollified. Her expression eased. "Sorry. I'm just—you scared me. You're bleeding."

He winced a little at that and she closed her eyes, rubbing them with a thumb and forefinger. "Let's start over, okay?" She looked up. "Roman Novik. What are you doing in my neck of Siberia?" She smiled slightly, a gentle acknowledgment of their friendship, the kind he'd seen her give her brother when she was trying to hide fatigue. Then she stepped close and wrapped her arms around his waist.

Oy.

He took a breath, hoping she couldn't hear how his heart pummeled his chest, as if trying to escape. *Keep it cool, Roman.*

He put his arm around her in a one-armed hug, hating the fact that while, to her, it was an "I know we're old friends" gesture, to him it ignited all the hopes he'd been trying to douse for over a decade—especially the last two hundred klicks.

Of course, she fit perfectly into his arms. Just like she always had.

And she smelled great—part lilac soap, part Sarai. He resisted the urge to smell her hair and instead stepped away from her.

Remember the mission. Right about now he wanted to strangle David Curtiss. If Roman was lucky, he'd only end up chipping ice and sweeping streets and *not* in gulag. What had he been thinking?

"I'm here because of the coup."

"Were you trying to stop it?" Sarai turned on the hall light. "Is that how you got hurt?" She reached up toward his wound. He jerked away.

"I'm just trying to get a look at it." She withdrew her

hand. "It looks like you have some glass in there. I'll need to irrigate and dress it." She took him by the elbow, pointed him down the hallway. "I promise I'll try not to hurt you."

Yeah, right.

"Sarai, we don't have time—"

"I thought you were in Khabarovsk." She flicked on a light to an exam room and led him inside. He felt like a twelve-year-old boy being led into the principal's office. Where was his voice? His reflexes felt like they'd been slathered in honey.

Then again, like some allergic reaction, Sarai always had a calming…even paralyzing effect on him.

How did she know he was in Khabarovsk? For some reason, her knowledge of that information shook him.

Certainly she hadn't been tracking him like he'd been her over the years. "I am, I mean, I was…. Oh, stop, Sarai. Listen to me. I'm not just passing through town and happened upon your clinic. I was looking for you."

She turned, a frown creasing her face.

"There's been a coup in Irkutsk."

"I know." She turned away and patted an examining table. "Sit."

I know? She knew about Bednov's deadline for foreigners? Then, did that mean she would come along nicely? "I'm not sitting. I…you should be packing."

She looked at him, frowning, and shook her head. "I'm going to clean you up." She gave him a benign smile, then she crossed to a cabinet, opened it and began pulling out supplies—antiseptic, an irrigation tray, tweezers, a needle. "Besides, I'm fine."

Evidently. He felt his chest tighten, yet he moved toward the exam table, propelled by the hypnotic hold she had on him. He slid on to the table just as she turned toward him, hands gloved, holding a tweezers and a sponge.

"Hold still. I need to get the glass out. And then I'll clean it."

She stood so close he could feel her breath on his chin. He studied her face as she cleaned his wound. Tiny crow's-feet around her eyes betrayed her years of stress and sacrifice. And she seemed thinner under that bulky sweatshirt, but maybe stronger all the same. He somehow knew that she would have changed, but this woman seemed even more determined, more resolute. He supposed years on the edge of civilization made her harder.

Oh, great.

"How have you been?" he asked softly. She didn't answer, but dropped a piece of glass into the tray she held.

"You didn't tell me how you got injured." She took a bottle and ran fluid over his wound, catching it in the gauze pad, then mopping up the excess before it ran into his shirt. The silence of the building seemed to echo between them, and a chill ran under his parka, where before had been a thin layer of perspiration.

"I hit a deer." He didn't add that he'd had to track it into the forest and destroy the injured animal. Nor that he'd hit the windshield and had been sporting a killer headache for the past three hours.

Or maybe he should attribute the headache to sheer dread over what he had to say next.

Please, Sarai, try not to be…so…independent.

Mother Teresa had nothing on Sarai Curtiss for pure guts and stubbornness.

"This might hurt a little," she said as she dabbed on antiseptic. He closed one eye against a slight sting. She glanced at him, smirked. "Oh, don't be a baby."

Oh, don't be a baby.

Without a second's warning, memory swooped in for the kill.

He'd been playing street hockey with David, who checked him hard. He'd smashed into a park bench, skinning his leg down to the ankle. Sarai had draped one of his arms around her shoulder and helped him home—and he'd let her. Then, because she knew how, he'd also let her dress it.

She'd called him a baby.

He'd pulled her into his arms and showed her indeed, how ridiculous her statement was.

He looked up at her, blinking against the press of memory.

Her mouth opened slightly, and he noticed her blush. "I didn't mean that." She gathered up the used gauze pads. "I'll do the stitches in a minute."

"Okay. But hurry. We need to get out of here."

She turned to him, frowning. "I told you, I'm fine. What are you talking about?"

He stared at her, a sick feeling in his gut. "What are *you* talking about? Of course you're leaving, right?"

She stared at him, blinking.

Oh, no. He sighed. "Sarai, I'm here because David sent me. Bednov put out an order for all foreigners to leave Irkutia within seventy-two—" he checked his watch "—no, make that sixty-three hours and seventeen minutes. Or you'll be arrested as an enemy of Russia."

Sarai said nothing. Just stared at him. Then light filled her eyes and…she laughed.

"You think this is funny?"

"Roman. I so can't believe you." She shook her head. Trust David to turn one little skirmish—okay, *martial law*—into a reason for her to go back home to America and get a "real" job as he'd said last Christmas. This little outpost of hope felt more real than any carpeted, air-conditioned clinic in Suburbia, U.S.A. She picked up the suture tray and returned to the exam table. "I mean, really. I know you owe David from that stunt at Epcot, but I can't believe you'd actually let him talk you into coming to Smolsk to try and drag me out of Russia. Do you think I'm stupid?"

He opened his mouth, as if in disbelief, and she only briefly glanced at it—stamping down the accompanying memories—before she picked up a needle and syringe. "Yes, I know about Epcot. Now hold still, I need to numb the area."

"Stop."

She nearly jumped as he grabbed her upper arm. "Roman, you're going to get us hurt! I'm holding a needle for crying out loud." She took a deep breath and set the needle down, pushing her heart back down her throat.

Or maybe her racing pulse had more to do with his grip on her arm. And the way his eyes sparked—so utterly macho, so utterly in control. So very Roman.

Except, she'd noticed from the first that this wasn't the same charismatic young man she'd fallen for a decade before. He wore hardness around his eyes, and an unfamiliar clench to his jaw. She'd known him as an idealistic college graduate, hoping to change the world. He'd charmed her with his smile, his humor, even his faith, so young, yet so vivid. For a short time she'd believed that together they might make a difference.

Sadly, the only difference he'd made was to break her heart.

Judging by his expression, that playful Roman had died under the double-edged choices of his job. Before her sat a man she didn't know—a soldier, with sharpened edges, dark eyes and danger emanating off his demeanor like a hue. Just the man she feared he'd become. She suddenly felt like crying.

"This is not a joke, Sarai. David did ask me to come, but because you're in real trouble. Governor Bednov has declared martial law. And if you don't leave with me tonight, you're going to get trapped in Irkutia…and arrested."

She took a breath and stepped away from him. "Yeah. Hardly. First of all, for your information, I treated Bednov's son tonight, and while, yes, we were unsuccessful, Bednov knows what I do here and my work matters. He's not going to shut it down."

Roman shook his head.

Her voice tightened and she shook her arm out of his

grip. "Secondly, I've been in countries before that had political coups, and survived just fine."

He raised his eyebrows and, just for a second, she had the urge to slap him.

Fine. She held up her hand in surrender to his unspoken point. "Listen, this is all going to blow over. Besides, Smolsk is about as remote as I can get. Bednov is not going to send an army of FSB regulars out here to arrest me."

"But I could."

She felt her mouth open and hated herself for showing shock. "You wouldn't."

He swallowed, sighed, looked away and for a second she glimpsed the young man who had begged her not to leave, even if it had only been on her answering machine. "I don't want to." Then his eyes hardened, as did his voice. "But I might have to if you don't come nicely."

A beat of challenge passed between them, and she felt the last of her dreams swan dive. He'd arrest her?

Like a criminal?

Ouch. Her chest felt as if a caribou sat on it and for a moment she felt light-headed. "Roman, I have work to do here. This clinic is due to officially open in three weeks. I can't leave now."

"You can come back."

She couldn't contain her disbelief. "It took me nearly a year to get a visa the first time. Do you seriously think that, especially after martial law, they'd let me return anytime this century?" She stepped away from him. "Look around you. My clinic has an ER, an operating room, a delivery room, five rooms upstairs for overnight patients. I have an equipped ambulance, a defibrillator, an ultrasound machine, an X-ray room and even a dental chair. Do you have any idea the headaches and cash it took to get this stuff here?" She shook her head. "Roman, I leave town for even a week and this place will be stripped clean. The mafia will piecemeal out my supplies to the highest bidder, and if I ever make it back in, I'll be starting from zero—*if* I can even get it started again."

"You're not safe here."

She looked away, closed her eyes, fighting the angry prick of tears. "I'm just as safe here as anywhere. I'm needed here." She wanted to add that God had put her here, but Roman wouldn't understand that, would he? He knew nothing about personal sacrifice for the sake of the gospel.

"I can't let you stay here."

She met his eyes, the ones she'd once thought held love, even her future, and saw only resolve.

She swallowed hard and picked up the needle to numb his wound. "Fine. Arrest me. But hold still first."

He caught her wrist halfway toward his head. "You've got to be kidding me."

She stared at him, disbelief huffing out of her. "Are you scared of me?"

He narrowed one eye, but said nothing.

"C'mon, trust me, Roman. If it's one thing you can count on, I'll do my job. Right. Even if it costs me my freedom."

He didn't meet her eyes as she numbed his wound and administered five stitches.

She finished in silence, snapping off her gloves. "When was your last tetanus shot?"

"Sarai, listen to me. I'm only trying to hel—"

"You can sleep in one of the upstairs rooms, if you want." She turned toward the door, milliseconds away from tears. She could hardly believe her brother—and the man she *once* loved—would so belittle her dreams, her life's purpose. Did they seriously think that after being held at gunpoint in a refugee camp in Somalia, or choppered into a burning village in Chechnya, that she would be the slightest bit ruffled by a little disturbance in a city two hundred kilometers southeast?

She found her composure by the time she hit the hallway, and broke out in long strides.

"Sarai!"

She didn't turn. Wouldn't turn. Ever. "Go back to where you came from, Roman. I don't ever want to see you again." Her words would have carried more emphasis if they hadn't cracked at the end.

She entered her office and slammed the door, locking it as it shuddered.

Roman slammed his fist into the door. "Why do you always have to be a martyr!"

"Go away!"

She heard him hiss, perhaps holding back a few Russian adjectives. Well, she'd heard them all before, and frankly, with his chosen profession, she wasn't surprised.

Okay, so maybe that wasn't fair. David had kept her apprised of Roman's desire to be God's man in his profession.

Still, he had so much potential to be more...and perhaps that was what hurt the most.

And she *wasn't* a martyr. She was just doing something no one else could do. She didn't exactly see people lining up for her job, did she?

If people like her didn't stick around when life turned into a battlefield, who would?

Sarai sank to her knees with her back against the door, pressed her palms into her eyes and refused to cry.

Chapter Five

"I sat in the hall all night staring at her locked door." Roman ran his palm against his eyes, fighting the tug of sleep. "She's simply overjoyed to see me."

On the other end of the cell phone line, Vicktor gave a snort. "You have all the fun."

Yanna's sat–cell phone toy had saved Roman a few minutes ago when she routed Major Malenkov's call to his jacket pocket. Only, eight a.m. Khabarovsk town time translated to five a.m. on the Smolsk clock. Three hours he'd been sitting there on the cold concrete floor, trying to talk Sarai into opening her door.

It would help if she gave him a response other than muffled sobs. She'd been quiet for more than an hour now, however.

He felt like a real hero. Flying across three time zones so he could be the bad guy. At least in Sarai's eyes.

And soon, in the FSB's eyes, also. Because the clock was ticking. Malenkov had ordered him to check into the office by the end of the day. Roman didn't even want to calculate the hours he had before Malenkov discovered that unfortunate glitch.

"Sarai offered me a cot in one of her convalescence rooms, but I have this gut feeling she's just waiting for me to snooze off so she can ditch me."

"C'mon Redman, aren't you overreacting?" Vicktor said. Roman could hear him on the other end take a sip of coffee. The guy had a regular java addiction after his short-term gig working for the Seattle Police Department. Roman could use a shot of caffeine right now, if only to ease the headache that knotted his brain.

"No. I don't think so. At the very least, she's not talking to me. Do you believe she actually thinks David and I concocted this mess to get her out of the country?"

"Bednov's edict is probably in the news."

"If I leave to get a newspaper, she'll bolt."

"She lives for that clinic. If anything, she'll chain herself to her examining table."

Roman smiled. Yes, Sarai would do something like that. He'd practically had to threaten to handcuff her and drag her away from Red Square the day of the Moscow coup.

Until, of course, he'd nearly gotten killed.

That event had changed things with head-spinning velocity. She'd nearly given him windburn exiting from his life.

"Well, then, you'll have to turn the Redman charm on overdrive."

"Sadly, I think she's immune."

Vicktor laughed. "Roman, the fact is, the problem with you and Sarai is that you are too much alike. Driven. Focused. Sadly, you're focused on different things."

"Yeah, like I want her alive."

The humor evaporated from Vicktor's voice. "I think she'd say the same thing about you."

Roman stared at the closed door, hating how those words dug into the crannies of his chest. "What's the latest on our dead American?"

Silence. Apparently Vicktor didn't want to change the subject.

"Listen, you of all people should know that I'm doing my best to live out my Christian life the only way I know how. What more does she want of me? I don't understand her, and she certainly doesn't get me."

"I think she gets you just fine. The problem is you can't accept it."

"That's not why she left me."

"Then why? I remember you two back then. You were inseparable. Do you remember the night you took her to the Moscow circus?"

Yes. It had probably been the last full and refreshing breath he could remember. Everything seemed a blur since then.

"You told me that night that you were going to marry her," Vicktor said quietly.

I would have. Except, she didn't want me.

"I don't know. I guess she was afraid I'd get killed. But let's take a good look at who's been the one to risk her neck over the past decade. If anyone is on a suicide track, it's Miss Save the World."

"Well, you're both going to be dead if you don't throw her over your shoulder and hightail it back here. You're lucky. Malenkov is tied up all day in meetings, but I can guarantee you he'll come hunting you when he sets foot in the office. I suggest you be here."

"I know." Roman sighed, glanced again at Sarai's closed door. *C'mon Sarai, loosen up.* "So, did Utuzh give you a report on our dead guy?"

"Oh, yeah. The smell—you were right. Not vodka. He had acute kidney failure. If he hadn't been murdered in the casino, he might have ended up dead in North Dakota. And the stuff you freaked out over—good instincts. Uranium. HEU, the same stuff your Smirnov had, at least the same substance. Whether it came from the same source is difficult to determine."

"He must have ingested it somehow."

"I don't think he used it as pâté on his black bread, Roman."

Roman shook his head, feeling the knot in the back of his neck tighten. "What did he have in his stomach?"

Vicktor paused, perhaps reading the report. "Vodka. Fish—fresh-water Kombola. Some bread."

"Run a check on everywhere he stayed while in Russia. Talk to the hotel, see what local café serve Kombola."

"Roma, if the guy ate contaminated food, wouldn't we have others who were sick?"

"Maybe we do." Roman instantly regretted his tone. "Listen, I'm just...tired. Maybe, also, find out if there are any decommissioned reactors near the cities he stayed in. And, question the Alexander Oil guy when he tries to claim the body."

"*Ladna.* I'll call you. Try and get back here before you get into real trouble."

"Yeah, well, tell that to She Who Locks Herself in Her Office."

Vicktor laughed as he hung up.

I could use a little help, God. Roman ran the back of his hand across his whiskered jaw. *No, better yet, I could use some answers.*

Like, why Sarai, a woman who at one time smiled every time he walked into the room, couldn't stand to be around him longer than ten minutes. He was just trying to be the man God wanted him to be—he just wasn't doing it *her* way. She should take it up with God, not him.

He was perfectly happy with the profession God had chosen for him. Being a cop felt right, and he did it well, or at least, had until recently. Yes, there may have been a blink in time when he considered being a missionary. A blip, really, when he'd helped Sarai at an orphanage and thought that perhaps, maybe, he could invest his life into saving people's souls, rather than their skins. However, God didn't want everyone to be a missionary, did He? He needed cops, too.

Roman closed his eyes, leaned his head against the wall. He shouldn't have put so much hope—against his better judgment, he might add—into seeing her face. Into thinking that all this time she might have kindled a respect for him. He'd let foolish dreams soften his heart, and she'd landed a stinging blow with her reaction.

He could understand her disappointment, even reluctance to leave all she'd worked for…but to believe he'd try to sabotage her career with a fabricated story?

Did she think so little of him, and his respect for *her?*

Again, false expectations. She probably hadn't thought of him but once over the past decade—when she laughed with David over Roman's Epcot fiasco.

That's all he was to her, a big joke.

A fool.

He closed his eyes, feeling the hard panes of the concrete floor drill into his spine. He should have curled up, snatched a little shut-eye. But, like the fool he was, he'd sat with his gaze glued to her door. As if she was some sort of criminal. Well…she was. Or would be soon.

But could he arrest her?

Even to save her life?

She already hated him…he could hardly make it any worse. Except…the thought of her in handcuffs made him ill.

That, the fact that he hadn't eaten in about twelve hours, and the smell of cleanser and antiseptic redolent in the hall did wonders for his stomach.

C'mon, Sarai, open the door.

He stood and stretched his cramped muscles. Probably, she'd had the good sense to crawl under her blanket and get some sleep while he'd been sitting here like an idiot. Served him right. This entire trip had idiot written all over it. Or maybe, Love Sick Fool.

Whatever. He should take Vicktor up on his hint, throw Sarai over his shoulder and shove her on the nearest transport, even if she went kicking and screaming.

That would be better than arresting her.

Maybe.

He braced his arm against the wall, stretching his calves. Then he broke into a quick walk down the end of the hall.

He had to admit, Sarai had built an impressive place here using her Russian resources. Compared to Western facilities, the clinic had primitive written all over it, from the white-washed concrete walls, the cracked floors, even if they were clean, and plainly attired rooms. All the same, he noticed all the essentials for an ER trauma in the room at the end of the hall, and wondered how often she had had to use it.

She had ambition. And guts. He knew a bit about what it took to get supplies—especially medical supplies—into Russia. She needed the resources of Solomon and the courage of King David.

Obviously the Sarai he'd known—the one who loved to watch Russian movies, who made a mean stir fry and beat him in chess—had morphed into this driven, all-work-no-play medical soldier.

He had a good reason for his frontal assault into his career. Like trying to escape a heritage of failure his father left behind. But Sarai came from a family of achievers, of heroes. So, what was her excuse?

He was leaning against the ER reception counter when he heard it—the squeak of hinges. Sarai poked her head out of the open door, checked the hall and then slid out, pulling it quietly behind her.

The little sneak.

How he hated when he was right. Especially about Sarai. Please, couldn't he be wrong, just once?

"Sarai!" He took off in a sprint down the hall.

And, wouldn't you know it, she did, too.

"Sarai!"

Great, he'd seen her. And why hadn't she seen him? Because she wasn't a trained spy, that's why. Because she lived her life in the open, honestly. Because she dedicated her life to helping others stay alive…and didn't risk it unnecessarily. Most of all, she didn't do maniacal, over-the-top things like spend the night like a bull dog outside another person's door.

Okay, so she *was* waiting for him to leave. But she wanted to get home, get a shower, and the last thing she needed was Roman following her to her two-room apartment only to notice that she still kept the picture of them together at Gorky Park.

In fact, she kept it next to her bed.

Yeah, that would certainly communicate *Over You* wouldn't it?

She stepped up her sprint, cut toward the main doors and slammed through them.

She could nearly feel Roman's breath behind her as she tore out into the street. The sun had just begun to sear through the trees and buildings along Ylista Pushkina, but shadows still pooled in the ice-rutted surface of the parking lot. The wind felt fresh and cold on her tired face, and smelled crisp, of early winter. She ran to her Toyota Camry, an import she'd picked up in Irkutsk.

Why did he have to be such a diehard? He and David were two peas in the same pod—they ought to be brothers. Another good reason for her *not* to fall for Roman.

Again.

She poked her car key into the lock, turned it.

Roman slammed his hand against her door before she could open it. He was breathing hard, and frankly looked a little green as he turned to her. "What are you doing?"

She lifted her chin. "Going home."

"Super. I'll drive." He held out his hand for her keys.

She closed them in her fist and shoved her hand into her pocket. "No way. I want you gone. Out of my life. Skedaddle, which is English for *Das Vedanya.*" She couldn't believe she was actually wrenching those words out of her mouth emphatically, without flinching. If he didn't look too close, he'd never know she'd spent a good portion of the last three hours crying in frustration and fury. And maybe a little over her broken heart.

Because, wouldn't it have been nice if he'd been looking

for her to tell her that he loved her? Oh sure, in her wildest dreams.

"I'm not leaving, Sarai."

"And you're not coming with me." She stared at him, painfully aware that he hadn't a minuscule of tenderness in his eyes. Yeah, he'd changed. Forgotten her. Wiped her clear out of his memory. Well, what did she expect…it was one short summer, and he was young, painfully handsome, a hero with a smile that could make her forget her own name. He'd probably moved on a few times since her.

Funny, David might have had the courtesy to mention that.

"You're coming with me. Gimme the keys." Roman reached out for her, but she backed away.

"You'll have to wrestle them out of my rigor mortised grip."

He raised his eyebrows. She smiled, not nicely.

"Don't make me do something you'll regret."

Her smile vanished. "Get away from me."

He winced. "Sarai, you are the most stubborn woman I've ever met." He sighed and ran a hand over his hair, mussing even more. "I know I'm the last person you want to see. Ever. And I know what you think of me. I promise you, if you give me five minutes to prove to you that I'm not lying…and then let me get you out of here, I'll never bother you again."

He looked away when he said it. As if annoyed with the fact that he had to bother with her now.

Inside, she heard the slightest cry of pain. What was it

about him that being in his atmosphere felt like she was ripping the skin off her heart? But, finally, she knew the truth.

Roman didn't love her. And she certainly shouldn't be hanging on to the hope that he would. They lived in different worlds. And he seemed content to keep it that way.

"Fine."

He stared at her. "Fine?"

"Fine." She barely kept the choked sound from her voice. "I need to go home. We'll go there and watch the news." While she threw his picture off the balcony.

He nodded.

"And then, you'll leave me alone. Forever. Right?"

He swallowed, looked over the top of her head. "Right."

Right.

"I'm driving, so hop in."

He narrowed his eyes. "You promise you won't leave me in the parking lot?"

She pulled out the keys, not looking at him. "Get in."

He crossed around to the passenger side, his hazel eyes on her as she opened her door. She reached across and let him in, arguing with herself for keeping her unspoken word.

They drove in clenched silence to her apartment. An early winter wind picked up litter and dirty snow and tossed it down the street. Her flat, located in a four story Khrushchev-designed brick building, had four entrances. Outside, it looked like it had been recently bombed, bricks littered the foundation, doors hung on one hinge, the garbage Dumpster overflowed with debris. Two stray dogs lifted their heads from their huddle under a broken merry-go-round in the snowy yard. Sarai parked, put a steering wheel club on the car and locked the vehicle.

The western cities of Russia had adapted quickly to European standards—remodeled flats and standards of cleanliness and repair. But in the villages, she felt lucky to find a flat with running water and electricity, let alone indoor plumbing.

"I'm on the third floor," she said as she pushed open her entrance door and in the darkness climbed from memory the chipped stairs. "Watch your step—the third step is out."

Roman followed her in silence. She reached her apartment, opened the outer steel door, then the inner one.

"I'm glad to see you've taken security precautions," Roman said quietly.

"I'm not stupid, Roma. I told you I was safe."

He sighed. "That's your opinion."

She closed both doors, locked them. Roman stood in the narrow hallway of her apartment. "I like it."

She shrugged out of her coat, hung it on a hook near the door. "Yeah, well, I don't spend a lot of time here." She slipped out of her boots and grabbed a pair of slippers.

"I was serious." He, too, slipped off his coat, then toed off his shoes. "Reminds me of my place. Only neater."

"Oh." Somehow that only hurt. More evidence that he'd become the man she feared…one-dimensional. Hard. Barren.

Then again, what did that say about her life? Homey

didn't exactly define her life—or her flat. Not with her two hard-as-stone sofas, a tiny Formica-topped table shoved into the corner and a black-and-white television with aluminum foil wrapped around the antennas for reception. Her kitchen had enough room for a sink and a stove. She kept her refrigerator in the family room.

"Help yourself to something to eat. You might find some bread in the fridge, or maybe some apples. Sorry. I haven't cooked here lately."

She strode over to her bedroom door and closed it before he could see inside.

Roman headed to the television. Crouching before it, he turned it on, playing with the reception. She couldn't help but notice his wide back, the muscles in his arms that tightened the sleeves of his thermal shirt. He'd gone from a boy to a man since she'd seen him last…no, he'd gone from boy to soldier.

She stifled a small shudder. She felt like she might be staring at a stranger. A strange man, in her apartment.

"On second thought, I eat at a café in town. Let's catch some breakfast."

He turned, and for a second, she glimpsed a tiny smile. "Perfect. Let me find the news while you change."

He turned back to the television, and she shut herself into her bedroom, cleaning up, then changing into a flannel shirt and clean jeans.

On the other side of the door, she could hear the television, the chatter of fast Russian. She hardly ever watched the news…or television for that matter. It wasn't only that she didn't have time, but after a day trying to decipher the language, she couldn't bear to have it seep into her down-time.

The sun had risen and light now pooled on her green down comforter, a luxury from home. She sat on the bed to pull on her socks, and her gaze fell on the picture of Roman.

"Let's get our photo taken."

It had been one of their first dates—a real date, without David tagging along as chaperone. She'd been in the city less than two weeks, and somehow Roman found her free moments and filled them with his smile, his magnetic charm. He took her to Red Square, explained the monuments of the Fearless Leaders. He translated for her as they toured the Museum of Military History. He bought her ice cream and flowers and made her feel...respected. Even special.

She'd turned into a pile of besotted mush around him.

At Gorky Park, she rode the Ferris wheel, gazing upon the Kremlin and the Volga River from her perch. A slight sweat lined her palms from the height and when Roman put his arm around her, she leaned into it. For safety.

He felt so strong next to her. Like he'd never let anything happen to her.

If only she'd seen through her romantic idealism to the truth—Roman might be charm and charisma, but he also embodied danger, recklessness and heartache.

The more she let him into her heart, the more she knew she'd never be safe.

Denial became her friend until the day of the coup. When

Roman appeared, bloodied and angry, ready to fight for his country and freedom. She knew he'd never change his mind.

He just wasn't sold out for God like she'd hoped.

At least that was what she told herself as she fled back to the States, to medical school and her goals.

Lord, I don't know what you've done in his life over the past decade. I mean, I know from David that Roman still seeks you. But, you brought him back here for a reason, and I pray you make that clear to me. Help me be a vessel for good and growth in his life. Even if he does drive me crazy.

She wiped away a tear as she reached out and turned his picture down.

In the family room, Roman lay on the sofa, his hair wet, watching the news. "I took the liberty of using your sink. Hope that was okay."

And he smelled good, too—a little bit of soap, a little left-over perspiration and way too much Eau de Roma. Drive her crazy was right.

She sat on one of her straight chairs. "So?"

"Evidently, Governor-elect Bednov has taken over in Governor Kazlov's absence. They think he might have been kidnapped, but no one has made any demands."

Sarai shook her head. "I can't believe it. I thought Russia was past all this."

Roman harrumphed. "Don't believe everything you read in the news. Russia still has old Communists at the helm. And they'd like nothing more than a reversal to the old ways."

"Bednov's a good man."

Roman gave her a look that made her feel like a kindergartener. "Hardly. He's a Party man. I know. He was a friend of my father's."

"Your father was in the Communist Party?"

"Yes. Until he realized he'd been a fool. And then they took everything from him." Roman tightened his jaw. "Just trust me. When Bednov says he's going to do something. It gets done."

"But he campaigned for peace."

Roman tucked his arms behind his head. "He campaigned for a strong Russia. You need to learn to read between the lines."

The newscaster came on with an update of the violence in Irkutsk. Tanks patrolled the city and a building burned, black smoke darkening the morning sky. Sarai listened with bated breath at the casualty toll.

"Seven dead, including one of Kazlov's assistants." She shook her head in disbelief. "That's horrible, Roman, but I still don't hear anything about your so-called foreigner evacuation. I know a plot by my brother when I see it." The telephone rang.

Roman sat up.

Sarai reached for the receiver. "It's my phone. I'll get it."

He pursed his lips and leaned forward, his forearms resting on his knees.

"Sarai, it's Anya." The sound of Anya's voice, so in control, yet so concerned radiated through Sarai. "We just got a call from Khanda. There's a boy there showing the same symptoms as Sasha. They need you."

Sarai nodded, glanced at Roman. "Okay. Can you and Genye pick me up? I'll be downstairs waiting."

"No." Roman pounced to his feet and, before Sarai could react, snatched the telephone from her grip.

"Hey!"

"This is Roman Novik. I'm with the FSB and Sarai's leaving with me this morning."

Sarai didn't wait for Roman to get a response. She leaped at him, grabbing at the telephone. "You can't do this!"

He held her away from him with one arm, almost laughingly as she fought for the phone. "No. I'm sorry, she can't meet you."

Fine then. Sarai turned and bolted for the door. Rage filled her steps as she grabbed her keys and her jacket, and flung the door open. She opened the second metal door and slammed it behind her.

Locked it.

Roman burst from the apartment and nearly impaled himself on the door. "Have you totally lost it? What are you doing?"

"My job!" Sarai stepped back, away from his reach as he pushed his arm through the slats and made a grab for her. "I came here, Roma, to help save lives and I'm not letting you or David or my parents keep me from doing it. I don't know why you seem so set against me, or my work here, but you'd better be gone when I get back."

Then she turned and raced down the stairs in her slippers.

Chapter Six

"We have a problem, Governor."

Light from the hallway seeped into his darkened office, only seconds in advance of the voice. Alexei Bednov opened his eyes and leaned up from his desk chair. His headache hadn't eased, even with a couple shots of vodka, a few pain relievers and an hour of shut-eye.

From the look on Fyodor's face, his headache just might get worse.

"Shto?"

Fyodor came in, shut the door. His drawn expression could barely be seen in the dim light, despite the press of early morning against the curtains. Outside, Bednov could still hear the occasional siren. "Riddle is dead. He was supposed to check in yesterday from Khabarovsk."

Bednov stifled a curse. "He had a shipment with him."

Fyodor said nothing, and this time Bednov let the curse out, a long hiss in the darkness. "Where is he now?"

"In the ME's office in Khabarovsk. The local FSB found him and called Alexander Oil."

"Gregori Smirnov sparked the curiosity of an agent in Khabarovsk, and I'll lay odds that agent will pick up Riddle's scent." Bednov shook his head, leaned over and turned on a desk lamp. "Have you sent anyone to pick him up?"

"Not yet."

"Good. Don't. Wait a few days, and then you go. See what they know and bring Riddle back. The last thing we need is Khabarovsk sending someone out here to sniff around. A dead agent on our soil would be hard to explain, even now."

Fyodor nodded. A thin man, he looked sickly in the light. "Um, Comrade Bednov, I wanted to tell you how sorry I was about your son."

Bednov nodded, but said nothing. Sasha served at least one purpose—he earned Bednov the sympathy of his province—probably the nation. It served as a sufficient alibi. If anyone ever figured out he'd planned the so-called coup to divert Kazlov's kidnapping and keep Kazlov from contesting the election results, or worse—arresting Bednov if the unthinkable happened and Kazlov won. Not that he would, after the incentive Bednov had given the vote counters. But now, he could grab power without so much as a frown from Moscow. Public sentiment would sweep away accusations and only confirm his denials, and soon he'd have everything in place to broaden his scope of power.

Sasha's timing couldn't have been more convenient if he'd planned it that way. Stupid, useful kid.

"How's our guest?"

"He's angry. And demanding his freedom."

Bednov snorted. "Take him to Chuya. And make sure he's in solitary confinement."

"Why don't we kill him?"

Bednov switched off the light. Yes, that was much better. Now, perhaps, his headache might ease enough for him to untangle his next step. "For the same reason they didn't kill the Czar and his family when they first took him. Because he still had information that they needed. If we want to pull this off, we must run our government as smoothly as possible. The last thing we need is to attract Moscow's concern."

Fyodor nodded, turned as if to leave.

"One last thing, Fyodor. Have you found the doctor yet?"

Fyodor stopped with his hand on the door handle. "I'm working with the embassy to put out pictures of all the foreigners. They are eager to help. Meanwhile, we've sent agents to Smolsk."

"Fyodor, you told them that it must be an accident, correct?"

Fyodor nodded. "Yes, I did, Governor Bednov."

"Your sister is the most infuriating—don't laugh, David, it's not funny. She locked me in her apartment." Roman held his sat phone to his ear as he paced Sarai's flat. He'd watched her drive away from his perch on her third-floor balcony just off her bedroom. Of course, she had to be the ultra-safe girl and install a balcony grate—effectively trapping him inside the flat. "I can't believe you talked me into this!"

David sounded like Roman had ripped him from something—raucous music blared in the background and although David wasn't shouting, Roman had to in order for David to hear him. "Do you have any idea where she might hide an extra key?"

"Don't give up, Roman. There's news on my end that Bednov has already arrested two oil execs who were trying to depart on their private jets. Says he's holding them under suspicion of kidnapping. But the chatter on this side of the ocean is that Bednov might be behind Kazlov's disappearance. Keep your head down."

"I'm not going anywhere unless I can find a key." He paced through her bedroom, aware that it smelled like her—fresh soap, a hint of lilac. She might have some sort of body lotion or something… Yes, there it was on the nightstand. Along with…

He flipped up a picture frame and time stopped.

She still had this? Right here, where she could look at it every morning, every night? He felt just a little light-headed and sat down on the bed.

The day of their first kiss.

Why did she so easily find the cracks in his heart? He still remembered holding her face in his hands, the way her eyes widened as he searched for permission in her expression and then—

"Roman, try in the kitchen. In a decoy sugar bowl. That's where my mother always kept one."

Roman turned the picture back down and stalked out of the bedroom. "She's got quite the setup here, Preach. She's worked hard at this clinic. I feel sick to make her leave it."

"I know. I'll do all I can from here to get her back as soon as possible. But my sources say that Bednov's serious. I know Sarai can take care of herself, but she has tunnel vision when it comes to a project. She'd rather sacrifice her skin than quit."

Or my skin. Roman walked out into the family room. Stopped.

On the television screen, framed neatly with the words "Foreigner at Large" flashed a fairly awful picture of Sarai Curtiss. It held for a moment, then flipped to another equally horrendous picture of a Frenchman.

"I can't believe this," Roman said almost inaudibly.

"What?" David yelled. Roman held the phone away from his ear, wincing.

"I just saw Sarai's picture on the television. Like...Russia's most wanted or something. What's going on?"

"I dunno. Maybe the embassies are trying to rope in their registered expats."

"I have to find her." Roman stalked to the kitchen and opened the kitchen cupboard. Inside, a number of containers hinted at success. He opened three before he hit the jackpot.

"I found the key. I'll e-mail you when I get back to Khabarovsk."

"Redman, thanks. May God give you wisdom. And providence."

Roman clicked off and pocketed his sat phone as he pulled on his jacket. He needed a truckload of divine wisdom if he hoped to find Sarai and get her out in—he checked his watch—sixty hours and counting. He opened the door, took the stairs two at a time, despite the shadows, vaulted the third step and slammed out into the street.

Thankfully, the town wasn't so large he couldn't sprint back to the clinic parking lot and pick up his smashed jeep in ten minutes or less.

Yes, yes! the clinic lights were on. And Sarai's Camry sat in the lot. *Gotcha!*

He burst through the doors, took a right and slammed open her office door.

Empty.

Breathing hard, Roman grabbed at his knees. His head felt woozy and he took a step forward, hoping he didn't go down. He needed to eat.

"You okay?"

Roman turned at the voice. A familiar voice. Tall, with bobbed blond hair, lines around her icy blue eyes and a look that made him feel like he'd traveled back in time to sixth form. Anya—as Sarai had called her—didn't smile. "*Da.* I'm looking for Dr. Curtiss."

"You're that FSB agent Sarai told us about."

She'd gotten to them first. "Yeah. And she's in big trouble. I need to find her. Now."

Anya raised her eyebrows. "Why?"

"I told you. She's in trouble. Your new governor, Bednov, is kicking out all foreigners, and if she doesn't leave in the next two days, she'll be arrested."

"By whom, you?"

Maybe. But he said nothing. Suddenly the room seemed to swirl, and he reached out for the wall.

"Sit down. I'll get you some tea." Anya disappeared as Roman cleared his head.

"No. I don't have time for tea." He followed her out into the hall. "Just tell me where she went."

Only, maybe he did need something, because another wave of dizziness washed over him. What was wrong with him? What if… Oh please, no. What if it was the effects of radiation poisoning? Finally?

He felt a cold sweat prickle his body.

He angled for an exam room. Okay, so maybe just two minutes, while Anya fetched Sarai. And some tea.

He sat on the table, rested his head on his hands. He knew he'd pay for Smirnov's crimes. Somehow. Regret lined his throat. It wasn't fair. Not after all he'd worked for.

"Here's your tea, young man." Anya came in, holding a cup, with a piece of black bread balanced on the rim. She watched him as he drank.

"You're not really going to arrest Sarai, are you."

It was more of a statement than a question. He glanced at Anya. "I'm with the FSB. I might not have any choice."

She sighed, crossed her arms. "If she needs to leave, why isn't her embassy calling?"

"They probably did. But she doesn't really stick around, does she?"

He got a hint of a smile.

"Her brother called me. He asked me to come get her." Roman wasn't sure why he might be passing this tidbit of covert information to Anya, but she hardly looked like a FSB spy. Besides, in the new era, even cops could have some American friends if they were careful. "Sarai and I knew each other years ago. I'm just trying to help her."

Anya made a silent O with her mouth, then pursed her lips and nodded. "I see."

Now what did that mean? "I'm just a friend."

"Then why did she run away from you?"

Good question. One he'd been trying to figure out for more than a decade. "She doesn't want to leave. But she has no choice. I just saw her picture on television, and soon they'll be offering rewards for information leading to her whereabouts."

Anya narrowed her eyes. "I don't know why, but I believe you. So you'd better be telling the truth." She pulled a piece of paper from her pocket. "She went to Khanda about two hours north of here." She handed him the paper, then, from the other pocket, Sarai's car keys. "Don't make me regret this."

Was Russia experiencing some sort of epidemic? Sarai could hardly believe her own diagnosis as she stared at ten-year-old Maxim Gordov. The village doctor, a young man who himself looked to be about twelve, stood at the foot of a double bed in the one-bedroom house. Under the green woolen blankets, and propped up by a homemade feather pillow, Maxim was shockingly yellow, his breathing shallow and giving off a sickly sweet scent. "I didn't know what else to do. It came on so fast. I just got the tests back this morning."

Sarai nodded, said nothing. Without the tests, for all Dr. Valya knew, little Maxim may have had the flu. But he should have been able to detect the renal failure in time to transport him to…where? Smolsk didn't have a dialysis machine. Maybe in Irkutsk… But if Maxim's case progressed like Sasha Bednov's, hope had died in the early morning when Max slipped into a coma.

His mother, Galina, stood in the doorway, her workworn hands covering her mouth, as if she couldn't bear to let out the groan that certainly formed in her throat. Her attire—wool *valenki* boots, a housecoat and a buttoned sweater over her thin body—identified her as a simple woman.

Maxim's father sat in the next room, head in his hands, moaning.

The weather mirrored their despair. The wind had begun to pick up, and Sarai had seen a wall of low-hanging gray clouds on her drive. This area of Irkutia province already bore the marks of winter—gray black snow along the roads, a blanket of pristine white over the fields, marred only by the occasional deer print. Ice dangled from the eaves over the door of Gordovs' wooden, blue-painted house like spears. Inside, the smell of coal smoke embedded the rug-covered walls, yet a layer of frost outlined the wooden window casing and a chill hung in the air. Sarai had kept on the *valenki* she'd taken from her office in the clinic. All the same, the home seemed a warm place, a cheery place.

So what did a ten-year-old village boy have to do with a rich governor's son?

She put her hand on Maxim's head, and frustration knotted in her throat. Perhaps she was just tired but she felt overwhelmed, helpless. She wanted to curl into a ball and sob.

Or maybe just surrender to Roman…and leave. Just run from the realities, the failures, the challenges.

Even if they got him on a plane to Moscow, Maxim probably wouldn't live out the day.

"Has he been sick?" She turned to Galina, who stepped into the room and crouched beside the bed, pushing back her son's hair.

"No. He's been fine. Maybe a bit tired lately. And he was sick a few days ago with the stomach flu, but that's all."

"No strep throat?" Sarai opened his mouth, flashed her penlight inside. Nothing to indicate an infection. "I'm going to set up an IV. Maybe I can flush whatever is causing his shutdown out of his system."

She didn't look at Galina as she prepped him and inserted an IV. She hung the bag from a chair. He didn't make a sound, didn't move.

"When did he lapse into a coma?" Sarai asked, checking his pulse. It was slow and thready.

"He had a seizure this morning when I woke him for

school." Galina's voice dropped to a whisper. "I was so afraid."

Sarai's throat felt thick. She looked at Valya. "Could I talk to you...privately?"

They stepped out into the street and, while the wind dug under her hat and a light dusting of snow floated from a steel gray sky, she told him the prognosis.

She stayed outside in the cold, her hands dug into her pockets while Valya returned inside. Even with two doors between her and the Gordovs, it didn't muffle the pain that radiated out, nor the effect it had on Sarai's spirit. Her throat burned.

Sarai pushed a hand into her stomach as she walked down the street, passing ramshackle houses fortified for winter. The smell of a storm hung in the air and snow fell thicker, accumulating beneath her boots. This area of northern Irkutia, smack in the middle of Siberia, wore snow cover from mid-October to May. The small town of Khanda had been formed during Khrushchev's reign as a labor pool to serve a local nuclear plant. Since the mid-nineties, however, when the reactor shut down, population sloughed off toward the larger cities, leaving the village hollow, devoid of life. Families like the Gordovs subsisted on tiny vegetable plots, and the lucky few found work at the various oil refineries that owned millions of *sotoks* of Siberian steppes. The Gordovs were lucky. Galina worked as a chef for one of the local oil companies.

No, not lucky. Not this day.

Darkened houses with their lifeless gaze watched Sarai

as she fought tears. She'd come to Russia to change the lives of kids like Maxim, and while she didn't hope to save everyone, the limitations of living on the backside of the world only churned up her frustration.

And now, just when she might be poised to make a difference, Roman wanted to yank her out of Russia.

She hoped he'd given up.

Not likely.

But she wasn't leaving. Not when there were people who needed her.

If she left, who would they have?

She turned and cut back toward the house, not sure what to say to the Gordovs. At least Maxim was past suffering. As if that might be any comfort to the parents of a dying child.

She stood at the entrance to their house, felt the grief inside and wiped her cheeks.

"I found you," said a quiet voice behind her.

Oh, no. How had he—never mind. Roman was a bloodhound for a living. She should have known that she'd never ditch him. Not unless he wanted to be ditched. She'd have to confront him. She closed her eyes. "Please, not now, Roman."

He reached out, touched her arm. "Are you okay?" The concern in his voice blindsided her and she felt herself loosening the chokehold on her grief.

"I'll be fine. Just…"

"Sarai." He forcibly turned her, tucked his hand under her chin and raised her gaze to his.

His hazel eyes clouded, and for the first time since

he'd forced his way back into her life, she saw emotion—concern, even empathy.

It only made the little knot of pain in the center of her chest release and spill open. Rebellious tears pooled in her eyes, and she tried to look away.

He didn't let her. "Sarai, what's the matter?"

She closed her eyes. "There's a ten-year-old boy in there who's going to die by tonight."

His "Oh, no," felt more like a groan. Then, because of the hero he was, he pulled her to his chest and held her.

She didn't resist, didn't pull away but put her arms around him. Holding on. Despite the stranger he'd become, he'd been the man who first made her feel protected. And in this pocket of time, she could admit she needed that right now.

"Sarai, I'm sorry." His hand ran down her hair, and she couldn't help but relish his strong arms around her. Or the fact that under his black parka she felt hard muscles and a strength that spoke of safety.

"Me, too."

She leaned back, looked up at him and tried not to let the concern in his eyes sink too deeply into her heart. *He's just a friend. My brother's friend. And...probably he's just trying to get on my good side.*

"Now do you see why I have to stay, Roma? Because more kids will die if I don't help them."

He was silent for a moment, then he looked away from her. "You can't save them all."

"I can try. If I don't, who will?"

Roman shook his head as if in frustration. "What's wrong with this kid?"

"He's got renal failure. And the weird thing is that it's the second case in twenty-four hours. Governor Bednov's son died yesterday of this very condition. I don't know why, but I can't help but wonder if they're related." She disentangled herself from Roman's too intoxicating embrace and found rest on a stump near the door.

Roman didn't move to follow. In fact, he stared at her with an odd expression. "Renal failure? Um, do you know what brought it on?"

"Not the slightest. Julia Bednov told me her son had been sick for a while, and she thought he might have picked up something at their dacha this summer. I'll need to ask the ME to do an autopsy on both boys."

Roman stalked away from her. "We need to talk about you locking me in your apartment."

Did they? "Sorry about that. But you need to stop with this…agenda. I'm not leaving. I thought I made that clear."

Roman said nothing, and she watched him stare away from her, out into the fields surrounding the village, his hands on his narrow hips, his wide shoulders reminding her of David, and just how much he trained for his job. Under all that fluffy jacket, Roman had the same build as her big brother.

One that meant he could force her to leave if he really wanted to. "Please, Roman, just go."

"Is that an oil field?"

What? Sarai frowned at him as he glanced at her over his

shoulder. "Yeah, I think so. A lot of folks in town work for Alexander Oil."

"Really." Roman wore a strange look as he came and sat beside her. His presence felt familiar. Although he'd turned into a stranger, he was still the man of determination she'd once known. She saw that much on his expression.

Apparently he could still be remarkably kind, too. "I'm sorry I ditched you," she said softly.

He dug a phone from his pocket. "Me, too. Because the clock is ticking, and I'm not sure I can get us out of here before you're illegal."

She let that statement absorb a beat before it registered. "You can't be serious. Have you not listened to one thing I said? What if there are other children in this village who are ill? I need to check them out, see if I can catch it before another child ends up like Maxim, or Sasha."

But Roman was on the telephone, and he only glanced at her. Jerk.

She stood, strode away from him.

"Yanna, it's me. I need you to check into something for me. Find out where all the decommissioned reactors are near Khanda, Irkutia. I think I may have stumbled onto something. Also, get me a list of shareholders for Alexander Oil."

Sarai watched him as he ran his hand through his hair, then rubbed his eyes. He looked tired. Even a bit pale. And no, she shouldn't worry about him. Not one bit.

He gave a wry chuckle and glanced at her. She looked away

but heard him as he said, “No. She’s still as stubborn as before.”

What? Sarai glared at him and he met her eyes. His chuckle faded. “Okay. Just…if you can route the call to me, that would be great. But listen, don’t get yourself into any more trouble. I’ll deal with it when I get back.”

Sarai returned to the stump, watch Roman rub his eyes with his thumb and forefinger as he talked.

“Yeah, well, maybe you can come visit me.” He glanced at Sarai. Smiled. And her heart did a strange leap in her chest. “Okay, I’ll tell her. Thanks.”

He clicked off, staring at his telephone.

And suddenly, she knew. “You’re not supposed to be here, are you?”

He huffed, and gave a wry smile, but didn’t look at her.

“You’re AWOL, aren’t you?”

“I’m just on a little…unauthorized field trip.”

“I cannot believe the lengths you and David will go to—”

“Sarai! Enough. Do you think I like dragging myself all the way out here in the middle of the night only to tick you off and get locked in your flat? Do you think I like chasing all over the world after you, worrying all the time if you’re safe or not, and wondering when I’m going to either have to bail you out—for the warm thank you of a slap across my face—or hear of your untimely death at the hands of local terrorists? You think that’s fun for me?”

She opened her mouth, closed it. Saw only the anger on

his face. Her brain had stopped on the words *worrying all the time.*

He worried about her?

No. Probably he worried if David was going to call him up and ask him to put his job on the line so he could save her not-needing-to-be-saved body.

"I don't need your help," she said softly.

"I know," he snapped, as he got up and looked away. "But just for once, will you accept my help, even if it curdles every independent cell in your body?"

She sighed, glanced at the house. Mr. Sacrifice for the cause. Well, she wasn't going to be the one who made him lose his job. "Just…wait here. I need to talk to Valya."

He only clenched his jaw as she got up, gave him a half smile and went into the house.

Chapter Seven

He had to have *kasha* for brains. Or perhaps the temperature had dropped so low his brain synapses had frozen up, because while one side of Roman's brain knew, just *knew* that her "okay, I'll go along nicely" routine had been an act, the other side made him stand out in the yard watching the snow blanket the tin roofs of the two- and three-room village homes. Even when he heard an engine fire up and a vehicle pull away, reality didn't whack him upside the head until he finally charged into the house.

Of course she'd gone out the back. Why had he ever considered her a calming force in his life? She felt more like a tornado.

He raced back outside, climbed into her Camry, hung a U-turn and floored it out of Khanda toward Smolsk. Where would she go? He popped on his headlights, and in the encroaching darkness saw taillights of the ambulance she'd driven as she lumbered onto the main thoroughfare.

Hatlichna! She was headed toward Smolsk. Maybe he had talked some sense into her and her pride just didn't want to admit it. Hopefully she would just keep driving straight and right into Buryatia province.

Yeah, and maybe he wouldn't be cleaning toilets in gulag this time next week.

Roman slammed his hand against the steering wheel. The car shimmied on the road and he slowed. Snow layered the road like icing and, as he drove out of town into the blinding whiteness of the encroaching blizzard, he had to double-grip the wheel. The heater couldn't keep up with the cold and he felt his feet begin to grow numb. Ahead of him, Sarai's taillights—at least he hoped they were Sarai's—cut through the gauze of snow like a blood-red knife.

He shook his head. At this rate, they'd get back to Smolsk sometime tomorrow morning…early. But in sufficient time for their window.

And maybe, hopefully, he'd have a job to go back to. A job that right now centered on finding the supplier of Russia's most dangerous—and toxic—commodity.

Highly Enriched Uranium.

Roman cut his speed as the taillights became clearer. Better to let her think that she'd left him standing in Smolsk. Then, at least she wouldn't do anything crazy like…

What? Ditching the one person who wanted to talk sense into her?

Or, maybe, fleeing from the one person who wanted to

derail her goals. Sarai had always been a driving force, someone who parted the waters and got the job done. But at what expense this time? Her freedom and probably his.

In less than two days, the pictures in the newspaper and on television would morph from information gathering to at-large posters. And, if Bednov turned serious, there might even be a reward.

In the middle of economy-ravished Siberia, reward money just might put food on a farmer's table for an entire winter. Buy the family a new cow, some warm clothes or coal.

Roman focused on the taillights. Where was she going? Hadn't she said she needed to stay in town and check the other children? Renal failure. Her words had triggered suspicions, and now he let them free to roam about his thoughts. Barry Riddle had suffered from renal failure. His passport had listed Irkutsk, and he'd been affiliated with Alexander Oil. However, Alexander Oil had wells across Russia, from Omsk to Yakutia to Sakhalin Island.

Still, what if Alexander Oil had property on or near a decommissioned reactor? Especially a reactor that might still have unused HEU in its storehouse?

The possibility probably merited a field trip, if not a sneak and peek, to the Alexander Oil offices.

Frankly, finding the HEU supplier might be the only way to keep him out of gulag. Sarai's lights ahead turned off to the right. Roman eased off the gas, slowed and took the turn at a crawl. Darkness had settled like a cloud, dissected only by his headlights and the thick snow. He kept back from

Sarai's car, hoping that her attention was so affixed on the road ahead she wouldn't bother to look behind her.

Because, obviously, she wasn't headed for Smolsk.

He tried not to let that fact dig a hole in his gut. Apparently, she had no problem cutting him right out of her life. Even after she'd discovered he'd risked his own neck for her.

Some things never changed.

Like, the way her eyes turned the darkest shade of sea green when she was upset. Or the way she wrinkled her nose when she disagreed, as if even his words might be odorous. Still, he couldn't help but notice that her freckles had never faded, and in summer probably made her look about twenty-one.

Or, maybe she'd simply be always about twenty-one to him. Because the woman who'd gone toe-to-toe with him, twice in the last eighteen hours, and ditched him, ahem, also *twice,* certainly wasn't the carefree ray of sunshine he'd fallen for in Moscow.

No, this Sarai version seemed driven. Even desperate.

As if she might be trying to prove something.

Well, weren't they all? Except, what did Sarai have to prove? She didn't have a legacy of alcoholism, of die-hard adherence to a passel of lies. She didn't have memories of watching his father go from refined businessman to drunken bum, of taking the blows when his father turned his disillusionment on Roman's mother. Or seeing his mother pack her things and leave.

Her father hadn't hit Sarai across the face when he found out his child had become a Christian. Or called her a traitor.

Thankfully, the Russian army had believed in the soldier they'd already spent two years in training, and two more in language training at Moscow University. Little did they know when they took Roman on for special operations training, preaching a new Russia, that he'd already found something else in which to believe.

Without David Curtiss and his grace-filled friendship, Roman might still be trapped in the hurt of his father's failures. Because of David's courage in sharing the gospel, Roman had hope in something better than the legacy his father had left behind.

And, for that reason alone, Roman zeroed in on Sarai's taillights, ignoring the swell of frustration as he pressed into the blizzard.

Sarai wiped her face with her gloved hand. It shouldn't be much farther, but if she didn't find Anya's dacha soon, she'd be in big trouble. She'd gambled—probably foolishly—by trying to find Genye and Anya's summer home to hole up in during the storm and during this supposed foreigner crackdown. She wasn't leaving, no way, no how, but Roman's words had rattled her.

Especially when he'd admitted that he'd worried about her. Enough to go AWOL.

She didn't know what the Russian FSB did to soldiers who disobeyed orders, but her limited knowledge of America's policy had her wincing.

Roman had put himself in danger professionally, and probably personally, because of her.

Go home, Roma. She wasn't leaving, but she hoped he'd gotten the message and left her.

As much as that thought tore a hole in her heart.

Do you think I like chasing all over the world after you, worrying all the time if you're safe or not?

Maybe she shouldn't focus so much on his words as his tone—exasperation. He sounded a lot like David when he'd pulled her out of Somalia.

Well, maybe she wouldn't be risking her life alone if Roman had been true to his Christian calling. Hadn't he told her that he wanted to be God's man, to change the world one person at a time? Hadn't he told her he'd give up everything for the gospel?

Sadly, she thought he'd meant in missions. Apparently, she and Roman had different definitions of "surrendering all" for God.

She leaned forward, gripping the steering wheel. She'd turned her lights on low beam—the high beams only made the snow seem like bullets spraying her. As she traveled north, jack pines and birch towered over the road, jagged arms that reached into the black sky and vanished. The wind swirled up drifts, cracked the trees and shook the ambulance. Although she had the heat on full, her toes felt cold, her nose an ice block. Inside her gloves, she balled her fists, hoping for warmth.

Please, Lord, get me to their dacha safely. And protect

Roma, wherever he is. She hoped he had the good sense to stay in Khanda.

So maybe that didn't say much about her own good sense.

She counted kilometers—thirty from the main highway—and slowed as she came up on thirty-six. She'd visited the dacha countless times in the summer, even spent a week with Genye and Anya once in the fall, enjoying *shashleek* and freshly harvested vegetables. Genye and Anya had winterized their dacha years ago, turning it from a summer garden home to a year-round retreat. And, they'd added two downstairs bedrooms, an upstairs bunkroom, a sauna and a main room. Stateside, she supposed it would be called a cabin. Stateside, it would also have indoor plumbing.

She crept along the road, plowing through the drifts, gunning the ambulance just enough to keep it from getting stuck, yet not fast enough to lose control. Dark branches, laden with ice and snow, streaked across her side windows. The sound raised gooseflesh.

Her stomach felt tied in knots. She hoped Genye and Anya had left some food behind.

She muscled the ambulance up a knoll, mentally calculating the half-click or so to the dacha, when her lights flashed on an object.

A deer stood in the middle of the road. Frozen and wide-eyed.

Sarai slammed on her brakes. The wheels locked up, she tried to get them to gain purchase, but the ambulance began to slide.

She worked the steering wheel, which laughed at her efforts. Helpless, she slid toward the deer. She watched, as if in slow motion, as the animal darted off into the forest.

She kept sliding. Slower, but with enough momentum still to careen off the road and settle with a poof into the ditch.

Sarai rocked back into the seat and slammed her hand into the steering wheel. Super. Just what she needed.

She put the vehicle into reverse, spun the wheels a bit, opened the door to check her progress and smelled rubber burning. She climbed out and surveyed the damage. Snow, up to the axles, nearly lifted the ambulance from the ground. She wasn't moving without a shovel, and maybe a tow.

Now what?

Silence around her felt soft and thick as snow sifted down from the blackened canopy. She heard only her heartbeat as she dug out her penlight, closed the car door, pulled down her cap and trudged into the darkness. She flicked the light on now and again to keep her bearings and hunkered her chin down into her jacket.

She tried not to let her thoughts tangle into the what-ifs. Like, what if she had seen the deer earlier? Or what if she hadn't left Khanda? Or what if she'd returned even one of Roman's telephone calls thirteen years ago?

Then he might be right here, in the ditch with her, helping her dig out.

No, she wouldn't even *be* in the ditch.

She hunched her shoulders against the cold and fought

the claw of sadness. Seeing Roman had only tightened the sharp band of regret around her chest.

No, not regret. Reality. He was sold out for his job. She was sold out for God. Anyone with their eyes wide open could see that difference.

Her legs felt nearly frozen by the time she found the dacha nestled under a canopy of poplar and aspen trees. The cabin wore a blanket of white frosting, and snow crunched as she climbed the steps and eased the door open.

Inside, time stood frozen, the remnants of summer caught in winter's grasp. She flashed her penlight into the main room. A batch of now-golden dill hung upside down near the window to dry crackled in the stiff wind that followed her in. A bunch of wilted daisies dusted the table top with their teardrop offerings. The place felt bone cold, shrouded under the blanket of winter. Sarai tried the light. Nothing.

Okay, this didn't have to be hard. One step at a time. She'd start a fire in the stove, then search for food.

Then hunker down for a few days. Just until the craziness in Irkutsk subsided and she could sneak back into Smolsk.

Besides, what did the Russian government want with a small-time frontier doctor in the middle of nowhere? Roman was overreacting.

Thankfully, Genye had stocked the wood bin, both inside and outside, before they'd left a month or so ago. Sarai filled the stove, found an old newspaper and lit it. It clawed at the wood, but the breath of winter had moistened it and the flame smoked out.

Sarai tried again, blowing gently, feeding in twigs. *C'mon little fire…*

The door slammed open, caught by a gust of wind. Ashes spewed out of the potbelly stove as Sarai turned, startled.

Froze.

When would he give up?

Chapter Eight

If Roman read her correctly, Sarai wasn't that displeased to see him.

Mostly displeased, perhaps, but he saw definite relief around the outside of her eyes as he shone his flashlight on her and closed the door.

For his part, relief took over his body and wrung him out, nearly buckling his knees. *Thank you, Lord.* He'd seen her car in the ditch, found her tracks and had pictured head wounds or even broken bones.

But no, here she sat, Miss "I'm fine on my own" making herself a cozy little fire. "Found you," he said as he came into the room, disguising well his unhinged emotions. She said nothing, just narrowed her eyes, watching him as he knelt next to her.

Or, maybe relief wasn't the right word for what he saw

in her eyes. Try, resignation. Good. She should get used to his following her. Like a lovesick puppy.

Oy.

"I wish you'd stop trying to ditch me." He picked up a log, looked it over, pulled out a compact pocketknife and peeled off a layer, cutting it into tiny strips. He tucked the bark around the paper and the logs she'd layered in the stove. "Matches."

She slapped them into his hand, still, silent. Uh-oh, not good.

He took off his gloves and lit the match, then the paper in several places. He blew on it gently to catch the kindling he'd cut. In a moment, the flames settled on a thick piece of pine and began to crackle.

He closed the door halfway. She sat back, tucked her hands around her updrawn knees, watching him. "Thanks."

He rubbed his hair. Snow flaked off it, but his scalp felt like ice.

"I don't want you to get in trouble on account of me." Her voice sounded muffled, and he realized she had rested her head into her arms.

She looked cold. Snow encrusted hair curled out of her cap. He reached over and wrapped his hand around the end, warming it with his hand.

"It might be too late for that."

"Fine. Then, sorry. But you made your choice. No one asked you to come and get me."

Well…that wasn't *quite* true. If he was honest, even if

David hadn't asked, as soon as Roman had discovered Bednov's deadline, he would have been on a plane and headed her direction.

As much as he hated to admit it.

"Please, Sarai, help me help you. They've already started to post your picture on the news." He reached into his jacket. "If you hadn't taken off, I would have shown this to you." He pulled out a newspaper. Inside, thumbnail pictures of foreigners in the Irkutia province filled the page A-4. "See?"

Sarai stared at it, a horrified look on her face. What was it about him that repelled her, but only made *him* want to pull her into his arms?

It had felt too good the first time, back at her clinic, despite its brevity. And the second, when he'd comforted her over her sick patient—she'd lingered just a little. Like she needed him, cultivating all his stifled protective urges. If he got too close to her again, he just might do something foolish, like kiss her.

No, that would be so much more than foolish because, while he might still love Sarai, painfully more than he had thirteen years ago, she couldn't stand him. And wouldn't that be fun, laying out his heart for her so she could leave it cold and alone when she left him—again. And again.

She's not the same girl you fell in love with in Moscow. And a man who ferreted out criminals for a living, reading hints and relying on his gut should face the Dear John truth.

"Don't you see?" he asked softly. "We need to get you out of here."

She folded up the paper and smiled sweetly. "I've been in countries before when my visa's expired or been revoked. The right people, the right strings pulled and I'll be reinstated in no time." She handed him back the paper, looked at the flickering flames. "Besides, why do you think I came here? I fully plan on laying low for a few days, so don't worry. You can be on your merry way."

He barely choked back his disbelief. "Your picture is in the paper. *Zdrastvootya?* What more do you need, a 'Wanted' label under it?"

She rolled her eyes. "If you leave now, you can make it back to Smolsk before the storm gets really bad."

Roman rested his forehead on his palms, fighting frustration. Well, at least she knew she should keep her head down. For now. One step forward… And, they still had forty-eight hours, right?

Hopefully, tomorrow he could talk her into more. "I'm not going anywhere. My car's in the ditch beside yours."

She shook her head, but he saw the smallest of smirks lift one side of her mouth. Such a pretty mouth…

"Stop. What do you expect? It wasn't like you left your flashers on. I nearly went through the windshield," Roman said.

"Forgive me, O Bloodhound. If I had known you were following me, I would have put out semaphores, of course."

He gave her a mock glare. "Where are we, anyway? I hope we haven't committed yet another crime."

She looked disgusted. "Anya and Genye's dacha."

He made a silent O with his mouth as he got up. "Got

anything to eat here?" He strolled over to the tiny kitchen composed of a two-burner gas stove, an electric oven and fridge and a small two door cupboard. Inside, he found cans of salmon, a bag of sugar, tea, crackers and a jar of raspberry preserves.

He took out the salmon and began fishing for an opener. He heard Sarai rise. The floor creaked as she moved into the kitchen.

"David tells me you're a captain now. Of your own Cobra team. That's pretty impressive." Sarai took off her hat and hung it on the rack by the door. She stood there, her hands woven into her jacket sleeves, and when he glanced at her, he couldn't help notice that she appeared tired.

"You okay, Sar?"

She looked at him, gave a half smile. "I always knew you'd go far."

He let those words settle into his chest. "Thanks. I'm amazed at what you've done, also. You've always…taken my breath away."

Oops. He hadn't quite meant that as it sounded. Or maybe he did. She swallowed, and he turned his attention to the can opener. For a moment, all he heard was the slush of his pulse in his ears.

When she said nothing, he sighed and dredged up words from the clog of emotions in his chest. He could keep this nonchalant, without giving too much away, couldn't he?

"I meant your aspirations were always so noble, I just couldn't keep up."

She pulled out a chair, sat. "It's not like you to just sit

around and do nothing. David told me about the Epcot thing." She paused, smiled. He watched it out of his peripheral vision and tried not to wince. "The thing is, it still took courage, and I know you're only trying to save the world, in your own way."

Well, maybe not the world. Just Sarai at the moment. The world would come later.

"I'll bet your dad is proud of you." She said it so softly, he barely caught it.

"Hardly." He tried to keep the bitterness from his voice. "He died, Sarai. Drank himself into a stupor and froze to death." He put the open can of salmon on the table.

"Oh, Roma. I'm so sorry." She reached out to his arm, and he tried not to let it undo him. "Did you two…reconcile before—"

"No. I never went to see him."

She said nothing.

He clenched his jaw, fighting a sudden rush of emotions. "How about I make some tea?"

"You're not him, Roma. I know you think you are, but you'll never be him. And I'll tell you why."

He didn't look at her as he found the teakettle. Snow would melt, make water.

"Because you're a Christian. And no matter what happens, your life matters. Maybe not the way I want it to, but you're a man of principle and salt and light in your world. I know because David tells me everything, and you're like a brother to him."

He glanced at her, dangerously aware of how much that

meant to him. "Thanks." Carrying the kettle, he moved to step past her, outside, but she caught his sleeve.

"I worry about you, too."

He opened his mouth, but nothing emerged.

"And, deep in my heart, I know someday you're going to die. And I won't be there to stop it."

He set the kettle on the table. She wanted to have this conversation *now?* What about ten plus years ago? "I'm not going to get killed, Sarai."

"You will. And then.... I don't want to be there when it happens." She let his sleeve go, looked away, as if that might be the end of the conversation.

Not quite. He pulled out a chair, straddled it backward. "And what about you? It's not like you don't go around risking your life. I think you have this knack for picking the hot spots in the world. Have you any idea how your brother—all of us—worry about you?"

She crossed her arms over her chest. "At least I'm doing it for the right reasons."

"I knew it! You still think I'm out to make a name for myself, don't you?"

Even in the shadows of the dacha, he could see her eyes flash. "Yes. Okay, I do. I think you're trying to prove you're not your father. That you're not going to end up like him."

"Thanks, Sarai, for that sensitivity, as well as your vote of confidence. Did it ever occur to you that I am just trying to be the guy God created me to be? Not everyone can save lives—and souls. Some of us are cut from a different cloth. Besides, don't tell me you don't get a little high when you save a life. Don't tell me that there isn't a piece of you that sees herself as a savior to these people."

"I don't." She sat back, folded her arms across her chest. "I'm here for eternal purposes. I share the gospel, I tell people that Jesus loves them as I heal them."

"You heal them."

"*God* heals them. For crying out loud." She shook her head. "At least, when I die, it'll be for a good reason."

"Oh, yeah, I forgot, you're a martyr." He rose, turned the chair around.

She looked away, out the window. But, when he glanced at her he saw that her chin trembled.

"I'm not a martyr, Roma." Her voice dropped and he heard tears on the far edge. "Don't you think that I get lonely. Discouraged? That I want to give up and just go home. And get married and…have kids…"

Oh. Wow. He froze, pretty sure that if he didn't, he might do something stupid, like pull her into his arms. Because her words felt raw and vulnerable, and the look on her face, as if she'd surprised herself, made his chest hurt.

Look what we could have had.

"Do you have anyone you want to get married to?" he asked softly. Was he now a glutton for pain?

She gave a huff of what he'd label exasperation, or maybe quick cover. All the same, it felt like a stake through his heart. "No. Of course not. I'm just saying that I'm not the girl that you and David and my parents label me—"

"No one is labeling you."

"You are. You think I'm just some sort of renegade doctor, risking my life—"

"Okay, that's true, I concede—"

"But I'm just trying to be the girl God made me to be. All my life I wanted to be a doctor. I saw it as my way to fulfill the Great Commission." She glanced at him, and he saw hurt in her eyes. "As if you'd know anything about that. The only reason you ever liked me, if at all, was because I was David's little sister and you thought I was easy prey. Guess you were wrong, huh?"

He opened his mouth, feeling gut punched. "That is not true. You know it. I loved you. And you shattered me when you left."

Oh, no, why did he have to say *that?* But she always knew how to ignite his emotions. Like a match to tinder.

She looked at him, her beautiful green eyes wide.

Yes, that's right, Sarai, I'm still in love with you. I never stopped and just being near you dredges up the feelings I've been trying to ignore…or dodge for way too long. The words formed in his thoughts, but stuck like gum in his chest. Please, let him not be so stupid as to let them out.

He grabbed the teakettle. "I'm fine now. It's over. I got it after you spent three months not returning my calls, and about thirteen years not talking to me. But in case you're wondering, I *did* love you. That was real. And so is my concern for you when I tell you that you're going to be in big trouble if you stay in Irkutsk." His voice sounded as if he were talking through a grate. Rough edged. Broken.

She looked up at him as he stood there—why wasn't he

moving?—and in her eyes he saw question. Doubt. And just a little anger.

Then, just like that she blinked it away.

Just like she'd blinked him away so long ago.

He should have expected as much. He stalked outside, into the snow and filled the teakettle.

She was so over him that it made him wonder if she'd *ever* loved him.

But before that thought could wound him, he stilled. Listened. Yes, voices. And the dart of a light.

He dropped the kettle, dashed back into the cabin. Sarai stood at the sink, opening the jar of preserves. She jumped as he slammed the door open.

"We have company. I want you to get into the other room and stay low." Oh, no, the fire had already betrayed them. How could he have been so—

"What on earth are you talking about?" She turned, opener in hand. "No one is out to get me."

"We don't know that, do we?"

She just stood there. He took two strides and scooped her up. The can opener fell with a clatter into the sink. "Roman!"

"*Tiha!*" He ignored the way she pushed against his chest and strode into the back bedroom. "Will you just trust me for once?"

"Put me down," she gritted, but her voice stayed low. Good girl.

He set her down in the tiny bedroom. "Stay here. Close the door."

Her eyes widened. "You're scaring me."

"Finally," he snapped. Then he closed the door behind him.

"Stop it, Julia." Bednov stood over her as she slumped across the kitchen table. The kitchen that he'd spent thousands of his hard earned rubles to remodel. Did she think that it wouldn't come without a price?

He barely stopped himself from grabbing her hair, yanking her to her feet. "You knew Katya had to be dealt with." He reached for the vodka bottle, took a swig before he wiped his mouth and capped it.

"She was only trying to help."

"She knew about Khanda. Do you think that American doctor won't figure out how Sasha got sick?" He shook his head. "You're so stupid."

She lifted her head, stared at him with red-rimmed eyes. Oy, she looked rough, with greasy hair, no makeup. And she smelled like a garbage Dumpster. "She took care of Sasha since he was a baby. She was like family."

"She was a liability."

He saw Julia's eyes harden, saw coherency for the first time in two days. "I know why Sasha died, Alexei. And I'll make sure you pay for it."

He hit her. She screamed, fell out of her chair onto the floor. He didn't need this. Not now. He'd worked too long, too hard for this time. His time. He left her there, crying, and went in search of Fyodor. He'd personally chosen Fyodor from the Spetsnaz. The former soldier would know how to track down the American.

And kill her before she discovered a link back to Bednov.

He'd do it for Russia.

And, if he planned it right, it wouldn't even be a crime.

"He's gone completely over the top, Anya," Sarai said as she peeled a potato. "By the way, that's American slang for 'lost it.' He thinks I'm going to be some sort of international fugitive or something."

Anya smiled at her as she picked up another potato. Her blond hair stuck out from under a white beret, and she still wore her sweater, despite the fact the fire had driven the chill to the far corners of the cabin. Across the room, Roman slouched in a fraying armchair, brooding as he read the paper in the firelight. Maybe he'd find a diabolical plot to kill the president somewhere in those pages.

"I think he's acting like a man in love." Anya smirked as she dropped another peeled potato in the water.

"You're being particularly nice considering the fact that he nearly jumped you and Genye."

Paralyzed by shock, Sarai could only listen as Roman crept out into the main room, waiting for her "attackers." She'd cracked the door enough to watch him pounce as Genye opened the front door.

They seemed pretty evenly matched for too long a moment as they rolled out onto the stoop and into the snow.

Her pulse jerked every time she remembered Roman stopping mid-punch, jarred by her scream as he pinned Genye, his armed cocked to drive his fist into Genye's jaw.

Roman had looked at her, and she'd seen something that

still rattled her. Fear. Cold, straight out, fear. As if she might be hurt.

Obviously he had no problem pouncing to protect her, even if it might be from her dearest friends. Although, was it protecting her, or completing his mission to kick her out of Russia? At the least, he proved he'd become nothing but the shoot-first-ask-later cowboy she'd feared.

She dropped the potato she was peeling into the pot. "He's not in love with me, Anya," she whispered, casting a look at Roman. Even now he seemed like tightly coiled danger sitting there, his long legs stretched out and crossed at the ankles, his arms thick in his thermal shirt. The glow from the stove turned the highlights in his golden brown hair to fire, softened the hard planes of his face. He'd always been cute, but over the years he'd turned hard-edged handsome, with a fierceness to him that both scared her and drew her.

Much like how she'd felt when he'd scooped her up into his arms. And, for the briefest of insane moments, she'd wanted to just stay there.

"He's just an old friend. My brother sent him here to find me." Sarai raised her voice. "To kidnap me and yank me out of the country."

"Not kidnap. As long as you come willingly," said a voice from across the room. He didn't look up from the paper.

"See. He's out to wreck my life." She picked up another potato. Behind her, she heard the paper snap closed, perhaps with even a little tearing. She couldn't help but smile.

"I'm going out to help Genye hook up the electricity or

something." Roman swept by, grabbed his coat and slammed the door behind him.

Anya raised her eyebrows as she watched him leave. "I think his pride might be a bit bruised."

"Or his ego. He's the most frustrating, determined, aggravating man I've ever—"

"Oh, so you're in love with him, too."

Sarai looked up, threw her potato into the water. "I'm not. Maybe I once was."

Fearing for Sarai after contacting Dr. Valya in Khanda, Anya and Genye had set out to find her. When the storm worsened, they'd headed north, to Anya's dacha, praying that Sarai had thought along the same lines. They'd brought with them warm clothes for Sarai and the key to their root cellar.

Anya rose, stood over the pot of borscht and cut her potato into it. "*Maybe* you were in love?"

Sarai gathered the potato shavings and dumped them into the compost basket. "Okay. Yes, *probably* I was. I mean, it felt like that at the time."

Anya stayed silent, picked up another potato. But her blue eyes lingered on Sarai's.

Sarai sighed, sat back down and wiped her hands on a towel. "We met the summer before medical school. I came over to visit David. He was going to Moscow University. The first time I saw Roman, he was playing street hockey with David. He had on a sleeveless shirt and a pair of sweatpants, and when he smiled at me I thought I felt the earth move. I should have sensed the warning then, but I fell for his charm like a teenager. He was right out of the military, going to school to learn English before he went off to their version of FBI school. But, you see, he was a brand-new Christian, so I thought, well, maybe he could use all that energy for something else."

Sarai twisted the towel in her hands. A candle flickered on the table, dim luminance in the darkness. Outside, night pushed against the windowpanes and hid the wind that rattled the door. "I guess I fooled myself into thinking that he wanted to do what I wanted to do—spread the gospel by helping people. I remember once, as we were riding the Ferris wheel at Gorky Park, he told me he wanted to do what it took to save lives and souls." She glanced at him outside, in the pale light of a lantern, cutting wood. He had strong arms and a stance that made swinging the ax a sort of mesmerizing dance. "I guess he was just trying to get me to kiss him."

She blinked away the memory of his success, of being wrapped in his embrace under a full moon while it waxed the Volga River. Yeah, at the time, she'd done a great job of lying to herself.

"The thing that hurt the most was that he seemed so perfect. Safe. I could see us together, wherever, working to save lives. He was such a great guy—compassionate, brave, sure about his faith. I got involved in the Bible League while I was in town, and we staged some outreach events, including one at an orphanage. Roman went along—I suspect to make sure I didn't get into any trouble—but he rounded up the kids and started a game of tag. I watched him, Anya.

He laughed and goofed around with them, and you should have seen their faces. A real live Russian hero, a soldier, playing with them."

Sarai's eyes burned. "He was tender, sweet and kind and I probably fell in love with him right then."

"And never stopped loving him." Anya set down her knife, sat across from Sarai. "What happened?"

Sarai pressed her fingertips along the corners of her eyes. And here she thought she'd finished crying over Roman Novik. "The Moscow coup. It was near the end of my visit, and somehow I knew that things were going to be over. I kept hinting that maybe he shouldn't be a soldier, that maybe he could join the Bible League. But he dodged the subject, with the skill of, well, a soldier. The day of the coup really drove reality home."

She closed her eyes, back in Red Square, hearing the explosions, the screams. "I was handing out Bibles near Lenin's Tomb on Red Square, and suddenly I heard tanks rumbling down the street. Then gunfire. I didn't know what was happening. I took off toward GYM—that department store on the other side of the square—and nearly made it to the entrance when suddenly someone jumped me. Right there on the cobblestones. Wow, that hurt, but not as much as it would have if I'd kept running. A Molotov cocktail—one of those bottle bombs—went off right next to me. All I remember is screaming, and then a soothing, calm voice in my ear, telling me not to be afraid."

"Roman's."

"Of course. He'd been looking for me, and I think he

might have saved my life." Sarai sighed, aware now that it was useless to try to stop crying. "Only, he'd been hit and was bleeding."

She'd sat up, dazed, hurt, and very afraid. And then she'd taken a look at Roman and her world dimmed. Right then she saw the future. Saw him beaten, bloody and then dead—in the line of duty. And knew that her heart would shatter into a bazillion pieces if she stayed with him.

"He's a soldier, Anya. And I can't change that. He's not interested in being a missionary. He doesn't give a second thought to risking his life."

Anya smiled, covered Sarai's hand with hers. "A lot like someone else I know."

Sarai opened her mouth. Closed it. Then, "It's not the same thing. I'd die for a good cause. Besides, I'm not in any danger."

Anya nodded slowly. "What exactly does Roman do?"

"I guess he catches bad guys. Risks his life, just like David, to save the world."

"Why?"

"I dunno. Because maybe that's what he's good at—"

Anya raised one eyebrow. "So, would you say he's called to be a cop? That God intended him for that?"

Sarai narrowed her eyes. "Stop, Anya."

"No, you stop. Just because you're supposed to be a doctor and missionary, doesn't mean everyone is."

"I know that."

"You don't believe it."

"I do."

"Just not for Roman."

"I asked him once if he considered being a missionary. He told me that not everyone is cut out to do that. But he *is* cut out for it. I know it. What's worse, he's going to die, and it'll be for no good reason."

Anya leaned back, arms akimbo. "Like, ah, saving the world?"

Sarai looked away, at the crackling flames in the stove.

"I think this has more to do with your fear of him getting killed than your disappointment in him. I think you fell in love with him because he was charming, but also brave. He embodied the kind of person you respect. Then, seeing him bloody really hit home exactly who he was, and scared you all the way to America and out of his life. And I think you carry your self-righteousness as a barricade to losing your heart to him."

Sarai opened her mouth. Ouch. When did Anya develop X-ray vision to see all the way to her heart? "That's not true. If he were here, helping me, we'd be risking our lives together. He just has so much potential to be more. And he's blown it."

"I'm thrilled you think so highly of me," said a low voice.

Sarai looked up. Roman stood in the doorway, wearing a dark expression.

Chapter Nine

"You know, some women might be *pleased* that they had a guy around to protect them." Roman stalked across the room and dropped the armload of wood into the bin. He turned, brushing off his jeans, his black parka.

"I don't need a—"

"Hero. I know." He shook his head. "Believe me, I know." He advanced toward her just as she bounced to her feet. "Sadly, you'd better get used to it, because like it or not, you've got one."

He left her standing there as he strode out into the cold for another load of wood.

"You okay?" Genye asked as he passed him.

Roman said nothing, letting the snow wash over him and cool the fine layer of sweat on his brow. He gathered the logs he'd spent the past ten minutes chopping and turned back to the dacha.

Sarai stood on the porch, wearing her parka, hunched against the wind. The wind caught her hair, ran it into her eyes. "Can I help?"

Nyet. "Yeah. Try to remember that I'm on your side."

She leaned against the railing as he tromped in past her. Only, she didn't follow him inside.

Women. He dumped the load, then cast a look at Genye, loading the fire, and stalked back outside.

The snow continued to fall, burying them in its frozen grasp. But under the gleam of the outside light the drifting of gentle flakes seemed wondrous in their softness. Sarai stood against the railing, staring out into the darkness, her hands in her sleeves. She was shivering slightly, but would she put on a hat, or even go back inside?

Nyet. Because she didn't think about herself, or her needs. Didn't realize that hurting herself hurt him, too. And hurt the people who loved and cared for her. She thought only about her precious career.

You could have been so much more. Sarai's words dug a hole through his chest. Again, not good enough. He should be scabbed over by now.

"Roman?" Her voice sounded sad, even resigned.

"What?"

She stiffened and he felt instantly sorry. Well, a little sorry. He came over beside her, turned and leaned back against the rail. She didn't look at him.

"Is it true that you were shattered when I left?" she asked.

He sighed, folding up his collar. "It's cold out, Sarai. Let's go inside."

She glanced at him, and the wind skimmed her blond hair back from her face. Red paths down her cheeks betrayed the tracks of tears and he felt something chew at his stomach.

"Is it?"

He clenched his jaw. "I was hurt, yes. But I got over you." *Liar, liar.*

She nodded. "Me, too." She looked back out into the cold. "The thing is, I saw our future, Roman, and I knew you weren't going to give up being a hero…and, well, I just think you could have been so much more."

You said that already, thanks. He shook his head, leaned up from the rail and stalked two paces from her. "I know you think I'm just after parades and medals, but the truth is, I'm good at my job. I'm not cut out to be the guy you want…a pastor?" He gave a scoffing noise. "Right. I can't string two words together on my reports. But I'm pretty good at untangling the right from the wrong and I usually get my man."

Not my woman.

"I know. David tells me." She looked down at the accumulating snow. "If I were to tell the truth, I know that what you do is good. I'm…afraid you'll end up bloodied in my arms."

"As could you. There are no guarantees in this life, Sar. You and I could get killed tomorrow, crossing the street."

He moved closer to her, smelled lilac on her hair as the wind turned in his direction.

She turned, stared up at him. Oh, she was so close he could trace the shades of green in her beautiful eyes, and if he leaned, just a little—

"I know that. But if you were doing it saving souls—"

"It would matter more?"

"I guess."

Roman lowered his voice. "Do you think David's death was any less noble than Paul's?"

She blinked at him. "Paul was a martyr. David died of old age."

"David was a warrior. But he fought the battles God wanted him to fight. He cleared out the promised land for the Israelites. And, if he'd died, he'd have been hailed as a hero. Paul fought battles also—spiritual ones. But the key here is that both did what God asked them to do. They were the men God wanted them to be."

Her eyes were on him, and he noticed she still had the habit of chewing her lower lip. He stared at it for a moment.

"Not everyone is supposed to be a missionary."

"But maybe you were." She grabbed his jacket. "You could have been."

"There are missionaries killed around the world all the time, Sarai. Being a missionary isn't going to keep me alive."

"I know. It's just…" she said softly.

And just like that, in a moment that should have had an accompanying lightning bolt, he figured it out. "You think that if I was out here, working with you, you could keep an eye on me. *Keep me safe.* Oh, Sarai. Please trust *me.* Not the man you want me to be, but the guy I am. I know what I'm doing." Her beautiful eyes clouded and he reached out to her, cupped her face with his hand. "And you have to trust that God knows what He's doing for us. Whatever you do, both in word or deed, do it to the glory of God. I believe God wants me to do what I'm doing. You have to trust me, and God, on that."

She stared at him with a frown.

He watched her weigh his words, and the truth felt hot and heavy on his chest. "Sarai, you don't trust God."

"What?" But her face betrayed the truth. "Of course I do."

"That's it." He wanted to do a head slap to accompany the explosion of understanding in his mind. "You might trust God for yourself, but you're not willing to trust Him with my life. Or even this ministry." He gave a harsh laugh. "How could I have been so stupid? You don't stick around the hot spots in the world because you're brave—I mean, you are—but it's because you're afraid that if you leave it'll all fall apart."

She made no effort, it seemed, to curb her glare.

He glared back. "Anya and Genye are more than capable of opening this clinic. Genye is a pastor as well as being a former soldier, and Anya trained for her medical degree in Germany. Please don't tell me that you can take care of the people in this area better than they can."

Her eyes smoldered but she said nothing.

"You're wrong, Sarai. You do need a hero. You just don't

want one. Even God. You won't drop the reins long enough for Him to have his way—"

"That's not true. Of course I trust God—"

"Prove it. Leave with me, leave this all behind and let God be in charge here—not Sarai Curtiss."

She winced. "That's not fair. You're just baiting me to get me to cave. Of course I trust God, Roman."

"No, you don't. Not with the things that really matter." He braced his hand on the railing, leaning toward her, his voice dagger sharp. "Not with your heart, you don't."

"Don't be ridiculous!"

But, as she ducked under his arm and fled back into the cabin, he read her expression.

Bull's-eye.

Roman stood at the kitchen window, staring at the wind-swept whiteness. Beyond him, the forest seemed colorless, the sunlight unable to cut through the torrent of flakes that seemed to come from all directions. Sarai paused for only a second on the ladder, fighting the urge to run back to the loft and bury herself under the comforter in the safety of the guest bed. Thanks to him—and his caustic accusations—she'd spent the better part of the night fighting her doubts.

Of course she trusted God. She was a missionary, for crying out loud.

Her brain felt sleep-addled, and her body craved coffee. She'd have to just ignore Mr. Smug.

That might be easier if Roman didn't have a physique

carved from a daily routine in the gym. The way he filled out his black sweater and a pair of Tommy jeans only upped his stun power. With her fuzzy brain, she knew she might be a goner.

Especially if he turned and looked into her soul again with those probing hazel eyes. He was downright dangerous when his voice turned soft and he leaned close, smelling of wood smoke and cologne.

You're over him, Sarai.

Yeah right. Tell that to her pulse.

She padded across the room to the kitchen, wincing when a floorboard creaked.

He didn't turn. "I know you're there, Sar. I heard you upstairs, pacing." He sighed, stared down at the cup he held in his hands. Tea. Probably green…the guy made eating healthy seem as easy as taking a breath.

Not her—she'd choose a bag of tortilla chips, some cheese dip and can of Diet Coke for breakfast any day of the week.

But this day, it would be coffee, and, thankfully, Anya had instant in her cupboard. Sarai lit the flame under the stove, then wrapped her arms around herself. She felt oh-so-lovely with her rumpled jeans, her frowsy hair and nonexistent makeup.

"Did you sleep well?"

A wry chuckle escaped before she could stop it. He turned, raised one eyebrow.

She didn't respond. Roman had stoked the fire in the potbelly stove. It blazed warm and inviting and she knelt before it, toasting her hands. It seemed so safe, so other-worldly to be warm inside this tiny cabin while outside the world turned white. *Thank you, Lord, for this place. And for Genye and Anya.* If they hadn't shown up, she might have had to sleep in her frozen ambulance. Her practical inner missionary knew she shouldn't be alone with Roman in the cabin overnight.

Genye and Anya's door remained closed. She heard the water come to a boil. Roman had turned back to the window, still surveying the weather. Sarai rose and filled her cup with water then added coffee, making sure it looked black. Very, very black.

She sat at the table, cupped both hands around the mug and blew. "So, I guess we're snowed in?"

Not that she particularly hankered to go anywhere, thank you. His little tirade last night didn't change her mind in the least.

In fact, if he so desperately wanted to risk his thick neck, she wouldn't judge him. Would no longer dwell on what could never be. He could return to his life of danger and bad guys and she'd wish him well.

Because she did trust God. She just like to help Him along a bit, that's all.

Roman pulled out a chair and sat. "Yes. We're snowed in for at least right now. I went out to check on the vehicles—they're dead. The engines won't even turn over. And it'll take a truck to get them out of the ditch." He rolled his eyes, but gave her the barest of smiles. "You really know how to plant it."

"I nearly hit a deer," she retorted a second before she realized the tease in his voice.

"Right." He took another sip of tea. "I'm going to wait until the snow stops, then we'll assess our situation." He cringed. "I know this doesn't matter to you, but you have only thirty-six hours left before you turn illegal."

"And you arrest me?" She let the question linger between them, giving him a hard look.

He didn't match it. "I don't know what I'm going to do with you."

Ouch. He wouldn't seriously arrest her, would he? She felt emotion build in her throat. He didn't dislike her that much, did he?

I was shattered when you left.

Okay, maybe.

"I have an idea," she said.

He raised one eyebrow in silent curiosity.

"I challenge you to a chess game. If you win, I'll go back to Smolsk with you, and if the law still stands, then I'll consider leaving."

His eyes narrowed, probably remembering their cutthroat games—and how often he lost.

"No. You will leave. Because by then the deadline will be passed and you'll be arrested by the first able-bodied FSB agent you encounter."

She crossed her arms over her chest, refusing to let his words move her. "And if I win, you go home—alone. And leave me be."

They stared at each other a long moment, then finally he

let the faintest smile curve his lips. But she saw it touch his eyes. And it made something hot curl in her stomach. "*Ladna.* You're on, *Sarichka.*"

They pulled the game out onto the table and Sarai set up her pieces, well aware that she just might be giving into her worst fears. Not heading out of Smolsk, because from her recollection, Roman had never beaten her in chess. No, her greatest fear was spending time with the man, letting the charm that embodied him seep into the cracks of her heart and find a foothold.

He came out strong on the first move with his white, king-side knight. Seemed fitting probably. Mr. White Knight charging out to save her.

She countered with a pawn, a classic, safe move. *Don't need you, pal.* And she hadn't lived in Russia for three years without honing her chess skills on and *off* the board. She wouldn't be leaving Russia anytime soon.

He met her pawn. Leaned back, smiled.

Okay, smarty. Her bishop charged out, face to face with his knight.

Roman leaned forward, studying the board.

He brought out his queen. Of course. He was trying to weaken her defenses, to intimate her, to decimate her confidence. Typical FSB move.

She wasn't going to let him have the upper hand. Moving another pawn, she set his queen up for capture. "Got ya."

"Ha!" He took out her first pawn. "Check."

"Where?"

"I can take your king, or your rook. You decide."

"Casualties are a part of the game." She sacrificed her rook and tried not to wince. Especially when he leaned back, two hands behind his head. "You still want to keep that bet?"

She leaned forward, her chin on her hands, then smiled as she pulled out another pawn.

Roman moved to capture it, and then possibly her knight.

Uh-oh. Roman had improved since she'd last played him. Coffee. She needed more coffee. Because she was *not* going to let him win. Not only couldn't she bear the gloat on his face, but going back to Smolsk with him would only prolong their time together.

And talk about losing the game…her heart might not ever be the same.

Maybe it was time to make a sacrifice. She moved her pawn and as she expected, he flicked her knight off the board. "Two moves, Sarai." He held up his fingers.

That's what he thought. "The game's not over, yet." She moved the pawn forward, where it stood between his king and her victory. "You could just concede now."

He took her pawn with his.

She tried not to smile. She still had a few tricks up her sleeve.

Moving her queen out, she took his pawn. "Check."

He leaned back, squinting at the board.

Yeah, that's right, pal. You made a mistake. Like trying to talk me out of doing what I know is right. Like trying to turn it into a control issue. I'm after what God wants. Regardless of what you think.

He moved his king toward the protection of another pawn. She saw him swallow.

She moved her queen into position to take out the pawn defending his king. Ha! "Now what are you going to do, Chess Boy?"

Roman moved his bishop out. Then he leaned back, and a slow smile creased his face. "Checkmate."

"What? How?"

"My queen, bishop and knight are all poised to get you. Choose your poison."

She sat back, her heart filling her throat. "I was one move away from winning! All I needed was to take out your pawn."

He shrugged. "Start packing, baby."

She leaned back, then knocked over her king. It spun and slid off the board, landed on the floor. Along with her future.

And, maybe her heart.

Especially with him looking all smug and cute with his hands folded across his chest, leaning back in his chair.

She hoped he fell all the way backward. "I need another cup of coffee." She lit the stove, then watched the water as it started to boil. "I know I said I'd go back with you but—"

"Sarai—"

She heard warning in his tone, but kept going. "First, I have to go back to Khanda and check for outbreaks."

"That's not your problem." She heard him stand up, pushing back his chair.

Sarai closed her eyes, trying not to let frustration pinch her voice. "I know. I'm sorry, Roman, but I can't go anywhere unless I know the kids are safe."

"You can't help anyone if you're a fugitive." His eyes said it all. Control, control. She felt like pouring the boiling water over his head. She turned away, shaking her head.

"What do you think caused the kidney failure of your patient?"

She glanced at him, frowning. Then she shook her head, rubbing her eyes with her finger and thumb, seeing purple stars. "I don't know. I had another case just a few days ago—I might have told you—Governor Bednov's son. He also had acute renal failure, and it came on suddenly. I don't know what could have caused it."

He drummed his fingers on the table. "What about radiation poisoning? We watched a film a few months back about the effects, and renal failure was one of them. Could that have caused it?"

She took the pot off the stove, poured out hot water, then added her instant coffee. "I don't know." Maybe. "There used to be a nuclear plant out this way—some of the villagers worked at it. But it's been closed for a while now."

Roman said nothing, but for a moment, she thought she actually saw his brain chewing the information. He nodded, rose. "How far is the nuclear plant from here?"

"I don't know. Anya probably does. She's had this dacha since her childhood."

"It's about fifteen kilometers from here by snow machine." Genye closed his bedroom door behind him. "Which is about the only way you're going to get out of here anytime soon."

Roman glanced at him. "You have a snowmobile?"

Genye nodded. He looked tired this morning, with frowsy hair and red-rimmed eyes. He stuck his hands in the pockets of his red bathrobe. "But it hasn't been driven in a couple years. And, you're not going anywhere in this blizzard. You won't see your hand in front of your face."

Roman closed his eyes and ran his fingers across his furrowed brow. Sarai read the signs of stress when she saw it.

She reached across the table and touched his arm. "C'mon, two out of three games. Loser makes supper."

Roman sighed and opened his eyes. "Let's just hope the blizzard breaks soon. Then, we'll see." And, for the first time since he'd appeared in her door frame, she saw a real smile hint at the corners of his mouth. Something sweet and hot came into his eyes. "But you can't beat me, you know. I'd like some American pizza."

She leaned back and folded her arms—mostly to challenge him, but really to keep her heart from jumping clear out of her chest. In an instant, she'd glimpsed the man who'd stolen her heart, the man who made her feel like only she could coax from him his gorgeous smile.

You can't beat me, you know. She had to wonder if he was right.

Chapter Ten

Day two trapped inside a five meter by ten meter cabin with Sarai felt like a prison sentence. Especially when everything inside Roman wanted to throttle her. Or maybe just take her in his arms and kiss her.

There he went again, acting as if they had a future.

If only she hadn't laughed so sweetly when he'd beat her two out of three times in chess. Or helped him chop wood and carry it in.

Or thrown that snowball at him.

Roman turned away from her, where she and Anya sat at the table, kneading pizza dough. He had no illusions that the pizza, especially minus the seasonings, would taste anything remotely like the stuff she'd taught him to make years ago. But he could live with less than perfect pizza when he saw her speaking in low tones to Anya, with her hair pulled back and her eyes free of the darkness that seemed to shroud her since he walked into her life two days ago.

He'd gotten an up-close look into her incredible eyes when he'd felt an icy trickle run down his back as he'd been chopping wood. In his peripheral vision, he spotted his attacker gathering ammo for another volley, and spun and tackled her.

She shoved the snow in his face.

He'd pinned her down easily. "Stop," he'd said, with a low growl.

She'd just laughed, breathing hard, her gaze on his.

He'd felt everything slow, then. Snow fell around them, landing on her face, her nose. It melted and ran down into her woolen cap, blending with her freckles. The wind brushed the trees, a murmuring audience to the scene in the snow. Her hair smelled clean, having been recently washed in Anya's sink, and he caught the soft scent of wool and wood smoke against her skin. Her beautiful green eyes seemed bright as she stared at him. A blush infused her cheeks.

"Let me up, Roma," she said softly. He barely heard her against the roar of his pulse. His gaze roamed her face, stopped on her lips. He could nearly taste them, soft and sweet against his.

Sarai. This was Sarai, pulling him out of his world, into a moment where he could breathe fully, could stop and just enjoy her smile. All he'd ever wanted—if he really thought hard about it—was a woman who trusted him. Who smiled when he walked in the door, who cheered when he succeeded and believed in him when he didn't. Who stuck around with concern in her eyes when he showed up wounded, and loved him enough to get under his defenses and patch him up.

She bit her lower lip. It yanked him out of the moment enough for him to see fear in her eyes. Had he changed so much that he frightened her?

Or maybe it was just the thought of him in her life that scared her.

"Roma?"

It took everything in him to clench his teeth and push away from her. He rolled back in the snow, glad for the ice on his neck. His chest felt hot and tight as she sat up next to him. The snow crunched as she stood. "C'mon, I'll make you that pizza," she said, and held out her mittened hand.

He closed his eyes. "I'll stay here. Just for a minute. You go ahead. I'll be right behind you."

She said nothing, but he heard her footsteps crunch away.

Right behind her. Perhaps that was where he was destined to forever be in Sarai's life. Her bodyguard. Her protector.

Not her husband. He'd never be enough for her. Why couldn't he figure that out?

She didn't want a man who dedicated his life to throwing bad guys out of her path, or tracked her down the dark alleys of her life. She wanted a man who would go to the ends of the earth with her, declaring salvation. A preacher.

What she didn't know was that he really didn't have it in

him. He didn't know how to save souls, to lead someone to Christ. It was all he could do to try to walk as a disciple, one day at a time and not to give into the urges of his loneliness, or the temptations of his profession. Plenty of his fellow Cobras knew he was a Christian. But to get into detail with them felt a billion times harder than just saying *nyet* to their off-duty activities.

No, he wasn't a preacher. The best he could hope for was that Sarai looked past his actions to his heart—he only wanted to keep her safe and be a friend to her brother.

Hopefully he'd do it without becoming a national traitor. Because, despite their brief snowbound interlude, Roman kept the stakes in the forefront of his brain.

He had twenty-four hours to get Sarai out of Irkutsk. And when the clock ticked down to zero, he'd have no choice.

If he didn't take drastic measures, he *would* have to arrest her.

One of them was going to a gulag.

He'd stayed there, in the snow, letting the flakes that peeled from the sky wet his cheeks as he stared into the black expanse that reached to heaven. "Lord, I don't know why you sent me out here. I know David asked me, but I didn't really consult you first. I'm asking you now, especially since I'm already here—what should I do? I can't let her stay, can I? How do I get her to see that she's really in danger?" Stubborn, blind Sarai. What would he have to do to get her to believe him, to trust him?

He just has so much potential to be more. And he's blown it.

"Lord, Sarai's words hurt. But mostly because I do want

to be everything you want me to be. You know I'd be a horrible preacher. But if you want more of me, help me to want that, too."

He wiped his cheeks with his gloved hand and felt the heaviness lift, just a little.

What did God want of him?

That question continued to ring his thoughts as he came inside and watched Sarai prepare his victory supper.

"Pizza's in the oven," Sarai said as she came up behind him. He felt her more than heard her, especially the way his skin prickled. He stepped away from her. "I'm going to take a sauna," he said without looking at her.

He strode out into the night. Snow still fluttered from the canopy overhead. He followed a trail out to a small shack, letting the smell of wood smoke lead him.

Inside, candles flickered against the wood paneling. The sauna house had two rooms, one that held a small table and samovar for tea. The inner room held hooks and a washbasin of cold water. Roman noticed that Genye had already stoked the stove, and he guessed the man was inside, sweating.

The sauna room was dark, with only the coals lighting the room with an eerie, hissing orange as Roman went inside. Genye greeted him with a grunt as Roman sat on the planks and inhaled the hot, thick air. He let it fill his lungs, cleanse them.

Sweat began to pour down his face, onto his chest, along his spine.

"I fixed the snowmobile. You're ready to go tomorrow, if you'd like." Genye spoke from out of the darkness.

"Thanks," Roman said, but felt a heaviness settle inside, a dread that filled his bones. Tomorrow, then, they'd leave, back out into the chaos of his world.

He cleaned up and exited the sauna with few words, and hiked back to the dacha. He saw Sarai through the window, working at the table, cutting the pizza. She looked up as he entered.

"You look refreshed."

Or wrung out. He smiled, however. "Smells good."

She shrugged. "I had to make it with bacon and dill. Not your standard pizza, but I hope it'll be okay."

He met her eyes. "I'm sure it'll be perfect."

He tried not to notice the blush, as if his words had touched her. As if she might be pleased that she'd made him happy. *Sarai, please don't.*

Thankfully, his heart took up a defensive position. It erased his smile as he brushed past her. "I talked to Genye. He said he fixed his snowmobile. If the weather clears, I'm going first thing in the morning to take a look at that reactor. I'll be back to take you to Smolsk by lunchtime. We'll be in Khabarovsk before midnight."

Sarai froze. He watched out of his peripheral as her blush shifted to anger. "I'm not going anywhere."

He glanced at her. "Yes, Sarai. I'm taking you to the nearest airfield and flying you out of here. I know you don't believe me, and it's been rather surreal today, but you have twenty-four hours to leave Irkutia. And I'm going to make sure you do."

"Because you're an FSB agent?" Her eyes flashed.

"No. Because I'm your friend."

She said nothing, but he saw a muscle tense in her jaw. Then, "You're not my friend, Roman. You're my keeper. My brother's errand boy."

He opened his mouth, then closed it before his tone could betray how her words sliced him. "*Ladna,*" he said and turned away. "Think what you want. I need to check out that nuclear plant. Be ready to leave by the time I get back." He glanced back at her. "And don't try any stunts. That ambulance is pretty well packed in, but Sarai, if you try to ditch me again, I'll track you down and find you. And haul you out of Irkutia over my shoulder if I have to."

He probably should have ducked, because the glare she gave him felt like a jaw-splitter. He tried not to wince. But she morphed so quickly from the girl who'd made him pizza to the one who wanted to scalp him with the knife, it was more than he could bear.

"I'm going with you to the nuclear plant."

"Oh, no, you're not. For one, it's a long cold trip. Secondly, I don't know what to expect."

"And you think either of those reasons scare me? Clearly you don't know me that well."

Oh, yes, he did. And that's what unnerved him. "You're not going with me," he repeated slowly.

She stabbed the knife into the cutting board. "Those are my patients who are infected, and if I can figure out why, you can't stop me."

Roman turned away from her and crouched before the wood stove. Opening the door, he grabbed the poker and stabbed at the wood. Sparks flew out of the grate and landed at his feet. "I'm not kidding, Sar. It could be dangerous."

He heard her tromp across the floor. She stopped at the foot of the ladder to the loft. "Oh, Roman, I'm not worried," she said.

Her tone made him turn. She was smiling sweetly. Too sweetly. "You see, I have a hero, don't I?"

Sarai pulled the comforter up around her face and tucked her nose underneath, breathing into the folds to warm it. A chill nipped the corners of the attic. The fire had to have gone out downstairs.

Or maybe the cold emanated from inside. Deep inside, where she'd harbored the last hopes that Roman still loved her.

Once, maybe, loved her.

Roman ground to a cinder any illusions she might have courted about his feelings. *I got over you,* he'd said.

Yeah, he had. Why not? It had been nearly thirteen years since she'd about-faced in his life.

Me, too, she'd retorted. *Sorry for that lie, Lord.* She hated the ache that gripped her chest. And it didn't help that her breathing hitched every time she glanced at him. He was a dangerous mix of charm and power, and those smoldering hazel eyes turned her mouth to dust.

Especially today in the snow. For the briefest of moments she'd thought he'd wanted to kiss—no. Her overactive imagination had her in his arms, right where she'd dreamed of being for so many years. And then, she'd seen herself holding on to him, crying, even begging him to give up everything he'd worked so hard for, just to be with her. How incredibly selfish. No, how incredibly naive.

Thankfully, he didn't harbor any naiveté about their future. He'd shrugged away from her without an inkling that she'd been about to grab him by the jacket and kiss him.

Being with him, even this short time had shaken her to her core. She missed the memory of his embrace, but also his strength, the way he had some sort of mental GPS trained on her—if she just looked over her shoulder he'd be there. He had hero written all over him, with his well-toned physique that bespoke confidence and ability. Beneath that, in his determination and sheer stubbornness, she saw commitment. He'd followed her for two days, putting his job in jeopardy.

He'd followed her after she'd ditched him, twice, and told her that he'd keep following her, even if he had to drag her out of Russia.

She closed her eyes, letting herself remember him as he'd been thirteen years ago.

Younger, for sure, with less experience in his eyes. And the way he held her hand—she could be anywhere in a crowd and somehow, Roman could zero in on her and appear. Like that time on Arbot Street when she went shopping with David's American friend, Mae. The renowned cobblestone street from the time of the czars was filled with painters, food vendors, music and plenty of local hoods hoping to separate her from her backpack. Mae, with her curly red hair and stunning looks, seemed to announce their tourist status, and Sarai prickled every time someone brushed by her.

She'd stopped to admire the work of a chalk artist when she felt the tug on her backpack, slung over her shoulder.

The thief moved so quickly, it took several seconds for Sarai to realize what happened.

He'd cut her bag right off her shoulder.

About her height and weight, the kid knocked over the chalk stand as he fled down the street. With her passport. Her visa.

Her money.

Sarai didn't think. She lit out after him, yelling. Years later, when she replayed the scene, she saw herself, a crazed tourist, yelling in Russian, "Give me back my umbrella!" But at the time, she thought herself brave, righteous and fierce. A woman who could save herself, who could face any foe.

Until she found herself turned around, out of breath and alone behind an apartment building. The thief had vanished. Around her, garbage Dumpsters overflowed with refuse. Dogs and pigeons circled the trash, and above her, from tiny balconies, laundry snapped in the summer breeze. She heard doors slam, the cry of a child.

She looked behind her and realized she was lost.

Certainly she hadn't run so far that she couldn't find her way back to Arbot Street. But, without money, or a passport…and where, exactly, did David live?

Panic tried a choke hold and she refused its grip. *Think, Sarai.*

Nothing seemed familiar as she wandered back toward Arbot Street. Or, in the direction she thought was Arbot Street.

Shadows darkened the alleys as the sun dipped below view, mocking her attempts to find her way home. The air gathered the night chill and pressed it into her short sleeve shirt. She passed a huddle of black-shirted youths, dressed in leather jackets and eyeing her with smirks. She wrapped her arms around herself, told herself to keep walking.

Steps echoed behind her.

Don't panic.

She picked up her pace, then broke out into a jog. She heard scuffling and leaped into a full run.

She turned the corner and discovered yet another narrow street packed with three-story apartment buildings. A dead end. A hand snatched at her shoulder, and she screamed, wrenching away from it.

Laughter. It sliced through her like a scalpel.

Then, another hand grabbed her arm, yanked her to a stop. *"Kakaya Zhenshina mwe nashli?"*

Sometimes, in the darkest corners of her heart, she could still hear his voice. *What kind of girl have we found?* Right then she knew the truth.

She wasn't fierce or brave.

She was afraid. So darkly afraid that she kept it packed down under self-reliance. Under bravado and her noble cause. Under pure foolishness. Because to acknowledge it would force her to admit that she needed someone besides herself.

Olive-skinned, with short dark hair and darker eyes, her attacker smelled of vodka. He shoved her against the door to an apartment building. Finding her other arm, he held her wrists in a viselike clamp that made her cry out. "Leave me alone."

More laughter. She looked past him, and her breathing turned to razors in her chest. Maybe six boys, all wearing crooked smiles.

"Please…don't hurt me. I'm just trying to find my way home."

She spoke in English, and knew that had been a mistake the moment they exchanged looks and grinned.

She closed her eyes and prayed.

"Otsan ot yeyo!"

She heard the voice, and for a second the words didn't register. Only the feeling of relief that seemed so powerful, it threatened to take her knees out. *Get away from her!*

Sarai opened her eyes to see Roman take down the hoodlum who had backed her up against the building.

She screamed as Roman sent his fist into the kid's face—one, two, three times. Until her brother pulled him off. "Let him go!"

Roman turned and his expression etched forever in Sarai's thoughts. She still revisited it whenever she felt so alone she wanted to crumble.

Roman didn't ask. Didn't hesitate. He pounced to his feet and crushed her to himself, holding on so tight it scared her a little. "I was so worried," he said into her ear, and his tone nearly broke her heart.

She closed her eyes, caught in the moment when she'd imagined herself brutally raped and beaten by a Moscow gang.

"Thank the Lord, Vicktor had a thing for Mae. He was following you. I swear, I'm never letting you out of my sight again." Roman put her away from him, breathing hard. He looked stricken, and in the fading light he looked fierce and dangerous in his jean jacket and black jeans. "I'm sickened by what might have happened to you." His voice sounded broken, and his eyes were wet. He didn't bother to blink them dry.

"I can't believe you found me."

He frowned, shook his head. "I'll always find you, Sar, I promise. I'd be lost without you."

As Sarai bracketed his face with her hands, she saw in his eyes a truth that she wanted to hold on to. She had his attention. His full, breathtaking attention. It felt sweeping, and she reacted with tears.

Roman mistook it for fear and held her.

But what she'd felt hadn't been fear, but relief. Deep, soul-filling relief. God had sent her a man who looked past the façade of independence and spunk and saw that inside, she feared so much. Loneliness. Failure. Weakness. A man who let her fool the world, even herself, but knew the truth.

She needed him.

Roman's voice was roughened with vestiges of anger when he finally spoke. "For every jerk out there, there are guys in Russia who are decent and honorable. Those punks won't get away with this, Sar. I'll make sure you're never afraid again."

Obviously, thirteen years later, he still operated on that principle—making sure that thugs like the ones who'd chased her down Trotsky Street ended up in prison. One by one.

Trying to prove that Russia wasn't a land of thugs and criminals.

Thirteen years later, she hadn't changed, either. She still wore the facade of tough girl. However, this time he wasn't getting under it. "Lord, why is Roman back in my life? What are you trying to do to me?" Sarai ran her hands over her eyes. They came away wet. Downstairs, she heard creaking, the squeak of the gas stove. Someone loaded wood, and her heart felt thick and heavy in her chest.

I'll always find you, Sar.

Maybe he'd kept that promise, also.

Chapter Eleven

"Where are you, Roman?" Yanna's voice dropped almost immediately after she answered the telephone. "You are in so much trouble around here that I think your face might appear on a stack of FSB's most-wanted playing cards. Malenkov knows you're AWOL. He's been on the telephone with Irkutsk all morning. They're putting an APB out for you."

Roman glanced at Genye, half-hidden by the open snowmobile cover. He couldn't believe Genye had gotten the machine to start. An ancient Buran, it looked as if it hadn't been running since the days of Brezhnev. Or Peter the Great.

However, if they got it moving, he'd already decided that he'd put Sarai on the back and just keep going. He'd seen an airbase on the road to Khanda, and with the right persuasion, he could get an AN-2 delivered, maybe even scrounge one up there. He didn't need a pilot, just the wings.

They didn't even need to get all the way back to Khabarovsk. Just over the border into Buryatia, or Tuva. He'd deal with the fallout—both Sarai's and Malenkov's—after that. At least she'd be alive.

And mad. He winced just thinking about it. "I'll be back as soon as I can, Yanna," he said into the sat phone. "What did you find out about Alexander Oil?"

"Two things. First, they own a number of drilling stations. The one near Smolsk is just one of them. Secondly, your dead American is an independently contracted site inspector. He's traveled around the region regularly for the past six years or so, checking the fields for leakage and other issues."

Had he gotten into a little nuclear fuel smuggling, too? It seemed that, regardless of the inspections and scrutiny they put on foreign tourists, someone always slipped through.

"There's more," Yanna said. "The two Americans Governor Bednov is holding for suspicion of kidnapping in Irkutsk are on the Alexander Oil board of directors. But most importantly, so is Bednov."

"He's on the board?" Wasn't that interesting?

"One of five. Three Americans, two Russians—a man by the name of Gregori Khetrov. He's a communications billionaire in Moscow, only right now he's sitting in Lubyanka prison, courtesy the FSB, on tax charges."

For sure the guy was crooked, but then again, so were

half of Russia's businessmen, a.k.a. former party leaders. "What about the reactors?"

"You're sitting nearly on top of decommissioned reactor number 213 in the Khandaski region. According to the manifest, all the HEU was transported from Khandaski three years ago to a reactor in Yakutia. Only, I can't confirm that it ever arrived. None of the lot numbers match up."

"Keep looking, Yanna. Maybe it was diverted."

"Maybe it's still at Khandaski."

Roman shot a look at Genye wondering how much the guy understood. "Great minds think alike."

"Listen, Roma, get to Smolsk. Vicktor and I have a little plan. He'll meet you at Sarai's clinic."

He felt a rush of gratitude for his friends. "Don't get into trouble, Yanna."

"Us? Get in trouble?"

He could hear her smiling on the other end. "By the way, David has sent me three e-mails looking for you. Maybe you should give him a call."

Maybe not. Roman had a few choice words for David that he should probably keep tucked inside his chest. He clicked off and stood over Genye as the man fiddled with the spark plug wires.

"Everything looks okay." He closed the lid. "Fire her up."

Roman braced his foot against the machine, grabbed the cord and gave it a rip.

It sputtered, then nothing.

"Again." Genye opened the hood, pumped the primer.

Roman pulled again. The machine coughed, he added some gas, then it roared to life. Smoke billowed out the back as it cleared the exhaust of age and rust.

Genye latched the hood and handed Roman an ancient helmet.

"Listen, you be careful, okay? I want Sarai safe." He wore a smile, but Roman saw protection in those eyes. And, after yesterday, when the guy had clocked him but good, he knew Genye meant it.

"*Konyeshna.*"

Genye nodded at Roman's agreement, then glanced at the house. Sarai was coming out of the door. "She might not admit it, but she needs you. Try to see that."

Roman stared after him as Genye turned and walked to the house.

"Ready?" Sarai entered the garage. She wore a clean pair of jeans—probably Anya's—wool valenki boots, her black parka, a scarf and a homemade green stocking cap that made her face seem tiny and sculpted. Her green eyes sparkled and for a moment he wanted to answer no.

Not quite ready at all.

If he had his way, in twenty-four hours she would be safe…and not talking to him again.

Which would be a thousand times worse than having her argue and tease and occasionally pout.

Being around her had made him realize why his life felt so eerily calm when she entered his atmosphere. Because despite her maddening determination, she had a smile that could stop his heart cold, and when she laughed, well, he'd just about die to hear her laugh. He'd barely won their chess games. In fact, he'd checkmated her by sheer chance the first time.

Not that she had to know.

Still, something about being with her cut through the buzz that permeated his life and focused it.

Gave it meaning.

"Get on," he said. She climbed on the back of the snowmobile and wrapped her arms around his waist.

Uh-oh.

Snow melded to her eyelashes and pelted her cheeks, and her pantlegs were soaked clear through. But, as Roman drove the snowmobile through a drift and they went airborne, Sarai felt something rocket loose and take flight.

Maybe her brain cells. For sure the tight knot of stress that came from the all-work-and-no-play routine over the last two, no, ten years. Okay, probably most of her life.

They landed in a poof of snow and Roman whooped as he gunned the engine. Sarai screamed, but she heard adrenaline and laughter in her tone as she tightened her clasp around Roman's waist.

Yes, she could get used to flying through the whitened, magical landscape, in and out of deer trails, thundering up and through snowdrifts, letting the machine drive her into the milky horizon with her arms around a man who looked both dangerous and delightful in his wool hat and whitened, snow-spiked hair. Crystals of snow gathered on his twenty-six-plus-hour beard, and his eyebrows looked iced over.

But his gaze seemed oh so very warm when he looked at her over his shoulder, slowing the snowmobile slightly. "You okay back there?"

"Fine!" She grinned. "Where did you learn to drive one of these?"

He gave her a one-eyed frown then turned his attention back to plowing through the snow.

Roman Novik, soldier. He probably had a plethora of talents she didn't want to know about. She sank her chin onto his shoulder, relishing the feel of his solid back, his strong arms muscling the snowmobile.

She had to admit, when Genye had uncovered the rusted heap in his garage, she'd nearly turned and fled. But with a little tinkering, he and Roma had coaxed it to life, and with it, her curiosity. Oddly enough, Roman agreed to let her come along on his field trip.

She had to wonder if he might be up to something.

He was *definitely* up to something. "It could be dangerous," he'd said.

At the moment, she didn't care.

They plowed through another drift and snow crashed into her scarf and down her back. "Ooh-rah!"

Roman glanced at her, smiling. "Having fun or something?"

She said nothing, just grinned.

They drove in silence, the engine cutting out conversation. Through the gray haze, Sarai saw oil wells to her south and west, some working, others frozen. The pungent smell of diesel cut through the crisp air, and even the exhaust of the snowmobile.

Roman angled north, as if he might know where he was going. She hung on, and for a moment, she even closed her eyes, trusting in his ability to guide them.

They went over a knoll and zipped down the other side. Roman slowed the machine. "There."

She followed his point, and her pulse did a small rush when she saw his destination.

A nuclear reactor.

"It's huge." She counted two smokestacks, and on either side, like a ring of iron giants, electrical towers cut into the gray sky. The plant itself looked like a factory, a huge box with few windows, laden with pipes. On one end, lined up like shotgun shells stood maybe a dozen three story silos.

Roman gunned the snowmobile right toward the plant, oh, joy.

Hadn't he ever heard of a little accident called *Chernobyl?* "I thought you just wanted to see where it was. Roman, I don't want to go any closer."

"Now you tell me," he said, but didn't slow. "I told you that it might be dangerous. You said you wanted to come along."

No, what she said was that she wasn't worried because she had a hero. But, as usual, she'd been in serious denial.

Now that she saw the reactor, a coldness started in her stomach, then spread out through her arms, and it had nothing to do with the snow still pelting her cheeks. "Roman, I'm serious."

He slowed the snowmobile. She looked beyond him and could see a road leading to the plant. Flanked on either sides of the road, a guard stand and entry gate indicated security. Beside it, a tall white monument—or sign, perhaps—topped with a red-painted concrete flame betrayed its purpose.

"Calm down, it's decommissioned," Roman said over the rumble of the motor.

"Then why are there still people here?" She pointed toward a truck just beyond the gates.

"It's decommissioned, but it's still operational—in terms of cooling the spent fuel. They cool the nuclear waste in rods in a pool of water for about seven years and then store them in those huge silos. I'm sure there is a skeleton crew monitoring the cooling." He pointed with his gloved hand. "Listen, no one will know we're here. It's scarcely manned, and all we're going to do is do a little poking around."

A little poking around? But before she could object, he revved the machine, and drove parallel to the road, cutting a wide angle around the plant, and stopped at the edge of a pine forest.

"If you want, you can stay here." Roman got off the snowmobile. "I won't be long."

She angled a look at the plant, then back at Roman. Let's see, stay here in the cold until he got hurt and left her stranded, or go with him and get arrested? Then again, once he returned he might just arrest her anyway.

She got off. "Lead the way, hero."

He nodded, then opened his jacket and pulled out—

"A gun?"

"Calm down, it's just a precaution." He tucked it into his outer pocket. "We'll have to hike from here, but I think the blizzard will hide our approach."

Oh, great.

She wondered if she should be ducking as they trudged out from the cover of the pine forest and crossed the hundred or so meters to the fence.

"I'm going to hoist you over," he said.

"I can do it." She dug her hands into the fence, but her thick boots refused purchase.

"Let me give you a boost—"

"You touch my backside and I'll kick you."

He stepped back, hands up in surrender.

She fought her way up, over and let herself fall into the snow on the other side.

He jumped up and vaulted it before she even climbed back to her feet. Jerk. She slapped away his outstretched hand.

He laughed.

She made a face at him.

Now he bent over as he ran toward a service door, as if hunching over might conceal the two intruders wearing black coats against a snow-white backdrop? For crying out loud…

Still, ten minutes later, they were inside the building. Silence felt thick, or maybe she just couldn't hear anything over the thunder of her heartbeat in her ears. The smell of gasoline and concrete permeated the walls, and she couldn't stifle a shiver. They were inside a nuclear plant.

She probably needed to get her head examined. Then again, that should probably be standard practice whenever she found herself in Roman's airspace.

"What are we looking for?" she asked.

"*Tiha!*" he said and put a finger to his lips.

Wait—wasn't he a federal agent? Why all the sneaky, sneaky? Shouldn't he be allowed to just stroll in, flashing his badge or something?

He moved out into the hall and scrambled to another door. She stayed glued to his tail and shut the door behind her.

They were in an office, and from what it looked like, an abandoned office. Like all Russian offices, pictures of the plant, including floor plans and egress routes hung on the wall. Roman shone his flashlight on the map, tracing his finger along a route.

"Here." He tapped it twice, then looked at her. "I think you should stay here until I get—"

"Not on your life, bub. I'm Velcro on you."

He raised one eyebrow, but didn't smile. "*Ladna*. But keep up."

Was he kidding? She'd probably run him over.

They exited to the hallway, and he did a James Bond, sneaking down the hallway, down stairs, through passageways until he came to a locked room. Yes, she read the radioactive sign on the door, even pointed it out to him, but he shrugged it away.

What, was he impervious to radiation poisoning? Hello, she didn't want her teeth and hair falling out at the ripe old age of thirty-five.

He opened the door, shone his light inside. It reflected off a pane of glass. *"Poshli,"* he said as he beckoned her inside.

She smelled the odor of danger as she closed the door into total darkness. Or maybe the smell was the redolence of her own fear. As Roman stood and slowly panned his light through the glass, she felt cold and clammy. And bald.

"What does *Vwesoka Obogashenie Oran* stand for? It can't be good. Especially with the symbol of radioactivity on it? And the word for "dangerous," *Opasnost?* What is it, Roman?"

He turned to her, bracketed his hands on either side of her face. "Calm down. It's uranium. Probably Highly Enriched Uranium, which was used to power this nuclear reactor. What I need to know is the lot number on those casks."

"Wait, you lost me at uranium—as in *radioactive* uranium? The stuff used in nuclear bombs?"

"The very same. And someone has been selling it to terrorists outside of Russia." He took off his hat, wiped his brow with it. Obviously, he wasn't real thrilled to be ten meters away from the stuff, either.

"The thing is, this uranium isn't supposed to be here. If indeed it is uranium. It might just be the containers."

He moved toward the door and she grabbed his arm.

"Have you lost it completely? You can't go in there! Not without protective gear and—"

"Relax, Doc—it's only radioactive if ingested."

"Oh, that makes me feel so very much better. Radioactive means *radioactive* in my book, Roman. Please, let's get out of here. I—"

He clamped his hand over her mouth and pulled her tight against him. Very tight, and protective-like. She could hear his heart pounding as they stood in the darkness.

Footsteps. Outside in the hall.

Please, please, keep going.

But, no. They stopped.

And that's when she felt Roman reach for his gun.

She just knew he was going to get killed one day and she'd be around to see it...or worse, get killed right along side him.

Why did she always have to be right?

Chapter Twelve

"Please, Sarai, just don't move." He placed his mouth very close to her ear, and his lips brushed her neck as he spoke. He felt her tremble, but she said nothing, just turned and dug her grip into the lapels of his jacket and pulled him closer.

He'd wanted her in his arms, but this wasn't quite what he'd had in mind—especially with potentially radioactive material behind door number one, and a Bad Guy behind door number two.

He put his arm around her, positioning her behind him as he heard the handle click. She seemed to read his thoughts, for she put her head down, right into his spine.

He gripped his service pistol with both hands as the door swung open. Thankfully, he had all seventeen rounds in it.

Milky hall light cut through the darkness, a second before a guard appeared.

No, a *thug*. An out-of-place thug with the demeanor of a mafioso in his leather coat, his high and tight crew, the look of suspicion on his face, and especially the .40-caliber Varjag pistol he aimed at Roman.

Briefly aimed. Because Roman kicked the gun out of his hands and followed with a cuff across the jaw.

Mafia hit his knees.

"Roman!" Sarai rushed out.

He caught her. "Stay back."

The moment cost him. Mafia had palmed his two-way. *"Pomagee!"*

Roman snatched it away from him, cutting off his call for help, and threw it against the wall. "Put your face on the floor, hands behind your head."

The man obeyed. "This is a government facility. You're trespassing."

Roman put his foot on the man's neck. "I'm FSB. Tell me, how many guards on duty?"

Mafia goon stayed silent.

Roman pressed down. "See, you don't look government. *I* look government—hungry, cold and just a bit desperate." He touched his gun to the man's head. "All I want is information."

"Roman." Sarai's voice held just enough shock to make him pause. "Please, let's just get out of here."

He shouldn't have brought her along. He relaxed his posture. "Listen, all I want to know is the lot number on the containers there."

Mafia stayed silent. Roman glanced at Sarai and shook his head.

Footsteps thundered down the hall. Sarai yanked his arm. "Roman!"

Now he really wanted to shoot someone—namely himself for putting her in danger. Alone, he'd have no problem sticking around and shaking the truth out of these punks. Instead, he grabbed her hand.

It was cold and small in his.

Poking his head out of the door, he saw two uniforms heading his direction. "Keep up!" he said as he bolted out the door.

"Perestan!"

He ignored the command to stop and pulled Sarai down the hall. They rounded the corner as two shots chipped off the concrete wall behind them.

Shooting? In a nuclear facility?

He stopped, waved Sarai on. "Run!"

She didn't hesitate, which he attributed to her fear rather than obedience.

As the first guard rounded the corner, Roman squeezed off a shot just over his head just to put a hiccup of fear into their hot pursuit. The man backpedaled, bumping into the second and Roman turned and sprinted down the hall.

The fewer shots fired, the better.

Sarai had already reached the back door and barreled through.

He followed her just as an alarm sounded. It deafened him and echoed out into the cold.

Sarai fought with the snow, her steps heavy and slow. Roman charged past her and scrambled up the fence, leaning over the top to grab her hand.

She took it, and he hauled her over just as a contingency of guards burst from the door.

Roman pulled her down into the snow and tucked her under him as shots whizzed over their heads.

"Why are they shooting at us?" Sarai said, her voice muffled and very high.

"That's a good question." Roman pivoted and returned fire.

The guards scattered. He hauled up Sarai by her armpits and half pulled, half pushed her toward the trees, shooting on the run.

As Sarai collapsed by a tree, breathing hard, Roman ducked behind the snowmobile and yanked at the cord.

Nothing.

Sarai gave him a wide-eyed look. "Start it!"

What did she think he was trying to do?

He pulled again. It sputtered, died.

And then, over the siren, he heard an engine roar. Sarai looked past him in horror.

"Company?" he asked as he grabbed at the cord. Please, *please.*

"Hurry, Roman!"

She stood, ran behind him, as if to help. Another gunshot drove her to her knees. "They have snowmobiles!"

Of course they did, probably nice ones. Definitely a mafia operation. Because, according to his last intel, nuclear plants in Russia weren't privately owned.

Then again, nowadays "private" meant adopted by a former Communist.

He felt Sarai grab the arms of his jacket in a death grip as he gave the cord another yank. He added juice and the machine spluttered and caught. Thank you.

"Yes!" Sarai leaped on the snowmobile. "Hurry!"

No, he thought he'd check the oil first. Roman climbed on and they roared off, him still standing.

He ducked as they jagged through trees.

"Roman, there's two of them. And they're gaining!"

He sat down and dug his feet into the floorboards. "Hang on!"

She didn't need the encouragement. She'd turned into a little backpack of terror, such was her grip on him. She ducked her head into his spine. "I don't want to die, I don't want to die."

It was about time.

He gunned the engine, flew around trees, through the tangle of brush. His heart lodged in his throat when he clipped a tree and nearly dumped them as he leaned into a turn. Sarai stayed glued to him.

Compared to the sleek machines of his pursuers, his snowmobile was a tank. He plowed through ice-caked drifts and heard their engines dying as he tunneled farther into the forest. He tightened his grip on the gas. The snow machine gave a little hiccup, revved into high and burst into a pristine indentation of virgin white. Was this a lake?

He angled toward it, tasting his successful getaway. Behind them, on the other side and through more trees, he could barely make out the tall smokestacks. The alarm still sounded, a muffle of panic behind the forest. The mafia boys' boss would be hearing about the break-in right about now.

If only Roman had gotten the lot number on the Uranium casings. But, at least he and Sarai were safe.

For now. But if Malenkov wasn't mad at him before…

He felt her hold loosen, and she lifted her head. "Are they gone?"

"I don't know. Maybe. We're going across this lake and into that forest. We'll lose them for sure on the other side."

He glanced back at her, and his throat constricted at her expression of fear, and the tears ringing her eyes. "Sorry, Sar. I didn't think it would go down like that."

"Well, what did you think would happen when you sneak into a government facility with a gun? That everyone would sit around and eat cake?"

He smiled. "I would have never let them hurt you."

She narrowed her eyes. "See, this is why you scare me. Because you don't care if you get killed."

His smile vanished. Didn't care? Is that what she thought? Sorry, but he had a lot of living left to do, thanks. He wasn't a martyr.

He left that kind of idealism for Sarai.

Sarai felt just one second shy of breaking into hysterical laughter or maybe crying. Her nerves buzzed just below the surface and nothing short of a hacksaw could break her death clamp around Roman's waist. But, beneath the fear, the shock, even the adrenaline, she felt the tiniest tinge of amazement.

He'd broken them into a nuclear reactor and raced out, guns blazing, hauling her up and over the fence like a rag doll. She'd have to be made of concrete and steel not to be aware of his strength, his cool head, the way he put himself between her and bullets.

Bullets!

She began to tremble as they drove down the embankment toward the lake. *Calm down, Sarai, you're fine.*

Fine? She was *not* fine. If she wasn't going to get her visa revoked before, Roman had just made it a thousand percent certainty.

Hopefully, that wasn't a part of some diabolical plan, and merely a byproduct of being in his personal space.

Along with the feeling of his protection. Starting with the tickle of his lips on her throat as he whispered to her in the facility, right before the heavy drama.

He scared her, he intrigued her, he made her furious…yet he also reached out to the scared woman inside and made her feel safe. Even with bullets whizzing past her head.

Go figure.

They sped out onto the ice, and she lifted her head and surveyed the landscape. On the other side of the lake, a pink-painted conrete house parted the trees. Two stories of grandeur, it looked like it may have been built for a Party official, probably the one who ran the nuclear facility. Now it stared dark and forlorn under the burden of snow.

Sarai looked behind them. Nothing but snow and forest

and gray sky. Relief ran through her like melted butter. Maybe they'd escaped.

See, she was starting to think like a criminal. She shook her head, easing her grip on Roman. "I can't believe you just did that."

"What?"

"Broke the law!"

"I didn't break the law…I just dodged it."

For crying out loud.

"I can't believe you, Roman. I'm around you for five minutes, and suddenly I'm in a Jackie Chan movie only with bullets. You're a magnet for disaster. Or is that special treatment just for me? What were you looking for, anyway?"

"Uranium."

"Then you should consider this mission a success. Or would you be happier if we were both deep crispified in there?"

"What I want to know is who was shooting at us." Roman slowed the machine. "Regular army would have had AK-47s. These guys had top-of-the-line Izmekh Varjag pistols…and the look of hired—"

A crack, like the sound of branches breaking, cut off his words.

He slowed the machine to a crawl.

More cracking, like the litter of applause and Sarai's heart blocked her throat. Ice. Cracking!

Roman must have read her mind. He gunned the snowmobile to the background noise of shattering ice.

"Faster!"

Roman leaned into the snowmobile, as if somehow making himself smaller might make him…lighter?

She looked back and her heart left her.

Ice opened in their wake, and only their forward momentum kept them above water.

"Faster!"

The cracking circled around them. Sarai watched in horror as a plate broke off in front of them, and the snowmobile nosed up. The back end slid toward the water.

"Jump!"

Adrenaline launched Sarai off the back, and she aimed for solid ice. Two steps and a leap.

Her body landed on the edge, her hands scrambling for purchase as her legs dunked into the cold water. A thousand shards of pain knifed into her legs at the contact. She screamed, kicked her legs. The panic propelled her onto the ice like a walrus.

She rolled over, scooting back to safety.

Roman!

She saw him behind the handlebars, his jaw set as he fought to get free from the press of the windshield. "Roman!"

The snow machine sunk deeper, only its skids above the surface. Roman clawed his way over the windshield, and his head cleared the water.

"Sar—"

The snowmobile bobbed, then slid into the blackness. And, as if tethered by a hook, Roman went with it.

Governor Bednov hung up the telephone. Sitting back in his leather chair, he steepled his fingers. The sun streamed into his office, and he heard the ticking of the clock behind him.

The hotshot FSB agent in Khabarovsk had come to Irkutsk. He'd most likely found Riddle's uranium shipment, although he couched it in terms of hunting for clues about the dead American. According to Bednov's FSB contacts, the agent had headed straight for Smolsk.

Bednov saw coincidence there—what was this FSB agent's connection to the American doctor?

He dialed Fyodor's cell phone. "Where are you?" He needed a drink. The image of Julia, her mouth swollen, passed out on the sofa again today made his stomach churn. She was starting to feel like a liability.

"I'm in Khanda. She was here last night. Left before the storm. But we waited in Smolsk all night and had her flat and her clinic under surveillance. She hasn't returned."

Bednov frowned and rubbed his finger and thumb into his eyes, seeing flashes of light. "Could she have left the country?" Not preferable, but he still might be able to track her down outside his borders.

Then again, without proof, what could she do? He'd simply make sure she never set foot in Russia, at least Irkutia, again.

Was she somehow connected to the FSB agent? Only, how? And if they were together and got out of Irkutia, they could do serious damage to his long term goals. "The Khabarovsk FSB has a loose cannon. He's in Smolsk, looking for clues to Riddle's death. He may even be with the American. If you run into him, you know what to do."

Silence on the end of the line told him Fyodor's reaction.

"Did you hear me?"

"Kill him?" Fyodor's voice edged on defiant.

"What do you think? Yes. Kill him."

"But he's an FSB agent. I could—"

"I'll protect you. I'll list him as a rogue agent, an enemy of the state. If you kill him, it will be in the line of duty."

Silence. "Yes, Governor." Fyodor clicked off and Bednov rested the receiver back in the cradle.

Chapter Thirteen

Roman felt the water close over him. He fought not to open his mouth and gasp. But oh, how he wanted to scream. Every nerve felt filleted, bare to needles of cold that turned his brain to ice. Momentarily.

Then fear kicked in and with it the heat of common sense. The snowmobile had snagged him by the boot, and he kicked to free himself even as he plunged into the depths.

He tore off his gloves, not really feeling his hands, and bent to pull at the laces. His lungs blazed. He grabbed, and the lace tightened into a knot.

The lake sucked him down. He felt his lungs leaking. *Lord, help, please!*

His knife. He grabbed for it, just above his boot, and barely felt it in his grip as he sliced at the boot laces.

Free! He yanked his foot out and kicked hard, shedding his coat as he fought his way to the surface.

He hit his head against the ice and nearly blacked out. But light beckoned and he kicked toward it, feeling his remaining air seep out. Two more kicks.

Shadow swept into his brain, clouding it like smoke. Tired. So very tired. He fought through the web of exhaustion pulling at him. Sarai.

Sarai.

The blackness swept over him. He felt heavy. So heavy.

Then, something pulled at him. He gave a feeble kick.

His head broke surface and he gasped. Air. Sweet precious air. Burning his lungs. He sucked it in and his vision cleared.

"Roman!"

Sarai lay on her stomach on the ice, holding the back of his shirt as he tried to tread water. But his arms felt thick. Sluggish.

"Roman, hold on."

The sun seemed so bright this side of the ice. Bright and spotty in his eyes. He reached out for the edge, but it broke off. "Back up, Sarai. You'll go in." His voice sounded strained, and he knew he should be alarmed.

"I'm not letting go of you." Her eyes found his, and despite his brain-frozen state, he saw something hot, even angry or maybe afraid. "Kick hard."

"I'm kicking. But the ice isn't strong enough to hold both of us."

Behind his words, he heard a low hum. Sarai heard it also and turned to look.

"Snowmobiles," he said. He willed her to look at him, and winced at the fear in her eyes. "Run, Sar."

She shook her head.

"Run!"

"I'm not leaving you!"

"You have to leave me. Go. With luck they'll come out on the ice, and they'll end up in the drink. You can get away. Go back to Anya's dacha."

"No! I don't want you to die." Her eyes filled.

"The feeling is very mutual. And if you stay here with me, the minute those snow machines come out on this ice, you'll go down. Run, Sarai."

"What if they follow me?"

He nearly cried with relief. "If they catch you, tell them I kidnapped you. Only don't speak Russian. Please, it's the only way."

She stared at him, her face tight, her expression horrified. Then, abruptly, she let him go, backed away and fled across the ice.

He was obviously already frozen because watching her go, his heart felt cold and dead in his chest.

Sarai ran across the ice, careful to veer away from the gaping patch of ice chunks their snowmobile had furrowed. She raised her arms, waving at them. *"Pomagee menye!"* She didn't look back at Roman, but prayed he stayed above the surface. *"Pomagetye!"*

Two red snowmobiles, with warmly dressed mafia thugs

mounted on the back came into view. She ran to the edge of the lake, waving hysterically.

They angled toward her. She glanced back at Roman. His head barely surmounted the surface of the water. He couldn't have had the strength to yell, because he'd be shouting at her if he'd heard her speaking Russian.

And if he knew her intentions. Get help, even if from the bad guys. Roman would just have to strangle her later.

They came closer and she ran toward them, her arms up.

They stopped their machines, and one raised a pistol. "Stop!"

"Please. Help my friend!" She pointed at Roman. His head bobbed, went under, then bobbed again. "He's the one who broke into your facility."

They glanced at her, then at Roman.

"Please! I'll tell you everything I know if you help him!"

"You'll tell us anyway."

"He's an FSB agent. Just think what *he* could tell you!"

For a moment, those possibilities, and the fact that she'd just handed him over to have information tortured out of him nearly doubled her over. It took all her resolve to stare at them, hard, challenging.

I'm sorry, Roman. But she didn't care what lines they had to cross. She wanted Roman alive. And she wasn't going to let him die if she could do something about it.

The thugs looked at each other and in mutual assent got off their machines. One opened a box behind his seat. He pulled out a webbed tow rope with a hook on the end and flung it at her.

She caught it and jogged back out onto the ice. "Roman, stay with me!"

He didn't even bother to turn toward her voice. She saw him sink under the water again. No!

She got on all fours, then shimmied out to the edge. He was fighting, kicking hard to stay up. His head broke the surface and she grabbed his shirt.

"Roman, I have help." She fed the towline into the water, around his shoulders and hooked it onto itself at his chest. He looked chalky white, frost and ice around his mouth.

"Hold on, hero," she said, her voice shaky, as she backed away. Roman held on to the rope, his gaze in hers. Dark eyes that she couldn't read.

She backed onto solid ice, sat up and began to pull.

He moved toward the edge. But she couldn't move him onto the ice. *Lord, please help me!* She dug in her feet, wrapped the webbing around her hands, leaned back.

Roman inched up, then fell back as her strength ebbed.

No. He couldn't die because she didn't have the strength to pull him out. No!

"Dye Menye." A shadow over her shoulder reached for the webbing. Mafia Man sat next to her and heaved.

Roman slid onto the ice, half in, half out. Sarai got up to go to him.

"Nyet." Mafia Man put his hand out to stop her. Then he pulled again and dragged Roman across the snow.

Roman's eyes were closed, his body unmoving.

Please, Lord, no. Sarai ran to him, checked his pulse.

Slow. But still alive. "Help me!" She rolled him over, slapped his cheeks. "Stay awake, Roman!"

He blinked, groaned. "Sarai..." His eyes closed again.

He'd die of hypothermia before they got back to the nuclear plant.

She looked at the two mafia boys, now heading in her direction, then behind her at the woods and...the *house!*

"Let's take him there." She pointed to the pink painted home. Hopefully, it had blankets, or furniture she could use to start a fire.

If she had to, she'd warm him up with her own body heat.

Thankfully, Mafia One and Two didn't argue with her, a feat she attributed to her doctor tone. So much for their not knowing she spoke Russian.

Unfortunately, she'd have to make good on her promise to tell them everything. That wasn't much, and if Roman lived, he might not be thanking her.

If Roman lived.

She sandwiched him between herself and Mafia One as they drove around the lake to the home. Then, the two men grabbed Roman's rag-doll body and dragged him by the armpits into the house. She heard him groan, a sound that had her rejoicing.

The door had a dead bolt lock, but to her shock, one of the two dug out a key.

They opened the door and dropped Roman inside.

"We need to get him someplace warm," she said.

They looked at each other. Then they picked up Roman

and dragged him through an entryway and into a family room with a stone fireplace.

A *nice* family room. With black leather seating and leopard skin pillows and a thick Kazakhstani rug on the floor. They dropped Roman onto it. Then they turned to Sarai. "Don't try anything. We're watching you," Mafia One said.

She ignored him and dropped to her knees beside Roman. He looked pasty, with gray lips and ice in his hair. And when she removed his only boot, he barely roused.

He did, however, react when she reached for his belt.

"Leave me alone."

"Not on your life. You need to get out of these wet clothes and dry off." She unbuckled his belt, but his hands came to life and caught hers. His eyes were still closed, but she heard a heartbeat in his voice. "No, Sarai. Find me something else to put on. A blanket or something." His hands trembled as he let her go.

Fine. She ran out of the room, brushed past the mafia duo and pounded up the stairs. She heard feet behind her, but didn't stop.

Three bedrooms. She yanked a bedspread off one of the beds, rolled it into a ball and raced back downstairs, passing the man who'd followed her.

Roman was sitting up, his eyes open but not focusing well because he blinked at her, as if he might not know her.

Yeah, well, he might wish that after she got done with him. Anger felt like an easier emotion to deal with than the relief flooding her veins. "Let me help you!"

"I can take care of myself." He reached out for the bedspread and she tucked it around him. "I'm going to take off these clothes, so you'd better turn around."

"I'm a doctor. I've seen men undressed."

"That I didn't need to know." Still, his voice felt stronger. "Just turn around."

She shook her head, turned and decided to build a fire before she clocked him. She ignored his groans as she layered the logs, the kindling, and found the matches. In moments she had fire chewing up the pine logs.

"Where are the guys who brought us here?"

Apparently he hadn't been completely out of it.

She turned around. Roman had the blanket clutched around him, shivering violently. "I'll get you another blanket." She ran back upstairs, past the guards, found the same bedroom and stripped the blanket from the bed.

As she turned, a picture caught her eye. A painting of a woman. A beautiful woman with mink-colored hair and piercing dark eyes. Eyes she'd seen before.

Eyes she'd seen broken with grief.

Julia Bednova.

Sarai went back downstairs and passed one of their guards-rescuers. He stood at the entrance, arms folded. The other stood in the kitchen, his ear to a cell phone.

They reminded her of her brother, David, when he'd served temporary detail in the Secret Service.

Roman leaned back against the sofa, his eyes closed. He shook violently. "Wow, I have to admit, I never thought it would hurt this much to be warm."

Sarai draped another blanket around him. "The pain is a good thing. It means you're alive."

He kept his eyes closed. "That's a new way to look at it."

She suppressed the urge to put her arms around him and merely sat back, pulling her knees to herself. The fire crackled, and she wondered how long the men outside the door would wait before they demanded answers.

Hopefully, until Roman stopped shivering. And until she stopped shaking.

He looked terrible. She couldn't hold in her emotions for another moment and tears filled her eyes, spilling down her cheeks.

Roman had nearly died.

Her sobs leaked out and she put a hand over her mouth to squelch the sound. Roman opened his eyes.

"Sarai…" His voice softened. "Sarai, come here."

He held one arm open. He still wore his jeans and she wanted to yell at him for that, but how could she when he looked so sweetly gallant?

She scooted over next to him before she let her brain engage.

He pulled the blanket around them and she sank close. His skin felt clammy, and she took the edge of the blanket, pulling it closer, wrapping her arm across him.

"Roman, I'm scared. I had to get help, but now the two men who helped pull you out are standing guard, right outside the door. They're going to question you."

Roman's teeth chattered as he nodded, and pulled her tighter.

"And you almost died." She put her hands over her face, trying to wipe out the image of him sliding under the ice.

See, he was going to get killed and it would shatter her.

I was shattered when you left, he'd said at Anya's dacha.

So he knew the feeling. Only, that made her feel worse, and more tears filled her eyes. She clenched her jaw, but a whimper shuddered out.

"Sar.." he groaned. "Don't…c-c-cry." He cupped her face with his hand, still wrinkled from the water. It felt like ice on her face. She didn't recoil, instead met his hazel eyes, seeing something inside them she'd seen long ago.

Something that had reached right through her layers, to the fears inside and calmed them. The look that told her that they could be soaking wet and in the clutches of a couple of Russian thugs, with her life spiraling out of control, and he'd do anything to keep her safe.

Run through gunfire, or maybe go AWOL and follow her to Siberia.

And, while she probably wouldn't be in this mess if he hadn't talked her into an unauthorized visit to a nuclear reactor, she also wouldn't feel the one-hundred-percent certainty that she wasn't alone. Maybe she *did* need a hero. Someone who would die for her. Despite Roman's charisma, his antics, even the way he drove her to her last nerve, Roman was precisely that hero.

So, why, exactly, had she left him?

His thumb caressed her cheek, and his gaze traced her face, her eyes, her nose.

Her mouth.

He moved slowly, as if caught in time, or slowed by fear, and she helped by meeting him halfway.

Roman.

He kissed her softly, his hand holding her jaw, then moving around behind her neck. Strong. Purposed. He pulled her closer and deepened the kiss.

Sarai let him. Roman. *Her* Roman. She felt something inside breaking free, something she'd kept locked for so very, very long.

She could admit that her rejection of him might be less about her disappointment about his career choice and more about sheer fear—after all, he did show up bloodied, the materialization of her worst nightmares, in Red Square, and he hadn't flinched at risking his neck, ever, in the ten-plus years since.

All the same, being in his wavelength again had scraped away the denial.

She still loved him. Heartbreakingly so.

"Roman." She pulled away, her gaze on his mouth. He stilled, and she met his eyes.

"I'm sorry. I…should have asked." He wore apology in his frown. "I just… I missed you."

Her chest knotted, words that she longed to say, should have said ages ago, filling her throat. She'd always operated on the belief that he wanted to go out a hero, in a blaze of glory. In a shootout, taking down the outlaws in the world.

But he'd been willing to sacrifice his life in the middle of Siberia, with no one watching so she might escape.

The man shivering in her arms was exactly the man she'd once loved—a man of principle, of passion.

A man who wanted to save lives, just like she did. Maybe he had become exactly the man God wanted him to be. Not Paul the Missionary, but David the Warrior.

She should give him more credit for working out God's call on his life.

"Roman, I saw something upstairs…something strange."

"A whirlpool tub with a—"

"No." She gave him a playful smack, and he smiled as he closed his eyes.

"A picture of Julia Bednov. The governor's wife."

Roman frowned, still not opening his eyes. "Bednov owns shares in Alexander Oil. I'll bet this place is on their property."

"Their son died of renal failure, remember?"

Roman opened his eyes. Stared at her.

"And Maxim, from the village, his mother was a cook in a local factory."

"Like a nuclear plant? Did she do some extra cooking for a certain governor-to-be and his wife?"

Sarai glanced at the door, lowered her voice. "She might have even brought Maxim along, maybe to work, or even play with Sasha."

"So, how would they both get infected with nuclear waste? The plant is far enough away that—"

"The lake."

His mouth opened, but no words came out. Then he closed it. And if he'd been white already, he paled even further. "Of course. It's probably fed by underground streams. Russia's standard practice is to submerge its used nuclear fuel in a pond to cool, but if any of the containers leaked, the waste would have been absorbed into the sand around the pond, and then into the underground streams and fed into the lake."

"Roman, I'm sure that you weren't in there long enough—" She put a hand over her mouth to stop herself, but tears came again.

Roman brushed one away with his thumb. "Don't cry, *Sarichka*. I'll be okay. I'm in God's hands, remember?"

At the moment, she didn't want to go there. Didn't want to talk about being in God's hands. Although God had saved Roman this time, she didn't know what was going to happen in the next hour, and she wasn't putting her hopes up too far. A person could get skewered believing too much.

Maybe, in fact, Roman had nailed the truth. She didn't trust God. Not at all.

"I always knew you'd die in the line of duty."

"That's the risk of my job, Sarai. I'm a cop. That's what I do. I always thought that's what Jesus meant when he said to 'take up our cross and follow Him.' To accept our mission in life wherever it leads, even if it leads to death."

He gave her a sad smile.

"I'll get you home. Get you tested. You'll be fine." Her voice sounded like it had come through a vise.

"Of course I will," he said softly and ran his hand down her hair. He'd stopped trembling, but she felt a tremor start in her soul.

"I always thought that taking up our cross meant that if we were going to die for something, let it be worthwhile," she said.

He leaned his forehead to hers. "Saving the world from nuclear terrorists seems pretty worthwhile."

Not if it meant she had to watch him die.

"I don't know what that verse means, Roman. I just know that I—"

The door slammed open. Mafia One filled the door frame, and he didn't look happy. "*Gotov?*" he asked.

Ready? For what?

Chapter Fourteen

He might actually get some sleep this night. Alexei Bednov replaced the receiver and stood up from his desk. Stretched. Julia was in the next room, sprawled on the sofa, watching television. Sauced to the gills. He'd found her in a slump on the floor in the kitchen an hour ago, and it had taken his last shred of kindness not to leave her there.

I'll get you, Alexei. Julia's voice rung in Bednov's ears.

Sure you will, sweetie, the governor thought. He smiled and poured himself a snifter of brandy. Now that the militia and FSB had restored order to the city, this day had been calmer. Curfew, certainly. But in time, he'd lift that. Restore government. Provisionally, of course.

This could work. He'd seen it in the cards years ago, knew that one day he'd be poised to reclaim all Russia had lost. Disillusionment with the capitalist way caused society to demand change, just as he knew it would. A person couldn't eat freedom. Of course, he understood the benefits of capitalism, and could live with the negatives, like Barry Riddle, and his two incarcerated investors.

He'd try them for murder. And then execute them.

If he could not execute them, he'd let them languish in a Siberian prison for a few years. That would keep their mouths closed.

He sipped the brandy. It coated his throat with heat, loosening the knot of tension in his chest. He smiled at the image of one FSB agent being wrung out by Fyodor. He'd wanted Novik in his custody for too long now—from the first day the agent had met Gregori Smirnov. It wasn't easy to find a courier who not only believed, but was willing to risk his health for the good of Mother Russia.

Fyodor would know what to do to make him talk. Especially since Novik—and the American girl—had broken into the Khandaski nuclear plant. By morning, Bednov would know just how much Captain Novik and his girlfriend knew. Little, probably. But enough to raise noses in other parts of the country.

Not everyone believed in a strong Russia. At least not in *his* definition of strong.

But here, in the province of Irkutia, they did. Because Alexander Evgeyovich Bednov was their leader.

He poured himself another snifter of brandy. His men had pulled the two from the ice. They could return them there when they finished. He smiled at that.

How convenient. He wouldn't ever swim in that lake anyway.

Roman decided he had to still be in shock, or partially frozen because that last shot to his gut should have hurt more than it did. As it was, his brain felt fuzzy, his eyesight cutting in and out.

Sadly, his eyesight cleared enough to see a guy who probably played the underground fight-club circuit backing up and rubbing his fist. Roman felt profoundly grateful that he'd kept his jeans on—even if they were heavy and cold on his legs. Imagine how fun it would be to be interrogated, his hands tied behind him as he sat in a chair in his skivvies. That thought followed with profound gratefulness that he could feel his legs, that he was alive.

At least, for now.

He blinked, trying to clear his vision, and got a fix on the tall, scar-faced, bald interrogator who seemed to be getting a second wind.

Joy to the world.

Roman licked his lip, tasted blood and sensed that it might be thick, although that, too, had gone numb. Fight Club circled him like a hyena.

"Irkutia is now under martial law. Your rights no longer apply, Mr. FSB. And—" he jerked his head toward the other room "—neither do hers." Fight Club leaned close, breathed fish into Roman's face. "We only want to know what you were looking for."

A hot sauna, some smoked salmon and some alone time with the girl in the next room.

Roman said nothing. The longer he held out, the more time Sarai had for Vicktor to show up in Smolsk, get worried and come looking for them.

Roman hung on to the hope that Vicktor had the sleuthing skills to guess Roman had paid a visit to the reactor. Too bad he'd lost his sat phone on the bottom of the lake. Or should he say, toxic pool?

"You know we'll ask her next. And believe me, she may be a doctor, but nothing is going to heal what we do to her."

Roman tried not to let the reaction out, past his gut, but he inadvertently clenched his jaw.

Fight Club grabbed him by the hair. "I'm not kidding. It's been a long time since I've been up close and personal with an American girl. Are they all the same?"

Roman shook his head out of the man's grip. "Leave her alone. And listen up. I'm an FSB agent, and if I don't check in you can bet they'll come looking for me." He'd been repeating the same information for nearly an hour—was it an hour? It could be ten minutes and his befuddled brain wouldn't know the difference.

He heard a growl behind him. Braced himself. But the man only grabbed him by the hair again and hauled him to his feet. "Maybe you should rethink your answer while we talk to your girlfriend."

Panic spiked through him, conjuring up images. "Leave her alone. She doesn't know anything. She's a doctor—I kidnapped her."

Mr. Fight Club chuckled, as if amused. Roman jerked his head and realized that maybe he wasn't as numb as he'd hoped. He surrendered as the man led him back to the family room. Fight Club opened the door, made to push Roman to the floor.

Roman heard a scream and saw feet rushing at him. He flinched, ducked and rolled as Sarai launched herself at his interrogator.

What was she doing? Trying to get herself killed? Obviously, Fight Club and his pal had underestimated her when they left her untied in the room. "Sarai!"

He rolled onto his back, saw Fight Club wrestling a poker out of her hands. Blood trickled down his temple, but he had fury in his eyes as he gave the poker a vicious twist. Sarai cried out.

Fight Club raised the poker above his head. Sarai covered her head with her hands just as Roman kicked the man in the gut.

He bent over, and a whoosh of air escaped his lungs. Roman kicked him again across the face.

They'd attracted attention. Mafia Two appeared—the dark-haired one with the cell phone, and a gun. He held it on Roman. "Stop," he said calmly.

Fight Club stood up, flicked a glance at Sarai, who had backed up against the wall with her hands still curled over her head. Then he kicked Roman hard, right above the kidneys.

Roman stifled a scream, but pain exploded in his entire body and for a second he thought he might throw up.

“Leave him alone!” Sarai’s voice cut through the blinding pain. Through his blurred vision he saw her leap to her feet. “He’s ill and still suffering from hypothermia.” He recognized her doctor’s voice, despite a quavering around the edges. “If you let him rest, he’ll be in better shape to talk to you.”

No, Sarai. I’ll just feel the pain again when I don’t talk. Only, he couldn’t seem to form words with his stiff lips.

“Please. Listen, I’ll tell you what I know. Leave him alone.”

No!

To reinforce her words, Mafia Two grabbed Sarai and pressed the pistol against her throat.

She went white.

Roman stopped breathing. Fight Club straddled him, hit him again.

“Stop, please,” Sarai said in a voice barely audible.

As he watched, they pulled Sarai out into the hall. A sacrificial offering.

He lay in a ball as the door clicked shut and wanted to cry.

“What are you going to do to me?” Her voice sounded tinny.

The man she’d hit held his hand to his head and glared at her. Her stomach felt floppy and weak, her legs trembled.

He reached for her.

“Stop.” The command came from the other man. He lowered his gun away from Sarai. “We’re to keep them alive until Fyodor gets here.”

Keep them alive?

Her head started a slow spin. She reached out for the wall. Keep them alive. Yes, that's what she had to do.

Sarai took a deep breath. Years of muscling past bullies who wanted to scalp her or steal her medicines had taught her to sort out her thoughts, think through each breath. She latched on to her anger, separating it from fear and steeled her voice. "I'm a doctor and he needs something hot to drink, or he'll die. I'm going to make him tea."

Bleeding Mafia stared at her. Her pounding heart filled the gap of time. Then, he pushed her toward the kitchen and let her go. "In there."

She ignored the frowns of the two men, especially the one she'd hoped to skewer, and prayed that she had the strength to walk past them, to enact her plan without crumpling into a ball.

Again.

She should have been quicker, braver. As it was, she'd only worked her courage to half the needed strength, despite being crouched beside the door for nearly a half hour. Who did she think she was—a super hero? They probably doubted she had it in her to pounce, but she'd had her ear to the wall, and every time Roman made a noise—a noise that ripped her heart a little further from its moorings—her resolve hardened.

She had to get him out of here before they killed him. She'd just have to resort to plan B.

Whatever that might be.

Lord, give me wisdom! Help me save us. How had she gone

from life securely in her grip to fraying fast and well into desperation? She had to admit, she never felt more abandoned by God than now. After all she'd done for Him, she thought He'd certainly step in. Hadn't she earned at least that? In fact, she had to wonder if she wasn't somehow being punished. Only, for what? Loving Roman?

No, that came with its own inherent punishment. A girl should have to sign a disclaimer, or waiver of damages when she got near him.

She should have read the clause about how he'd grind her heart into little bitty pieces of sorrow. She'd heard that last little groan he made and wanted to wail.

Trust in the Lord with all your heart.

The verse from her childhood made her pause right inside the kitchen. Mafia One nearly stomped over her.

"Sorry," she said, meekly.

Buy time.

Her heart filled her throat, and she struggled to swallow it back into place. She went to the stove and grabbed a pot of water.

"No tricks. Or your boyfriend gets hurt." Mafia One sat, grabbed a napkin and put it to his head. Sarai saw the action and winced.

Be apologetic.

The thought arrowed into her head as she filled the pot with water. Hopefully it wasn't ground water. As in *toxic* ground water. She put it on the electric stove to boil.

"I'm a doctor. Maybe I should look at that." She turned and advanced toward him. He raised his pistol. "Get back."

Sarai raised her hands, saw that they shook. Probably a good thing, because then neither of them harbored any illusions. She felt her heartbeat as a pulse at the base of her neck.

She turned, opened up a cabinet and began to search for tea. Mafia One still had the napkin—now dotted with blood—pressed to his head. Some doctor she was—first do no harm. See the things Roman made her do?

She found tea boxes—Indian tea, and green tea. English breakfast tea. And, wedged into another box, right behind the teas…*Moscovskaya yspokaivayushee sredstva.*

Sedatives.

Of course. Julia Bednov probably had them stashed throughout the house.

She grabbed the box and did a quick count. The size of sugar packets, the sedatives dissolved in water. She'd used them on a few occasions for grieving parents, or even agitated patients. For that matter, she'd even given a mild dosage to Julia.

Apparently, the woman needed the stuff more than Sarai realized.

With the right dosage, the mafia brothers would drop like stones and wake up with nothing more than a couple head knockers.

She took down a box of green tea and opened it.

Be friendly.

She turned and held up the box. "Want some tea?"

Mafia One narrowed his beady dark eyes. Then, praise God! He nodded.

Sarai smiled.

She found teacups and ladled in tea bags. And then, one eye on her captor, she ripped open a handful of packets and poured in the white powder. She shoved the wrappers up her sleeve, then poured the water into the cups.

Stirred.

"I'm taking this into Roman. I made one for your… friend, too. They're on the counter." She picked up a cup and saucer, turning to leave.

Mafia One stood, and stopped her with a grip on her arm.

"Try again, Americanka." He reached out, took the cup from her hand. "Take one of those."

Sarai looked at the cup in his hand, then shrugged and turned. "Suit yourself. They're all alike."

Then she walked past him, thankful that her hand didn't tremble.

But, inside she was doing a wild rumba. He'd taken the bait.

She heard him grunt at Mafia Two as she stopped by Roman's door and nudged it open.

She closed it behind her, praying.

Roman writhed on the floor, his hands behind his back, working at his bonds. He looked up and the relief on his face took her breath away. "Please, tell me you're okay. That they didn't hurt you."

"I made tea."

He blinked at her. Frowned. Stared at the tea. "I'm sorry, I have no idea what you just said."

"I made tea." She crouched next to him. "I'll untie you."

She fought her shaking hands, feeling his gaze on her.

"Did you just say you made tea?"

"I did. I…well—" she lowered her voice "—I put sedatives in it. So don't drink any."

He raised his eyebrows and then grinned. It felt like one-hundred-thousand watts of sunshine to her heart.

His hands came free. He rolled over and reached for her. In the brief moment before he slid his hand around her neck and pulled her to him, she saw a sheen in his hot eyes.

As if he'd been…crying?

He kissed her hard, an almost desperate release of emotions. Nothing gentle there. Pure fear and heartache rolled into his kiss. The intensity rushed through her, caught her unaware and left her unhinged.

Roman was afraid. That, she never, ever expected.

He pushed her away, holding her at arm's length. "How long before it takes effect?"

She glanced at the door. "I don't know. They're waiting for someone."

He nodded, grabbed for his shirt and pulled it over his head.

"You need shoes."

His bare feet looked cold and pale. She stood and cracked open the door. The two guards were sitting at the table, drinking. She saw a vodka bottle in the middle and cringed.

Hopefully, however, it would only accelerate the process.

She clicked the door shut and paced, rubbing her hands together. A fire chewed the logs. One fell atop another and sparks flew. The smell of smoke filled the room and made her hair and skin feel gummy.

Roman sat up, cupping his hands around the tea. "Uh, is this spiked, too?"

"Yes. I didn't want to take any chances." He took a sip and some of it dribbled from his wounded lip.

"Probably need something to calm my racing heart." Then he winked at her, and he looked so…*not* desperate, *not* afraid or like they were hostages about to get beaten up that she just had to give a huff of disbelief.

Trust Roman to find a silver lining in the thunderclouds.

"*Gatov?*" growled a voice as the door cracked open.

She cringed but stepped back from the door. Mafia One entered, a little shaky, but menacing enough to sent a bolt of fear through her. He pointed his gun at Roman. "Get up."

"No!" She grabbed the man's arm, not sure what she expected, but not ready to hear Roman suffer, again.

Mafia pushed her down, and she hit the ground, hard.

"Leave her alone!" Even in his fatigue, Roman had "hero" flooding his veins and he pounced to his feet, right between Mafia Boy and Sarai.

Sarai's stomach clawed at her throat.

Mafia One swung at Roman's head. And, as Roman dodged the blow, Mafia One stumbled.

Roman saw it.

He grabbed at the gun. It skittered out of Mafia One's hand and onto the floor.

Sarai squelched a scream and dove for the gun. She picked it up, both hands wrapped around the butt. "Stop!"

Mafia One ignored her. He swung at Roman, but Roman dodged and his fist landed in the door. Mafia One howled.

Roman one-two punched him and Mafia One landed at his feet. Out cold. Roman stared at him, then looked at Sarai. "Let's get out of here."

Sarai scrambled to her feet, ran out into the hall.

Mafia Two was slumped at the table, his hand around his gun. *Please, Lord, don't let them be dead.* Even if they sort of deserved it.

Roman appeared with a coat and a pair of boots. He shoved the coat on her and his feet into the boots, then took her hand. He grinned wildly, as if he might be a boy sneaking into the circus.

"Glad you're not my doctor," he said.

She mock-glared at him. "I should be. Then maybe I could get your head examined and figure out what it is about you that attracts trouble."

He pulled her through the house, grabbed a hat and coat for himself and shoved a fur *shapka* on her head. "It's you, baby. You attract trouble."

Oh, yeah, that's right. She attracted *him.*

They ran out into the cold, and it nearly took her breath away. Roman ran to the snowmobiles. "Think you can drive one of these?"

Sarai had already climbed aboard. Was he kidding? She could drive an F-16 fighter jet if it meant getting out of here and back to Smolsk.

And…then where? As she pulled the start cord and started the engine, she cut that question from her mind.

She wasn't leaving Smolsk. She was a doctor. With a duty.

She didn't care if that duty cost her freedom.

Or her heart.

Chapter Fifteen

He couldn't believe how much he'd completely misjudged her. As Roman urged his snowmobile into the grayness of twilight, his headlights barely illuminating Sarai's sled, he knew one thing.

She had been absolutely 120-percent correct. She didn't need a hero.

She'd saved *him*. Twice today, if his muddled brain sorted out the facts correctly. He still felt chilled, right through to his capillaries, but a warmth sizzled in the center of his chest, keeping his core warm.

Sarai had kissed him. In between the terror of nearly dying and the pain at the hands of Fight Club, for a brief snapshot in time, he'd held her in his arms, not once, but *twice*. And she'd kissed him.

Not tentatively, not fearfully, but eagerly. *Eagerly.* At least the first time.

The second was all about him, not being able to put a cap on the fear that he'd lost her, and even worse the fear that he'd caused her brutal rape and murder.

She'd been right to leave him. He let that thought bruise him for a moment.

No, better to think about her in his arms, safe, kissing him as if she loved him, as if she'd been sorry she left. He let that thought seep out of his heart, into his chest and to the rest of his chilled extremities. And, if she loved him, maybe he wouldn't have to arrest her. Maybe she'd leave, with him.

Happily.

Oy, that lake had to have really turned his brain into an ice cube because his synapses not only weren't firing but they'd sizzled right out. One—he wasn't going to arrest her. Two—she'd never leave happily. Maybe kicking and screaming, or at the best, begrudgingly. But there wouldn't be jigs of joy when she closed up shop in Smolsk.

She'd worked too hard, too long for her dreams. The thought of her leaving it all behind, destroying all she'd worked for had him feeling light-headed and nauseous.

He should pack up and go home, trust her instincts about him and Russia's visa laws. How many times did they kick foreigners out of Russia these days? Seriously?

Don't answer that.

The wind had returned, and along with it turned the snow into whirling dervishes that swept up before his sled and pelted him. His eyelashes felt frozen and heavy, and he could taste the cold chapping his lips. At least he could *feel* his lips.

Ahead of him, Sarai, using some sort of inner GPS, headed straight south. Toward the road to Smolsk. Roman estimated they had about three hours until they reached the town at this clip.

Hopefully, the Mafia boys—Bednov's boys?—had topped off their tanks that morning before their hot pursuit of Bonnie and Clyde.

He rolled around the ramifications of Sarai's theory. Bednov and his family had vacationed at their Alexander Oil dacha long enough for little Sasha to be infected with radioactive waste from the nuclear plant. And what if dead Barry Riddle in Khabarovsk had eaten contaminated fish? Then wouldn't Alexander Bednov also be sick? Not if he knew about the lake.

No, most likely the fish in Riddle's gut came from Lake Baikal, served up in some posh restaurant in Irkutsk when he'd had dinner with Bednov. But was that proof enough that Bednov was involved in the smuggling of nuclear ammunition? Namely highly enriched uranium?

Nyet. Although circumstances painted a suspicious picture, Bednov might be an innocent in all this. Doubtful, given his history, but possible. Which left Roman with a big *nol* when it came to finding the uranium supplier.

If only he'd gotten the lot number on those casks.

If only Smirnov hadn't offed himself—or been offed—in Moscow.

Yanna's words came back to him, like an echo caught in time. *"Gregori Khetrov is on the board of directors. He's a communications billionaire in Moscow, only right now he's sitting in Lubyanka prison, courtesy the FSB, on tax charges."*

He wanted to give himself a head slap—only, he'd probably dump the sled over. How could he be so stupid? Bednov and Khetrov were stockholders in Alexander Oil. Of course they'd take out Smirnov first chance they got.

If only he had his telephone—sadly it was being eaten by toxic waste at the moment—he'd have Khetrov put in solitary before someone could do him the same favor they did Smirnov.

Roman felt his adrenaline kick in. Bednov could have planned this entire thing—the coup, the ousting of foreigners—to seize control of his oil interests and to protect his smuggling operation.

A plot that only a conniver like Bednov could conceive.

And, if Bednov connected the dots, he'd figure out that the same beautiful doctor who treated his dying son just might use her incredible brain to link him to the toxic waste, then the nuclear plant....

But he wouldn't guess in a million years that Sarai knew anything about smuggling of nuclear materials. Unless, of course, she had a nosy FSB agent on her tail, one who dragged her inside said nuclear plant, only to get caught and his insides slightly rearranged by Bednov's thugs, who then passed that information onto Bednov.

Again, a great leap, but his chest squeezed.

He had to get Sarai out of Irkutia, pronto.

Except what if the Mafia boys called Bednov? He'd be on the next plane to Bali.

Save Sarai or nail Bednov? Now the knot formed right in the center of Roman's skull, and he winced. Couldn't he do both?

The options whirred before him. Didn't Yanna say Vicktor had hopped a plane for Irkutia? Roman could pass Sarai off into Vicktor's capable hands, then go in for the kill on Bednov.

You're after your own personal glory, Roman.

No, he wasn't. He was out to save lives.

A sick burning filled in his throat. How he hated when her words tunneled deep and unearthed doubts.

Apparently she knew him better than he knew himself. Because, if he was honest, he'd rather have his fingernails gnawed off by piranhas than die in disgrace like his father.

Besides, he owed Bednov a taste of his own medicine. The thought became a memory, and with it, emerged his father's voice. "We failed communism." Roman found himself back inside his father's dingy two-room flat the last time he saw him alive.

The man looked grizzled and pale, with a tinge of yellow to his skin that hinted at liver poisoning. The scent of vodka embedded his rumpled suit coat—the only one he owned—a piece of the past from the days when he had reason to wear it. Roman took the vodka bottle from his father's clasp.

"Right, Pa. Whatever you say," he said softly. He'd flown in for three days, mostly because his old boss—a militiaman and neighbor—had seen Gregori Novik slouched in the corridor, next to a potato bin. And temperatures in Irkutsk hovered just above zero. Roman had to get his father to help—the hospital, at least.

"We failed communism!" Gregori grabbed at the bottle, missed and went down chin-first into the floor. He lay there, groaning, and Roman sighed. Gregori hadn't been the same since Glasnost. Since his "religion" had fallen, along with the busts of Lenin.

Roman grabbed his father under the armpits, hauled him into the bedroom. He pulled off the old man's *valenki* and winced. The man's feet were nearly black.

Frostbite.

"Pop, I need to get you to a hospital—"

"Nyet." His father wrestled himself out of Roman's grip and flopped back on the bed. Roman noticed the gray tinge of the sheets, and the smell emanating from the center of the bed. How had his father gone from respected munitions factory director to rummy?

Alexander Bednov. Once his father's boss, he'd taken over the factory and sold off the pieces to the highest bidder, just like every former Party leader turned capitalist in the early days of perestroika.

Bednov had left his father jobless. Without a ruble to his name.

He'd also pinned on Gregori the blame for the missing capital, had even threatened jail time until Roman handed out rain-check favors to officials from here to Siberia.

Some, he still hadn't repaid.

Roman wrestled his father out of the dingy suit coat and pulled up the covers. Now what? He saw the faintest remnants of his mother's touch—a family picture hanging from a nail on the wall, a military pose the army had snapped of Roman his first week as a Brown Boy. Wallpaper, a rose-and-gold pattern she'd put up just months before she left, peeled from around the door frame.

She'd married someone else, a friend of Gregori's who had surfaced from the rubble with his own small empire. Roman could barely forgive her as she lay dying of leukemia two years later. Christ's strength had carried him through those black months. But Gregori never said goodbye. Just drank himself into numbed oblivion.

It felt like a century since their family had been intact. Roman had grown up in that flat, and in the back of his mind he saw happier times—the New Year's tree, his parents attending his hockey matches, the Communist flag hanging on the wall, right next to a picture of his father with Irkutia's General Secretary Varanov. Those had been days filled with hope and a future. Roman wandered through the flat, picking up garbage, empty vodka bottles, cigarette butts. His chest tightened as he fought waves of despair. He stopped in the family room and stared at a picture of his father, in his uniform, gleaming with medals, his arms around his wife and son as he stared stoically into the camera. Roman remembered that day. He'd been about twelve. His father had dressed them up, taken them in for a portrait. Roman had held his breath, trying not to smile as the photographer counted down the seconds until he replaced the cover on the camera.

Roman had wanted to be just like his father that day. And a thousand days after that, even when he went into the military. He'd be a Party man. A man who lived for Mother Russia.

Until he met David Curtiss. David, and the awakening of freedom in Russia, introduced him to a new way of living. A living that had purpose beyond a government, that outlasted leaders. A living that earned him a right hook across his jaw the first time Roman had mentioned it to his disillusioned father. The slap felt like a *pero,* a knife slicing deep into his heart, dividing the past from the future. A future that now meant that he'd never end up curled with a bottle like his old man.

Roman believed in Jesus and His ability to change him from the inside out, to make his life purposeful. To give him a real hope and a future. One that didn't include letting Bednov escape.

Roman blinked away the memories and stared into the stream of light cutting through the darkness, filtering the snowflakes.

There had to be a way to nab Bednov *and* save Sarai. It started with getting Sarai to trust him, to believe that he only wanted the best for her and to get her to abandon her death grip on her clinic and leave with Vicktor.

The only remaining alternative would be to arrest her.

He still couldn't quite get that thought into his brain without wincing.

But he couldn't leave. Not with Bednov still in power. Even if he left Irkutia, Bednov's men would track him and

Sarai across Russia, and beyond. Sarai wouldn't be safe until Bednov was brought down.

He gunned his sled, drove even with Sarai, and she slowed slightly.

"Sarai! Are you cold?"

She looked at him. Shook her head.

They were out in the open and under the starry sky, the clouds having been emptied by the blizzard, with the moon pouring down light. Idle oil wells made eerie outlines. They'd long passed Alexander Oil headquarters. The road would appear soon. Roman estimated thirty or so kilometers to Smolsk.

The cold wind leaked in under his hat and burned his ears. His breath puffed out ahead of him, streaming behind him. He focused his brain on a hot cup of tea and a warm bed. Make that sedative-free tea.

And repaying Bednov for the crimes against his family, and all of Russia.

Roman would somehow be the patriot his father hadn't been.

Sarai watched Roman hunch over as he tunneled into the night. She'd fudged the truth—she felt frozen clear through, and couldn't feel her legs, let alone her toes. The only things hot were her hands—thanks to the handlebar heaters on this polarius snow bike—and her heart.

Or maybe pure shock generated the heat inside.

She'd just knocked out two guys, saved Roman's hide and was now fleeing for her life.

Forty-eight hours in his life and he'd turned hers upside down. Who, exactly, had she become?

Please, *please,* reach Smolsk soon. She focused her thoughts on something warm—her comforter, hot tea, maybe Roman's arms around…

She shook the thought away. Despite their kiss, they had no future. Not as long as Roman insisted on being a cop instead of… No, that wasn't fair.

For the first time, as she'd gotten an in-her-face glimpse of the dark side of his job, she knew that God had to have called him to his place in the world, just as He'd called her to missions. Roman was a man of honor, of discipline and sacrifice, of courage. A real hero, and a man who trusted God.

She cut her gaze back to him. He looked cold as he hunched over, fighting through the snow. Her doctor's concern stabbed at her. He shouldn't be out here in the snow, in the cold.

His pants were probably frozen to his legs.

He wouldn't be in this mess if she'd listened to him. If she hadn't gone racing off to Khanda. What good had she done there, anyway? What if her guess about the connection between Maxim and Sasha was wrong?

By returning to Smolsk and staying in Irkutia, she could be risking both their lives.

And, well, she'd already been there, done that today.

Her sled hiccuped and she jerked forward. Roman's sled pulled out ahead.

She felt the hum trail away, then the machine sputtered

and died. The sudden quiet, after the steady roar in her ears, felt strangely serene. Roman turned, then circled his snowmobile.

"What's up?" he said over the roar of his engine.

"I dunno. It just died." He looked like the abominable snowman, frost caking his hair, his whiskers.

"Must be out of gas." He had to have seen her shivering. "You're cold."

She said nothing.

"C'mere." He reached out, grabbed hold of her jacket and nearly pulled her off her snowmobile into his lap.

Up close, she could see that frost whitened his eyelashes, coated the ends of his hair.

"I'm worried about you," he said. He pulled her tight to him, circled his arms around her. "Maybe I need to find us a place to hole up, get warm."

Right here, right now, she felt warm. How she wanted to close her eyes and stay. Right. Here.

He'd nearly drowned, been pummeled by a couple of goons and was probably frozen to the core, and he was worried about her?

It surged a wave of longing, and regret, inside her.

"Roman, didn't you say there was an airfield around here?"

He put her away from him slightly and nodded. She searched his eyes and saw in them confusion. She summoned her courage.

"Maybe I should leave."

She wondered if he heard her. He said nothing. Stared at her. Frowned. "I don't understand."

He cut his engine.

In the silence that flooded into the wake, she heard only her heartbeat, and the mourning of her dreams. But for Roman, and all he'd gone through for her today…

"We could go there. Didn't you say we could requisition a plane? We'll leave Irkutia."

He stared at her, but the smile, the ooo-rah, even the hug she half hoped for was strangely absent.

"What about your clinic?"

Huh?

"I mean, well, don't you want to go back and check on it before you leave?"

He had to have been under that ice longer than she thought. "I, ah…"

He touched his forehead to hers. "Sar, I know how much the clinic means to you. We'll leave tomorrow. After you've checked on things and we've warmed up."

Warmed up? She felt something hot start in her throat and zing the back of her eyes. Now this was the Roman she'd hoped for. Someone who put her dreams ahead of his own. Someone who cared enough about her life goals to make sure they would be taken care of in her absence.

Finally.

"What if you're right and Bednov or someone sends militia after me?"

Roman's gaze was searching her face. "My number-one priority here is keeping you safe. That's all I care about. I promise you, I won't let anything happen to you."

He cared about her. It wasn't a declaration of love, but right now it could be enough.

She closed her eyes, leaned against him. She was cold. But only on the outside. Inside she felt warm.

And not lonely in the least.

"Climb on behind me."

Sarai shifted to sit behind him, locking her arms around his waist. She leaned her head against his coat.

Roman pulled the cord, then, when the snowmobile hummed, he glanced back with a reassuring smile. "Didn't I tell you once that I'd always make sure you were safe?"

Oh, too late. Because her hero FSB agent hadn't the slightest inkling that around him, she, and her heart, felt anything but safe.

Chapter Sixteen

"What do you mean they got away?" Alexei Bednov didn't care if his tone woke Julia. She needed to wake up, maybe attend to some of his needs. Bednov rolled out of his bed and paced the floor in his bare feet. Outside, night seeped into the room, fractured only by the display on his digital clock and the occasional blocks of light from flats across the street.

Julia lay sprawled beside him, her dark hair in mats on her pillow. He'd flipped her onto his shoulder and tossed her in bed a few hours ago. She still reeked of vodka and cigarette smoke, but he hadn't cared. He needed her only for what she could give him, however little.

Probably, he'd have to think past this moment, to what she could give him tomorrow, and the day after. Losing Sasha had changed her.

If she'd been sober, she'd have had nothing to do with

him. He'd seen the fury in her eyes during her rare coherent moments. She meant what she said. *"I'll make sure you pay…."*

He tightened a fist and turned away from her. She should learn from others the consequences of leveling threats against Governor Alexander Evgeyovich Bednov.

"How did they escape?" he asked.

He could hardly believe Fyodor's reply. "She drugged them."

Bednov ran his hand over his thinning hair, feeling physically ill, and sank onto the side of the bed. "You can find them, right? Get rid of them? I don't care how."

Fyodor sounded tired. "I'll find them, Governor. I might need some backup, however."

Bednov rubbed his hand across his forehead, trying to ease the knot from his frontal lobe. "Okay. I'll send some men. The FSB shouldn't be any trouble. I've put out a warrant for Novik's arrest. He'll end up like former Governor Kazlov."

"And the American girl?"

Bednov glanced at his soused wife. "With agent Novik out the way, who knows what will happen to her?"

Roman felt like an ice cube when he pulled up to Sarai's apartment. The wind had died to a rustle, the snow lay like frosting on the dirty roads, the rutted yards. The stars punctured the night canopy here and there, casting silvery brilliance along the icy roads.

He stopped and turned off the snowmobile, feeling like

he might still be moving. Behind him, Sarai shivered, blowing into her cupped hands, trying to warm her nose.

The door to the apartment building banged and Roman nearly jumped from the sled, ready to pounce on a late night drunk. The man wobbled out into the night and staggered down the road, dredging up one too many memories for Roman.

He needed to get Sarai inside, make sure Bednov's men weren't on her trail, then get someplace warm and clear his head.

Maybe he could also try to forget that he'd manipulated Sarai. She'd been willing to leave, and he'd turned her down. Which made him more of a heel than she realized.

He'd keep his promise to David…just not the way David hoped.

Roman got off the sled, tucked his arm under Sarai's. She leaned into his assistance, betraying her fatigue and he felt another stab of guilt. She wouldn't be bone-weary and cold if he hadn't dragged her out on his investigative hunches.

A real hero would have her on the first plane out of Irkutia, like she'd suggested.

"Roman, you can sleep at the clinic," Sarai said as they made their way up the stairs to her flat. Roman said nothing but took the key out of her stiff hand and opened the steel door. He closed it quietly behind him and locked it before he opened the next set of doors.

Sarai moved to step inside, but he blocked her. "Just…wait."

He moved in quietly, without the lights and listened.

Nothing but the thud of his own heart against his chest. He let a sigh of relief trickle out. "Okay, I think it's safe."

She came in, turned on the light. "Ah, heat." She pulled off her *valenki* and coat, but kept on her *shapka.* "I think I'll sleep with it on," she said with a soft smile.

With her hair still frozen around her face, her eyes framed by snow crystals, that slight smile found the still-functioning places inside him, and despite the guilt he felt, he reached out and pulled her to him.

He realized he was trembling.

She wrapped her arms around him. "We're okay, Roman."

He closed his eyes. For now. But what about tomorrow? *Please, Vicktor be here, take her away.*

She molded to him and hung on longer than he'd anticipated.

Longer, probably, than was healthy for him. Because, although he'd felt frozen a moment ago, he was thawing quickly.

He put her away from him. "I'm going to make you some tea while you change out of those clothes." He went into the kitchen before she could protest, and he heard her close her bedroom door.

Lock it, Sar. Because while he was a Christian, he was also a man, and right now he felt weary, cold and just a little overwhelmed. He didn't know how much self-control he could muster if she so much as smiled at him too broadly.

Especially since he had a dark feeling that after tomorrow he wouldn't be seeing too many of her smiles. Not once she realized he'd turned down her grand gesture for the personal glory of hunting down Bednov, international smuggler.

No, not glory. Justice.

Whatever. Roman went into the kitchen, put on the water and warmed his hands by the flame of the gas stove while it heated. He searched her cupboard and found a box of English Breakfast Tea next to the phony sugar bowl. The tea was steeping by the time she returned wearing sweatpants, a turtleneck, a University of Moscow sweatshirt and two pairs of socks. She'd pulled her hair back, into a ponytail, and without a hint of makeup, she looked like she might be twenty-one, and right out of college.

She leaned against the door and smiled at him. Sweetly.

Oh, no.

Roman backed up, folded his arms across his chest. *Lord, help me here to be the guy I'm supposed to be.* "I made you tea."

"Yes, you did." Only, she made no move for it. Instead, she advanced toward him. She had a small galley kitchen, with room for a tiny two-chair table, a small stove and a single sink.

He had nowhere to run. She came up to him, put her hands on his chest and looked into his eyes.

She had incredible eyes. And he saw right through them to the past, to the time when she'd told him she loved him.

He should have asked her to marry him. Instead, he'd held her face in his hands and kissed her.

Now, he only swallowed, unable to face the depth of

those feelings, and how much he'd longed for them. But someone needed to snap his fingers and wake them both up. They had the relationship of a cluster bomb—a blinding flash and lots of pain. Because, she wasn't going to give up her missionary life.

And he wasn't going to give up law enforcement.

Sarai leaned into him, raised her chin. "Thank you for the tea."

"Drink it, and then go to bed. I don't know what tomorrow will bring."

She wasn't listening. "Are you okay? You're shaking."

"I'm fine."

"You're cold. You need to change out of those clothes, get into something warm and get some rest." She opened yet another sugar bowl on the table and picked out a set of keys. "Help yourself to a room at the clinic. I'll bring you in some breakfast."

He held out his hand for the keys, noticed that his hand slightly trembled, and quickly closed his fist when she dropped the keys in.

She cupped both hands around his grip. "Roman, I have to tell you something." She looked up, her beautiful eyes glistening, and it tugged further at the knot of resolve in his chest. With everything in him, he wanted to wrap his arms around her, kiss her until they forgot Bednov and his thugs, children dying from nuclear waste and an icy three-hour ride through Siberia. He wanted to run his hands through her hair and pull her into the dreams he'd nurtured for the past decade.

No, more than that, he wanted to pick her up and disappear into the horizon with the woman he couldn't seem to forget. Who, even when he had risked her life, still poured all her energy into caring about him, tending his wounds and crystallizing all the whirring energy around him into calm. She alone was the one good reason he had for doing what he did. How he wanted to come home every day to her smile.

"Roman, I apologize to you for…blaming you for being who you are."

He frowned, trying to get a fix on her words.

She looked down and he resisted the urge to lift her face to his. "For years I said that you were only after glory. But after today, I know I was wrong. Yes, you risk your life, but I know it's because you're trying to be the man God wants you to be, and I can't stand in the way." She lifted her face, smiled at him.

He felt like crying. Finally, she got it. He cupped her cheek, ran his thumb along it. Opened his mouth, but nothing came out.

She put her hand over his. "I was wrong to walk away from you." Her eyes filled with emotion. "It wasn't your fault. I…was afraid I'd see you die in my arms, and I couldn't live with that."

He touched her forehead to his. "We're all going to die, Sarichka. God will determine the time and the place. The key is in living well, with purpose. That's all I'm trying to do, Sar. To follow God, and live each day 110 percent, doing what He wants me to do."

She ran her hand behind his neck, pushed to her tiptoes and kissed him.

He reacted on instinct, from the place of hopes and longings, putting his arms around her, pulling her tight and kissing her back.

Kissing her like a man who'd just remembered what it felt like to be young, and in love, with a hope and future before him. She melded her body to his, softening her mouth so he could kiss her deeper.

Danger, Roman. A voice inside him, the one he'd cultivated over the years of being a man of God began to speak. *Danger!* With everything he had in him, he pushed her away.

She slid slightly away from him, shock on her own pretty face. She closed her mouth, swallowed and turned the faintest shade of red. "I'm sorry. I guess I just… Probably I'm just emotional… It's been a long—"

He put his hand to her chin, angled her eyes to meet his and kissed her again, softly, just to stop her words.

"Sarai, I should leave."

"I'm worried about you. You could be hurt. I should probably go with you to the clinic, make sure you're okay." She reached for him, as if attempting to touch his ribs.

He caught her hands. "No." The light in her eyes dimmed slightly. "Sarai, I, ah, you're so beautiful. Even with David looking over my shoulder 24/7, I had a hard time keeping my wits about me whenever I was around you. I need to go. If I stay, or take you with me…well, although I'm a Christian, I'm still a man, and the Christian inside me is telling the man that I need to leave. Now. And as much as I'd like to stay, I want to do the right thing here."

He stared back into her beautiful eyes and summoned the courage to smile. "I'm going now. Be sure to lock the door behind me."

She nodded, and he let himself enjoy her slight smile, despite the guilt strumming at his heart.

Only, hadn't she just said she understood his calling, his career? Maybe she'd happily leave Irkutsk with Vicktor, and wait for him in Khabarovsk…

Yeah, and maybe he'd become the hero his father never was, and save the world from terrorists, and even establish world peace. He shook his head as he gave her a final look, then stepped out.

He was praying hard that Bednov's boys were still sleeping soundly at his dacha. Still, Roman mentally did the math. Probably he could expect them on Sarai's doorstep by morning.

There went his overactive FSB imagination.

Probably, after today they'd surmise she'd already fled the country.

Please, *please.*

Because, of course, she wouldn't be so stupid as to stay in Smolsk with the mafia on her tail? He wanted to head-slap himself. Where had his brain been an hour ago?

A smart FSB agent would bundle up the cute girl upstairs and secret her out of the country, double time.

Or, he could head to the clinic and see if Vicktor had arrived at the clinic yet, like Yanna had promised.

He mounted the snowmobile and braved the wind to The Savior's Hands Medical Clinic.

The building seemed cold and forlorn. Dark windows overlooked the yard as he pulled up. No movement. No reinforcements.

Which meant he was on his own. The cold found him—he'd been partially thawed after a few minutes in Sarai's flat—and he shivered. He needed some tea, maybe soup. And some shut-eye.

Most of all he needed a game plan, preferably one that included saving Sarai's backside and taking down Bednov.

He parked the snowmobile and found the key to the clinic.

It stuck only a moment in the lock, but long enough for him to catch the movement behind him.

Roman whirled and punched his attacker directly in the windpipe.

Roman Novik loved her. Sarai let that thought sizzle inside her as she downed the last of her tea. He still loved her. In fact, maybe he'd never stopped.

Well, neither had she.

Their love hadn't died, evident from the way he'd looked at her, kissed her when she'd practically launched herself into his arms. Their romance had just been banked for rekindling.

Sarai put her teacup in the sink, turned off the light and went to her bedroom. Tomorrow she'd pack her things and leave. Not forever. Just long enough for Roman to get her safely out of the province, and hopefully redeem himself with his boss. Then, she'd pull a few strings—or maybe ask him to—and then…

What?

She'd return, roll up her sleeves and start saving the world again? What about Roman?

She pulled up the covers to her neck and closed her eyes. They needed policemen in this town. After all, didn't they have their own mafia-gang problem?

She could live with Roman doing his police thing as long as she was around to stitch him up.

Mrs. Roman Novik.

Sarai Novik.

Maybe, little Sasha and Masha Novik.

Sarai smiled under the blanket, feeling tired, even giddy.

Maybe *she* needed a sedative….

"Thank you, Lord, for bringing us safely home." She said the words aloud, but quietly, suddenly aware of all she'd been through the past few days.

She felt alive and…not forgotten. God had sent her Roman to rescue her, even if she'd ended up rescuing him. For the first time in more than a decade, she didn't feel alone.

As if she might be able to take a full breath.

Unexpected tears filmed her eyes.

Roman did that to her. He made her feel safe, even though her world crumbled around her and she was captured by terrorists. Yes, he pushed her to her last nerve, but he also believed in her and respected her.

And protected her. Like earlier tonight, when he'd leaped to her rescue, putting his wounded body between her and her attacker. In fact, he'd put her safety before his own career—by going AWOL and following her to Khanda. Finally, he'd protected her with his honor.

Probably, it was time to trust him. He'd certainly earned it. Especially after she'd offered to hop a plane. She couldn't believe he'd actually turned her down, knowing how important it was to get her affairs in order. In fact, she had a sneaky feeling he wanted to stay.

She hoped it was because of her.

Why had she pushed him away for so many years?

Fear. And the fact that with him, she felt forced to trust in Someone bigger than herself.

Forced her to trust that God would be there when Roman wasn't. That, through everything, even the horrible moments, God still loved her.

He did, didn't He? Because, the Almighty had sent her Roman. The man who promised to always find her.

When he looked at her with his hazel eyes, she felt something inside her shiver with delight, and when he took her in his arms, she felt safe, right down to her cold toes. She let her imagination conjure up the expression he'd wear when she showed up tomorrow with a packed bag. The smile, the warmth in his eyes—it curled something hot and sweet in her stomach.

She'd just have to leave a list of explicit instructions for Anya and Genye. They could call her if they needed anything essential.

You don't trust God, Sarai.

Roman's accusation rung in her ears. Just because she wanted to make sure everything was done right didn't mean that she didn't let God be in charge. He'd given her this mission and it was her responsibility.

She could let go. She could.

Tomorrow she would. She'd start with telling Roman that she loved him. And then she'd leave town with him before Bednov's thugs could track them down.

Sarai woke early, despite a dreamless sleep that told her that she'd been exhausted through to her core. She hoped Roman had found a warm bed in the clinic and suffered the slightest twinge of guilt that she hadn't helped him.

Okay, he could take care of himself. That much she should believe.

He'd been right about her not following him to the clinic. She realized this when she couldn't wipe the schoolgirl smile off her face.

She showered, and triple layered in silk long johns, a turtleneck and a wool sweater. Just in case she found herself racing across the Siberian steppe.

She did a mental eye-roll. Three days with Roman and she'd turned into a pile of runny oatmeal. Evidently, nothing had changed in that department over the past thirteen years.

She gathered up her essentials—her Bible, visa, passport, a couple extra changes of clothing, toiletries and her picture of Roman. Then, shoving them into a carry-on, she hitched it over her shoulder and left for the clinic.

In the aftermath of the blizzard, the sun shone down and lit the snow-covered roads into a field of fiery diamonds. She drove slowly, praying for people she knew in town on the way to the clinic. *Please, Lord, don't let there be any disasters while I'm gone.*

She pulled into the clinic and noticed Roman's snowmobile, as well as the absence of Anya's and Genye's car. They were probably still snowed in at their dacha. And, worried sick. Hadn't they expected she and Roman back last night?

She'd leave them a note. And instructions. Maybe a few pages of instructions.

The clinic door was locked, and she said a silent thank you to Roman as she unlocked it and let herself inside.

The corridor felt gloomy and lifeless. She flicked on a light and went to her office. Probably, Roman still slept.

He deserved it, poor tired soldier.

She stopped to listen only a moment before she unlocked her office door. Her skin prickled in silent alarm and she attributed it to reflex, the residual jumpiness of being taken hostage.

She opened the door.

Screamed.

Whoever was hunched over in her office chair scrambled out of the blanket and to his feet.

Tall, with dark hair and even darker eyes, he had his gun leveled at her before she could blink.

Sarai screamed again, dropped her bag and reached for the ceiling.

Chapter Seventeen

Roman heard Sarai's scream and launched himself off the cot, toward Vicktor, whose eyes were probably still adjusting. Roman took down his friend with a grunt that had them both seeing stars. Vicktor kicked at him, scrambling out from underneath his grasp. "Roma, I wasn't going to shoot her."

He didn't answer, just found his feet, turned and pulled Sarai into his arms.

She shook and he buried his face in her hair. "Don't you think she's had enough scares for the week?" he snapped at Vicktor.

Roman felt Sarai's hands on his chest, but refused to give into her push to free herself. Behind him, he heard Vicktor sigh. "Sorry, Sarai. But after Roman's story, I didn't know who to expect."

"What, do you think I'm going to jump you? This is a medical clinic, for crying out loud!"

Probably, Roman had been right to hold on to her, because the anger in Sarai's voice—or maybe half fear, half indignation—told him she just might have taken a swing at Vicktor.

And Roman wanted Vicktor on *his* side when they sprung the news on Sarai that she'd be leaving with Vicktor today. *Only* Vicktor. Trouble was, after last night Vicktor still had trouble swallowing, due to Roman's line drive to his Adam's apple…something he hadn't forgiven Roman for. Yet.

Roman held Sarai away from him, but kept his grip on her arms. Her eyes were wide, tracking between Roman and Vicktor. She'd gone ominously silent.

Then, "What are you doing here?"

Roman swallowed, cut a glance at Vicktor. "He's going to take you out of here."

Sarai's eyes widened. "Wait a sec— You… I thought you were—"

Roman shook his head and stepped away from her, wondering if that swing now might be meant for him. "I must stay and investigate what we found yesterday. Bednov's connected to all this, and we need to find out how."

Sarai continued to stare at him, mouth half open.

"You need to leave, Sarai," Vicktor said quietly. But he used his firm, detective's voice. No pleading. No softness. Probably the tone Roman should have used with her from hour one.

She looked at him, then back at Roman. "You—no wonder you didn't want to fly me out last night. You *knew* he'd be here! You weren't worried about me, or my clinic. You were worried about getting the bad guy."

Roman's face twitched.

"I can't believe you." Sarai's eyes had filmed and she wiped them, apparently not giving quarter to her hurt feelings. "And here I thought you'd come to Irkutsk because you were worried for me."

"I am—"

"You make me sick. I knew you were only after making a name for yourself. I don't know why, but I have this nauseating feeling that you were just using me to further your career." She looked him in the eyes, and he saw the depths of her hurt a second before she blinked it away. Her voice turned cold, calm. "Shame on me for not figuring that out." She shook her head. "You wanted to know why I left, Roman. Well, here it is—because you only think of yourself. In the end, it's all about you." Her voice dropped. "I sure hope it was worth it." She stalked past them, to her desk. "Get out, both of you."

"Sar—" Vicktor started.

"Get out! I need to make some notes for Genye and Anya."

She braced her hands on her desk and Roman saw her tremble. He felt sick, and his stomach writhed. "C'mon, Vicktor."

Vicktor stood unmoving, a frown on his face as he watched Sarai. "Roman's on your side, Sarai," he said quietly. "You can trust him."

"Get out," she said, her tone softer. Roman barely overcame the urge to pull her back into his embrace.

"We'll be outside when you're ready to go," he said and motioned to Vicktor. His friend followed him out.

Roman heard the door lock behind them.

Vicktor leaned against the wall, his hands on his knees, and blew out a breath. "That didn't go well."

"She's mad, but she'll get over it."

Vicktor looked at Roman. Vicktor had hard, dark blue eyes, and an angular face that hid emotions well. Now, however, it showed a hint of sadness. "No, she won't. She might forgive me, but I read the look on her face, and well, I'm sorry, Roma. I know you well enough to guess you were hoping for more."

Roman said nothing, just slid down into a squat, his face in his hands. He hadn't expected more, but yes, after last night, he'd hoped.

Hoped that she would, indeed, trust him. Trust that he was trying to do things God's way, even if it didn't look like her way. Although, at the moment, even he wondered. *What, exactly, am I supposed to do here, Lord? Give me wisdom!*

He tried not to think of her in his arms, that fragile moment when she'd believed in him.

It didn't help his confusion that Vicktor hadn't completely bought into Roman's idea and harbored his own notions of how to take down Bednov. But Vicktor didn't know Bednov like Roman did.

He had a gut feeling the newly elected governor was about to abuse his power in new and lucrative ways.

You used me to further your career. The words stung, and he winced.

No.

I hope it was worth the cost.

Roman swallowed back the sick taste of failure in his throat. The cost. In this case, Sarai. No, in all cases, Sarai. When he'd lost her years ago, he'd never healed from the regret. It drove him, irked him.

Forced him to prove himself, over and over, that the job was worth it. That the sacrifices of home, and family—and her respect—were worth it.

Maybe this hadn't been about filling his father's shoes after all. In fact maybe it had more to do with Sarai. What if he flung himself head first into danger—with the hope that he went down in glory, instead of dying a cold, quiet death—so she'd see just how wrong she'd been about him? That her accusations were false and that he wanted to follow God's call, just as much as she did…only differently? That he'd die for what he believed in, just like she would?

But, whatever the case, it all boiled down to him following his own pride. And, especially of late, said pride had led him into humiliation.

Apparently Sarai wasn't the only one who wanted to be a martyr. At least she had her focus right. He thought of the verse he and Sarai had debated over, the one that seemed to define so much of his life. Matthew 16:24 "If any man will come after me, let him deny himself, and take up his cross, and follow me. For whosoever will save his life shall lose it: and whosoever will lose his life for my sake shall find it. For what is a man profited, if he shall gain the whole world, and lose his own soul? Or what shall a man give in exchange for his soul?"

Roman's father had given his soul to the Communists, and found it hollow. Roman glanced at Vicktor. Vicktor had given his to revenge and had only recently found salvation—after seeing the woman he loved nearly killed by a disillusioned KGB agent.

Roman had to wonder, perhaps, in this case, if he didn't fit the description of disillusioned agent.

No. He had gifts and talents, the ability to think on his feet that made him the top of his Cobra unit. God had given him those gifts, and until recently, favor with the powers that be. He hadn't given his soul away. It belonged to God. So then why did he always feel like he just couldn't quite get it right?

Maybe the verse about picking up his cross and following Christ wasn't so much about accepting the mission God called him to, that seemed suited to him…as it was…following Christ. Wherever he led. Regardless of the cost.

Costs, like…his pride.

Costs like not apprehending the man who'd destroyed his father's life. He had made a promise to David…and Sarai. To keep her safe.

What do I do here, Lord?

He heard sniffling in the room behind him. Roman looked at Vicktor, who gave him a sorry look.

So much for him being a hero. Sadly, a hero was all he'd ever wanted to be. A hero to the motherland, a hero to his father. A hero to Sarai.

I don't want a hero. I just want a man who loves God.

He loved God, didn't he? Not everyone was supposed to be a missionary.

But maybe you were.

Roman closed his eyes. Sighed. And for the first time, he let that thought settle into the crannies of his heart.

Sarai had been right about one thing—he'd never seriously considered being a missionary. Just gone with his gut. And God had blessed him anyway. But what would happen if he let God lead?

Pick up your cross and follow…

He did want to follow Christ. Because, unlike his father, he knew that the cause he believed in wouldn't crumble. On the contrary, it was the one sure thing in his life.

Roman smelled his own sweat as the truth sank deep. He hadn't been following Christ when he'd come after Sarai—he'd been following his heart.

He sunk his hands into his hair. *Lord, help me to follow you, whatever the cost. Because I do want to be the man you want me to be. Please, help me know what you want me to do here. I surrender my future into your hands.*

He sighed again, and in the wake of his thoughts, inside his knotted chest, he heard a familiar verse. *For I know the thoughts that I think toward you, saith the Lord, thoughts of peace, and not of evil, to give you an expected end. Then shall ye call upon me, and ye shall go and pray unto me, and I will hearken unto you. And ye shall seek me, and find me, when ye shall search for me with all your heart.*

He didn't know if it might be memory, or the breath of

the Holy Spirit weaving truth into his heart, but for the first time since hopping a plane for Irkutsk, he felt real peace take root.

Like the peace he'd felt with Sarai, as he'd held her in his arms, only warmer, more solid.

Peace that pierced the ever-increasing static around him.

Maybe if he'd stop hanging on so tightly to what he thought he wanted—being a hero—he might find God knew more about his deepest longings than he—

The wind banged the door in. Roman jumped to his feet, peeked around the corner, feeling Vicktor's breath on his neck.

Nope, not the wind.

"Oy." Roman pushed Vicktor back, against the wall. "We're in trouble."

Vicktor arched one brow, drew back and palmed his pistol. "You know these guys?"

Roman braced himself to spring.

Why had she trusted him? Or believed that he'd changed? Sarai felt sick as she thrust the last of her open case files into an accordion folder. Angrily, she wiped the tears from her eyes, furious that she'd let Roman inside her heart, again.

What did she expect from a full-time, sold-out FSB agent? He probably had his heart surgically removed years ago.

Why had she kissed him? Three times, if her memory served her correctly.

She shouldn't read honor into his holy "Man of God" act last night. That had been part of his game.

He probably had plenty of ladies back home to take his mind off the frontier doctor with too many freckles.

She felt a tinge of guilt over that last thought. David kept her abreast of Roman's love life—nil—but then again, Roman might only be feeding David a line.

He seemed to be especially good at that.

Sarah scribbled out a note to Anya and Genye, not quite sure if she'd made up her mind to leave, after all. Vicktor wasn't as easily swayed as Roman. Although Roman willingly made personal sacrifices to get the job done, Vicktor had a quiet resolve to him that made him dangerous. Frankly, she was slightly afraid of him.

Roman knew that. Yet, he wanted to dump her off into Vicktor's arms. While he stayed behind and took on the bad guys like some kind of Clint Eastwood.

She clenched her jaw against fresh tears. Jerk.

And who knew when she'd be back again? Just like that, he would uproot two years of her life. Couldn't Roman just leave her alone to fight her own battles?

A crack sounded, sharp and parting. Sarai jumped, heart in her throat.

A gunshot?

She held her breath and listened. More shots, and crashing. Cursing, in Russian, and a shout.

She ran to her door, opened it.

Her blood turned cold in her veins. Roman and Vicktor. Rolling around on the floor with the men who looked painfully like the thugs they'd left behind at Bednov's place. How had they found her?

Or, were they after Roman? Of *course.* His crimes were finally going to destroy her dreams. Once the authorities linked her with the break-in, they'd revoke her visa in a New York minute.

So much for coming back to Irkutsk to finish her work. Putin would have her name on an embassy automatic denial list before lunch. She'd never set foot in Russia again.

She slammed the door and locked it, leaning against it and breathing hard. Okay, think. This couldn't be that hard. She hadn't lived and moved and finagled supplies into Russia to surrender at the first sign of trouble.

First sign? No, that had been when Roman showed up on her doorstep. Sarai rubbed her temples. *Think!*

Governor Bednov. He knew her. Owed her. No, she hadn't saved his son, but she'd come to their aid. Helped his wife through her grief.

He'd at least listen to her. She'd explain that she'd had nothing to do with Roman's illegal activities, remind him of the good she was doing. He'd sway to her thinking… Especially if she—she grimaced at the thought—offered him a piece of her organization. Medical supplies siphoned off, sold…

But, for the good of the ministry, of spreading the gospel, surely…?

Sarai closed her eyes, shutting out indictments. Tracking across the room, she picked up the telephone and dialed Irkutsk.

Julia Bednov answered the telephone. And, by the sound of her slurred voice, she'd drunken a vodka breakfast. Sarai imagined her diet would change little in the near future.

"Julia? It's Sarai Curtiss, the American doctor."

Julia's tone improved, and Sarai heard interest. "Sarai. *Dobrayi Vecher.*"

Good evening? So maybe Julia hadn't stopped after dinner, kept right on until morning. Sarai wound the telephone cord around her finger, trying to shut out the sounds of scuffling in the hallway.

"Julia, I need to talk to your husband. I'm in trouble."

"Ah. *Da, da.* I know. No one is safe." Julia sighed. Long. Loud. Then giggled, in a strange voice.

No one is safe?

"They took him, you know. My Sasha. They took him away and buried him."

"Julia, I'm sorry about Sasha. I think I know what made him sick. I found another boy who was ill from a village near your dacha. Maxim, the son of your cook."

"Max?" Julia's voice dropped, slurred more. "I know him. Such a nice boy."

Sarai closed her eyes, willing Julia's attention. "Julia. I think there are more like them. Sick children. I need your husband's help to stay in Russia. Please. I need to talk to him."

"No," Julia's voice softened. "You must leave."

Sarai's stomach dropped. "What? Why? Julia, I can't leave, not—"

"Leave, Sarai. You're in danger." The line went dead.

Sarai stared at the telephone. Okay. So…

Pounding on her door made her jump. "Sarai! Let me in."

Sarai folded her arms across her chest. "Go away!"

A rumble outside made her freeze. She went to her window, pulled back the curtain and stared through the bars.

A tank.

In the courtyard of the clinic.

A tank?

"Sarai! Let me in! Bednov's found you."

Bednov? Wait…Sarai rubbed her temples, confused. She'd only just called Julia, how…? She sank into a chair. "What?" How could Bednov be after her? He had to be after Roman.

Horror felt icy cold in her veins. What had Roman done?

More importantly, what were those soldiers going to do to him?

Why had she let him back into her life? He was exactly the terrorist he claimed he was hunting.

A terrorist in her ravaged heart.

She should have locked the door three days ago and refused to come out. Well, she wasn't leaving now. They'd have to pry her out like an oyster.

On all fours, she crawled to her desk, climbed under it, and pulled the chair to cover her. She curled her arms around her up drawn knees. She was just a doctor. A simple frontier doctor.

Why was it she always managed to land in the middle of a war?

"Go away, Roman, go!"

And take your tanks with you.

Chapter Eighteen

"You gotta do something fast, Roma, or I will." Vicktor's knee crushed the spine of Mr. Fight Club—Roman tried not to find satisfaction in that—and held his hand back in a submission hold as they crouched behind the admissions counter.

How had a quiet morning with the sun just beginning to dent the morning gray pallor turn into heavy drama? Armed soldiers hunkered down outside the doors, and his old friend Mafia One lurked behind cover of a darkened exam room, having escaped Roman's clutches. Roman smelled diesel exhaust—evidence of military vehicles outside—and sweat slicked the back of his neck.

"Certainly this much manpower can't be to get one American out of Russia," Vicktor said.

"That's what I'm afraid of. Look at these guys. They're not military. They're too old, too experienced. Either Special

Forces or mercenaries. And, I'm betting the latter. I have a sick feeling they're after me. Especially after the break-in at Khandaski. They found me through Sarai."

"Or, they found her through you."

Roman clenched his jaw. "Thanks for pointing that out." He crouched beside her office door, gave it another pound. "Sarai!"

"Go away!"

Roman met Vicktor's gaze, tasting failure.

"Comrade Novik!" The voice boomed thought a megaphone into the building. "You and your hostage come out, and no one will get hurt."

His hostage? Vicktor made a face, mirroring Roman's dread.

"Am I the hostage? Or is she?" Vicktor nodded toward the closed door.

"I don't know. But Bednov—or someone—is serious about getting their hands on both of us. And that can't happen. We need to get Sarai out of here. I have a sick feeling, Vita, that if we surrender her to that rabble out there, she'll become a face on Amnesty International's Web site."

Vicktor glanced at his hostage, applied pressure and received a satisfactory grunt. "What do you want with the American?"

Fight Club gritted his teeth, refusing an answer.

Roman turned away while Vicktor encouraged his response.

"I don't know!" Fight Club ground out. "Governor Bednov asked us to find her. She's an enemy of the state."

"*You're* an enemy of the state," Vicktor retorted, but his face wore a pensive expression.

Roman checked the clip on Vicktor's service pistol. "We can't hold them off. They'll toss tear gas next, or worse, and none of us will walk out of here alive. You know that."

Roman saw Vicktor wrestle with the truth. They'd both witnessed Russia's version of hostage negotiations—or lack thereof, up close and deadly in Moscow. They'd sort out the bodies—emphasis on *bodies*—after they charged.

"I have an idea."

Vicktor said nothing, just met Roman's gaze.

"We're going to arrest her, and you're going to walk her out of here, under FSB protection," Roman said.

"Bednov's men will arrest me."

"No—you're here legally—with a legit paper trail. Killing you would only raise too much suspicion. They want me." Roman glanced at Fight Club. "You wait until she walks out of here, safely. Understood? She'll still be in FSB custody. Then, I'll surrender. Think of it as a trade off."

"Roma, you can't do this. You put yourself in their hands, and I don't know how long it'll take for us to free you." Roman read Vicktor's expression, and saw the lingering unspoken words: *if ever.*

"There's no other way. I should have done this three days ago, when I first got here. But I let my pride and my emotions get in the way. Now we're all in danger." He sighed. "Give me your handcuffs, Vicktor."

Vicktor wordlessly reached onto his belt and unsnapped his cuffs. "She'll never forgive you. Especially if Malenkov makes us put this on her permanent record. She'll have to leave Russia forever."

Roman stood, glanced again at Vicktor. "After the dust clears and you're safe in Khabarovsk, tell her that I really was on her side."

Vicktor nodded, his expression stony.

Roman kicked in Sarai's door.

He heard Sarai scream, but couldn't see her in the semi-darkened room. "Sarai?"

Muffled hiccups, coming from under the desk. He crouched. She had her chair pulled in against her and peeked out at him with wide, scared eyes.

Those eyes zeroed in on his heart and he felt nauseous. As if someone had sucker punched him. "Sar," he said softly. "You have to come with me. For your own good."

"Get away from me," she said, her tone sharp. No crying now.

He reached for the chair, hating himself. "No. Come out, or I'm coming in to get you."

She gripped the chair with whitened hands.

C'mon, Sarai.

He gritted his teeth against his own disgust and yanked out the chair. She cried out, and he didn't want to know if he'd hurt her. But she leaned back, kicking hard, aiming for his jaw.

"Sarai!" He grabbed her leg, dodged a kick, then another and pulled her toward him.

"No!" She swung at him, connected with his check and he shook away a flash of heat.

"Stop it!"

"Get away from me!"

"Don't do this. You're going to get hurt!"

She hit him again before he grabbed her hands and clamped them together. She was crying now, and he felt like it, too. Vise-gripping her wrists, he reached for the cuffs and snapped them on. When he let go, she made to hit him again. He dodged it, but wished he'd let her. It probably would have made them both feel better.

Or not. At this point, nothing would make him feel better. Ever.

She scooted back then, breathing heavily, staring at her cuffed hands. Silence pulsed between them, and he heard only their breathing, and his breaking heart.

"I hate you," she said softly. Then, she lifted her eyes and looked at him. Tears ran down her face, her hair askew from their struggle. "I really hate you."

He wondered if he could breathe, his chest felt so tight. But, he forced out words, and they sounded weak and ragged. "I know."

He hated himself, too.

Then he reached out, grabbed her by the arms and pulled her to her feet. She jerked away from him.

"Vicktor will take you out of here," he said.

She looked at him a long moment, frowning, silent. He couldn't read her expression. He pushed her gently out into the hallway. Vicktor stood up, a foot still on his captive's neck. Sarai had her head down, refusing to look at either of them.

Roman handed Vicktor the gun. "Take care of her."

Vicktor nodded, then touched her elbow. "*Poshli,* Sarai."

Roman traded places with Vicktor, subduing Fight Club. At least until they got outside. And then, well, hopefully the mercenaries would move in quickly, before Fight Club could revive their old relationship.

"I'm an FSB agent here on assignment and I'm coming out with the American!" Vicktor's voice sounded confident. Firm. He held Sarai like she might be a criminal, shot one last look at Roman and marched out the front door.

Roman tried to watch, but the ranks closed behind them. *Please, Lord, protect her, and Vicktor.*

And then the mafia boys rushed him.

"You let her go?" Bednov cursed into the cell phone as he stared at the television screen, watching the duo walking out of the building and climbing into an FSB vehicle. The dark-haired agent leading the girl held his badge high, evidence of official custody.

He had no doubt the renegade Captain Novik had cooked up this scenario with his FSB pal. Bednov's head spun and he sat, hard, on his sofa. With the American in FSB custody, he could hardly order his men to gun her down, at least with the world watching.

The camera panned back to the entrance, and he experienced slim satisfaction that the next shot betrayed a cuffed—and bleeding—Roman Novik.

Bednov rubbed his hand across his forehead, and it came back slick. Julia stumbled across the floor, on her way to the bathroom. She looked sickly in her pink satin bathrobe, her hair knotted, her mascara in trails down her once-pretty face. He barely recognized her.

Which would make it easier to dispose of her. Eventually. But soon enough so that she couldn't destroy his long-term plans. *I'll make sure you pay…*

She closed the door to the bathroom without looking at him.

"What do I do with him?" Fyodor's voice sounded drawn. "Take him back to Irkutsk?"

Bednov wrestled through the cotton of his brain for a game plan, something to discredit…no, make Novik suffer. It wasn't enough that he be killed. Novik needed to be an example for anyone who thought they might cross Bednov. Especially now. He stared again at the screen, at the rabble of men that he'd picked to protect him and his interests—Russia's interests—in the new era.

They had to take him seriously. Fear was power…Stalin had taught him that.

"Take him to Chuya," Bednov said.

Silence on the other end of the phone made him smile.

Sarai felt like a refugee. No, an international criminal. Or maybe both. She wrapped her arms around herself and shuddered, just like the AN-2 Russian air trap that flew her out of Irkutsk, into the sunrise. Across the aisle, Vicktor, her captor's accomplice, stared out the window.

She remembered the cold fear that had nearly crumpled her as she walked through an assembly of ragtag soldiers into the frigid air and blinding sunshine. Some wore uniforms, others simply submachine guns and etched war faces. They'd watched Vicktor pass holding his FSB badge, silent in their suspicion. She felt her skin prickle at the memory of the fear that one would jump out and yank her from Vicktor's grip.

At the time, she didn't know what she preferred.

Especially when she saw a television crew documenting her darkest moment. Just what she always wanted, her face on national television as a criminal. Maybe the international wires would pick it up and her parents could participate in her misery.

When they arrived at Vicktor's car, he'd opened the door and gestured her to climb in, saying nothing in the way of condolences or apology. He'd pulled away with a dark look on his face, and she'd glanced away from him to watch as the horde poured into the clinic.

Toward Roman.

For a second, something inside her felt weak, and floppy, and she thought she might faint. What had Roman done? And what was going to happen to him? The very fact that she let those thoughts slice through her anger told her what a fool she'd become to fall for him again.

They'd driven in silence to an airstrip outside Smolsk, where Vicktor removed the cuffs and escorted her onto a small airplane.

Silently. Pensively.

It made her very, very afraid. "What's going to happen to Roma?" she asked aloud, now, in the airplane, rubbing the places where the cuffs had chafed.

Vicktor seemed not to hear her.

Maybe she didn't want to know. Maybe Roman even deserved it, the way he'd wrestled her into handcuffs, yanked her out of her life without even a nod toward her feelings. She didn't even have her duffel bag, her passport, her Bible, her picture…

No, she certainly didn't need the picture.

Tears rimmed her eyes and she blinked them away. She was sick of crying.

"Where are we going?"

Vicktor glanced at her. "Khabarovsk. You'll be safe there. You can get a new passport and visa in Vladivostok."

"Then what?" She felt suddenly small, even naked.

Vicktor had incredibly dark scary eyes, yet when he smiled, she saw a hint of deep compassion. "Then, we'll see. I'm sure God has something for you to do there."

She frowned at him. Something for her to do? But her life, her mission was in Smolsk. She wouldn't be happy doing anything else.

She felt something heavy lay on her chest. Was she happy in Smolsk? Really happy?

Lonely. Afraid. Overwhelmed. Occupied. But happy?

Frankly, she hadn't been happy since she left Roman in Moscow. Yes, she'd always wanted to be a missionary. But more than that, she wanted to be used by God. For her life to matter.

None of that included happiness.

Like she told Roman, she didn't exactly understand what it meant to deny herself, pick up her cross and follow Christ, nor the part that said, *For whosoever will save his life shall lose it.*

She had denying down to a science, however. She'd followed Christ to the four corners of the earth for the sake of the gospel, and nearly lost her life on more occasions than she wanted to count.

Maybe losing her life wasn't about actually *losing* her life, but the things she thought she needed to make her life complete.

The clinic. Her legacy.

She'd prayed for God to use her to minister to the people of Smolsk. Roman's angry tones swept into her mind. "*Anya and Genye are more than capable of opening this clinic…*" Could it be that God had been at work this entire time to get her out of the way?

Regret filled her throat. How could she have been so arrogant?

Worse, how could she have not seen that God had not only been trying to get her surrender, but had given her the one thing for which surrender might have been sweet?

Roman.

Roman, silent as she accused him of selfishness, Roman holding her when she was cold, terrified and exhausted.

Roman, his eyes glistening as he looked in her eyes and snapped on handcuffs. To save her life.

What if, in losing her dreams, she found that God satisfied the needs inside her she didn't want to admit she had?

Needs like protection. Like safety. Like…being cherished.

Maybe Roman had been right. Picking up her cross meant not only sacrificing what she loved, but also following God…

Out of Smolsk.

Into the world, wherever He led even if He led her into Roman's dangerous, exhilarating, very scary life. Into new worlds, new opportunities to save lives.

Trust in the Lord with all your heart. The thought filled her mind, lifted her gaze out of the window, above the clouds, toward the heavens.

I want to, Lord. Help me to trust you. To follow you, whatever I have to surrender. She closed her eyes at the last and felt her chest tighten. "What are they going to do to him, Vicktor?" she asked again.

Vicktor said nothing, looked out the window.

Sarai unbuckled, got up and sat next to him. "Vicktor," she said softly, her voice tremulous. "What are they going to do to Roman?"

Vicktor sighed, closed his eyes. "I don't know."

Fear speared through Sarai, separating her feelings, crystallizing them into one clear truth. She loved Roman. Always had. Always would.

"Please, Vicktor, don't let them hurt him."

Vicktor opened his eyes, said nothing and stared out the window.

Chapter Nineteen

So much for staying out of the gulag.

Roman had been inside a few government correctional facilities over the years. He felt pretty sure this one was off the map. Way, way off the map, maybe even into Mongolia. Or it could be in northern Siberia for all he knew because he'd worn a blindfold since they'd tackled him—what, a day ago? Or two days?

Sensory deprivation had loosened his hold on time and space. When they untied the blindfold, he'd found himself standing in the middle of a concrete-block room, thin milky light shafting from a square window near the top of the wall. A forlorn chill emanated from the walls and found Roman's soul.

Two men faced him, and he didn't recognize either,

which was probably good, because hopefully they didn't have any ancient grievances against him.

One held a billy club. Roman tried not to focus on that as he stood and took a personal assessment, a sort of starting point. His eye still felt bloated, and his lip fat from Fight Club and his friends' less-than-compassionate take down. He'd surrendered easily, trying not to anger them, but Russian mafiosi weren't terror artists for their tendency toward mercy.

Probably, he had a cracked rib, too, because it hurt every time he breathed deeply.

Like, when he sighed over his nonexistent future.

Billy Club man stood silent as the other, a man the size and menace of a professional wrestler, took a step toward him. "Strip," he said. It sounded more like a grunt and had the same effect as a punch.

Roman swallowed. "Hard to do when I'm still cuffed."

From behind, he heard movement and in a moment, his hands came free. Oh, joy.

He could do this. Not think of the moment, or the shattered pieces of his life. He could go back to that place where he'd last felt peace, praying that God would use him, surrendering his future into God's hands.

He'd focus on God's voice, the one that reminded him that the Almighty had hope and a future for him.

Roman submitted silently to the customary search, gritting his teeth against humiliation, even as they marched him down the hall in his bare feet and scanty prison clothes. Somehow, he felt like they'd skipped something…like a trial?

However, he'd surrendered to Bednov's hands. And he, better than anyone, knew the legal loopholes in Russia.

It was quite possible that even Yanna, a genius hacker who knew how to find the blueprints of Putin's private bomb shelter, would never find *him.*

The prison reeked with the smell of urine and sweat. Fractured shadows from dingy bulbs lit the long concrete corridors. Solid black doors drilled into the walls evidenced habitation, but Roman didn't want to imagine who might be encased inside.

Billy Club walked him past the doors, and Roman felt slight relief in that. They stopped as the other guard unlocked a set of barred doors, and when they opened it, relief turned to a cold sweat.

General population. Inside the room, he saw row after row of thin mattresses, some with bedding, others bare. Sitting on them, in various degrees of repose, were prisoners.

Eyes riveted on him and he took a deep breath. Winced.

"Take good care of him, boys. He's FSB." Billy Club turned and winked.

Roman flashed him a smile. What would David call this? A witnessing opportunity? Roman walked into the room.

The lock turned behind him, and he steeled himself.

No wonder they hadn't bothered to torture him. A FSB agent in general population hadn't a prayer of survival. And, probably, that was Bednov's plan. By the time Vicktor got home and activated his release, or at least a transfer, Roman would be a bloody—and dead—pulp.

Roman didn't move, but did a quick and silent count.

Thirty men, at the least. And it looked like they didn't do a housecleaning very often, because he saw at least one man in the corner, unmoving. Hopefully he wasn't dead.

Roman backed up, eliminating a surprise attack from behind.

The men were bored. He was entertainment as well as fresh meat.

It happened fast. Two came at him in a tackle, and Roman kneed one, met the other with an uppercut. They grunted and went down, but another two jumped him.

He knew he'd go down, he just hadn't expected the ferocity of their attack. Nor the fact that he had it in him to fight back. He fought like he had as a kid, ferociously, with the edge of desperation. He swung, rarely missed and endured punishment as he struggled to stay alert.

I hate you, Roman.

Sarai's cold voice, zeroed in and centered him. He fought with the grief of knowing what he'd done to Sarai, to his future. He fought because he hadn't anything else left in him.

He fell to the floor, tasting his own tinny blood in his mouth. Faces blurred as he covered his head. Pain wrapped itself around his brain. Then sweet darkness closed in on him.

He awoke sprawled facedown on what he supposed might be a mattress. The redolence of unwashed bodies and sweat filled his nose and he coughed.

Everything hurt. He forced his eyes open and wasn't sure if they worked because he saw only darkness, as thick as pitch. He moved his hand, found his face, and it felt slick.

He groaned, then reached out and found a wall. Sitting up, he scooted back until his back hit the cool concrete. It went to the hot and painful places and balmed his aches.

"Who are you?"

The voice came out of the darkness, a gravelly voice, although strident, with the lacing of suspicion.

"Roman. Novik. I'm a…" Last time, his profession had gotten the tar beaten out of him. "Patriot."

The voice on the other side of the room harrumphed. "*Konyeshna.* Me, too."

A political prisoner? Roman touched his nose, winced. Could be broken. "Who are you?"

"Dmitri Vasilovyech Kazlov. Governor of Irkutia."

Roman blinked, scraping up an image from his memories. Gray hair, wide face, deep-set eyes. "Governor?"

"The rightful governor. And Alexander Bednov knows it."

Roman heard anger, despite the weariness in his tone. He searched it for deceit, aware that they could plant anyone here in the darkness. On the other hand, he could be alone, completely, for the rest of his days. Roman wasn't sure what emotion he should hang on to—suspicion or gratitude.

"I've been in here for nearly a week," Kazlov said. "Tell me, what's happening out there."

"We thought you were dead."

"I probably will be soon. Bednov needed me for strategic information." He sighed. "What's happened?"

Roman tested a rib and winced. "There was an 'attempted' coup—probably planned by Bednov to divert suspicion—but he stopped it and took control. He's ousted all foreigners and has declared martial law. He says you were kidnapped, presumed dead."

Kazlov turned quiet.

Roman debated his words, not sure if he might be digging his own grave. Especially if the man in the darkness was a plant, and not the former governor at all. Then again, he'd never see sunlight again. Maybe by handing out information, he'd shake Bednov's confidence, force him to make a mistake, even pack up shop. And, hopefully, Vicktor would be watching. "Did you know about his smuggling operation? The HEU, from the inactive nuclear plant in Khandaski near his Alexander Oil property? I have my suspicions he was smuggling it out."

Kazlov was silent. Then, "Yes. How did you know?"

"One of his couriers turned up dead in Khabarovsk with a container of HEU."

Kazlov said nothing for a long time. "We've been watching him for a while. But because of the campaign, we couldn't arrest him unless we had proof—"

"Otherwise it would look like you were setting him up to lose."

"Moscow, and the world, has us on a tight leash, watching. Too bad they were looking in the wrong direction."

Roman didn't comment.

"Bednov discovered that we knew and decided to take

us all out. From the enormity of his ploy, he must have had a small army working for him," Kazlov continued.

"Mercenaries, sir, for sure. He has the money to pay for help." Roman pressed the soft tissue under his swollen eye. "I met a couple of his men when I broke into Khandaski. Found the HEU that was supposedly shipped to a commissioned reactor."

"Which I'm sure is why you ended up here."

"Bednov knew I'd catch up to him. His son died of radiation poisoning, something he got from their dacha near the plant."

Roman heard Kazlov shift.

"How did you find that out?"

"A friend. A doctor who treated him."

"Where's your friend now?" Kazlov asked, his voice low.

Roman closed his eyes, seeing Sarai's tortured expression. *I really hate you.* "I arrested her, put her into FSB custody and sent her out of Irkutsk with a fellow agent. The FSB in Khabarovsk will protect her. And, I'm hoping they'll figure out Bednov's plan."

"You *arrested* her?" Kazlov's shock sounded authentic.

Roman winced, feeling freshly shamed. "She had the same reaction. Told me she hated me."

"Who are you?"

Oh, yeah. "I'm FSB."

"Oh. That explains the visit to general population. They worked you over pretty good. You were groaning."

Roman leaned his head back against the wall. "I'm surprised I'm still alive. And, I think I have all my teeth."

He heard a snort from out of the darkness. "Welcome to cell block 16."

"What do you mean you can't find him?" Sarai paced Vicktor's tiny apartment, amazed that a person could share such a tiny space with an animal the size of an Asian elephant, namely Alfred, Vicktor's Great Dane. She gave Alfred's rump a whack, hoping to rouse him from the sofa where he sprawled. He only opened an eye. She sat on the arm and refused to give into frustration. "Please, Yanna, keep looking."

Seven days she'd been in Khabarovsk while Yanna and Vicktor searched for Roman in the gulag archipelago. Seven days of hearing her voice echo, "I hate you." Seven days of waking sick to her stomach with worry, wishing she could rewind time, go back to that moment in her apartment and tell him she loved him.

He was the hero she didn't think she needed. But, oh, did she need him. She needed his smile, his friendship, even his irritating protection. Somehow, with him believing in her, she felt like the person she'd been trying to be for over a decade. Brave. Strong. Someone who saved lives.

Please, Lord, show us how to save his life.

"He's dropped off the grid, Sarai." Yanna stood at the window, her long brown hair silky in the evening glow. She wore workout clothes, but Sarai knew she hadn't been to volleyball practice other than to check in for nearly a week. The clothes were a decoy for anyone tailing her.

"Bednov has everyone under his thumb. No official contact to any of the agents working in the region until the government simmers down. And Moscow is backing him because he was 'legitimately' elected."

Vicktor came into the room, wiping his hands on a towel. He'd made them Plov for dinner, one of Sarai's favorite Russian rice dishes, but she couldn't eat it. Not when she thought of Roman cold, lonely…bleeding? Please, please not dead.

Sarai rubbed her hands on one of Vicktor's oversized sweatshirts. Thankfully, Yanna had turned out to be about her size, although the tight low-rise jeans definitely looked better on the exotic brunette with a taste for French fashions than a blond crunchy granola pioneer from Siberia. Sarai felt rough-edged and overwrought with each passing day.

Thankfully, her brother, David, would arrive tomorrow. He'd pulled in favors that rivaled a head of state to get an emergency visa to see Sarai. "Roman told me he thought Bednov had ulterior motives, that he was the head of some big smuggling ring—"

"He's probably right. But, without proof, it's only heresay. We can't nail him."

"What kind of proof do you need?" Sarai ran her hand absently along Alfred's nose. The dog belonged to Vicktor's father, but had taken a liking to Vicktor's sofa while his father was in long-term physical therapy. Sarai was thankful to see that the old cop, who'd been shot in the line of duty nearly two years ago, working his way back to the world.

"We need testimony. Documents proving Bednov's connection to the smuggling. A money trail." Vicktor leaned against the door frame. Out of his dark and cold cop uniform, and wearing a pair of faded jeans and a Seattle Seahawks sweatshirt, Vicktor looked less imposing, in fact, she'd even say handsome, in a steel-edged, danger-lurking kind of way. No, he wasn't Roman, with tousled brown hair, and hazel eyes that could find all her vulnerable places. He didn't have Roman's ruddy five-o'clock shadow, or his charming catch-a-girl's breath kind of smile. But the two cops had a similar build, one that made a girl feel safe. And one, she hoped, that would help Roman stay alive.

Wherever he was. *Please, please, Lord, look after him.*

Sarai stood up, paced in a small circle. Darkness pressed against the windows, and outside she heard the wind blow. Thanksgiving was two days away. Sarai knew she should be feeling grateful, thankful for so much. But she hadn't been able to contact Genye and Anya, hadn't the faintest idea if there were more children suffering from renal failure…

"Testimony?" Sarai stopped, stared at Vicktor. "I have an idea." She gave him a wry smile. "But you have to get me back into Irkutsk."

Vicktor narrowed his eyes and even Yanna laughed. "You're kidding, right?"

Sarai's enthusiasm felt hot and sweet in her veins. "No. I'm not. I know how to find Roman. You'll just have to trust me."

Vicktor quirked one eyebrow, his smile vanished. "Like you trusted Roman?"

Ouch. "Okay, I deserved that. But, give me the credit for wanting to save his life. I love him. I don't want anything to happen to him."

Yanna turned from the window, stared at her. "What did you say?"

Sarai met her dark eyes. "I love Roman. I should have seen that years ago. But I know it now and I'll do anything to make sure he's okay. Please, just listen to me."

Yanna crossed her arms over her chest. "I'm listening."

Chapter Twenty

Bednov opened the door and unbuttoned his coat. "Julia?" The flat sounded quiet, but then again, maybe she was passed out. Again.

Although, the past three nights she'd sat in sullen, or furious, grief, watching reruns while he tried to straighten out the mess Captain Novik had concocted. Thankfully, the Khabarovsk FSB hadn't believed a word the American doctor had told them or they'd be on his doorstep.

He'd talked personally to the head of the FSB in Irkutsk, who'd confirmed it with a call to the head of the Cobra division in Khabarovsk. Captain Novik had become an enemy of the state. And, they'd surrendered him to Irkutia custody.

They'd never see him again.

Bednov yanked off his suit coat and opened his bedroom

door. Froze. Julia's *schaff* was opened, her clothes—or some of them at least—missing.

He stalked to her bedside stand. Her passport was gone. He slammed the drawer closed and dug his cell phone out of his coat pocket as he stalked through the flat. "Julia!"

The kitchen, the beautiful kitchen he'd made for her, echoed his voice. A bouquet of fresh flowers sat on the middle of the kitchen table, a weekly delivery he thought he'd canceled the previous week.

He stared at it. And went weak. Bracing his hand on the table, he dialed the cell phone. But in his gut, he knew it was too late for security to track her down.

Someone had lied to him. Maybe it was Malenkov, maybe even his own FSB head in Irkutsk.

Probably, however, he'd lied most of all to himself when he thought that Captain Novik wouldn't cause him more trouble.

Fyodor answered.

"I want him dead," he said quietly. "Tonight."

Sarai put down her popcorn, clapping as the dogs ran out of the center ring. The room darkened and Roman put his arm around her. She settled perfectly into his embrace. Sweetly, sighing softly.

"What are they saying?" she asked as the announcer came on.

"They're introducing the high-wire walker." Roman saw himself point to a spotlighted man on a wire high above their heads. The man climbed on the wire, held out his hands

for balance. Even from here, Roman could see him fight for control.

Sarai sucked in her breath. "You'd never get me up there. My hands are slick just thinking about it."

Roman took her hand and she giggled.

"What if I was up there, carrying you across?" The words seemed not to come from him, but behind him, or through him. But Sarai stared at him, her eyes wide. He swallowed.

She leaned back, pushing away from him. Then, suddenly, she slapped him. "I would never trust you!" Turning, she fled.

Roman stood, "Sarai!"

Laughter around him, at him felt shrill and sharp. He winced.

Suddenly the spotlight turned on him, illumining her escape, his breaking heart—

The door to his cell opened. Light shafted into the room. Roman put up an arm to deflect the light and blinked out of the nightmare, clawing for comprehension.

Not again. *Please, Lord.* He ached to his toes, and yesterday, he'd seen a new guard eyeing him. It made his skin crawl to know he'd become a target of their warped humor.

"Get up."

Roman started to move, but the guard—the new one, tall, lanky but with determination written in his stride—strode toward Kazlov. "Get up." He nudged him with the tip of his AK-47. The elderly man grunted, then glared at the guard as he got to his feet.

"Where are you taking him?" Roman pounced to his own feet, hiding a grimace of pain.

"Wanna join him?" The guard's voice held challenge—and something else. Roman couldn't decipher it.

Kazlov met Roman's gaze, and he felt the truth broadside him. His mouth dried. *Is this it, Lord? Is this what you want?*

Roman put himself between the guard and the governor. "Enough. This man is a political prisoner. You're not going to do this."

Billy Club stood at the door, filling the frame and blocking the light. "Step back, FSB. This isn't your fight."

"It is. He's innocent, and you know it."

Billy Club shrugged. Roman lowered his voice, speaking to the lanky guard. "You know this is wrong. This is murder. If you truly want Russia to be free, you need to respect life, not take it."

Something—hesitation?—flickered in the younger guard's eyes. Roman met his gaze, held it.

And ye shall seek me, and find me, when ye shall search for me with all your heart. Roman heard the words reverberate deep inside. *I'm trying, Lord.* He didn't blink but felt his resolve weaken as his choices found his heart. *I'm sorry, Sarai.*

The lanky guard turned suddenly. "Take him, too. He's only going to cause us trouble."

Billy Club's gaze fixed on Roman. *"Ladna."*

Roman put his hand under Kazlov's shoulder, helped him limp out of the cell. Even the dingy hall seemed bright to Roman's eyes and he blinked, trying to get his bearings. Kazlov stumbled as they walked down the hall, and Roman heard nothing but their shuffled steps and breathing. So this was the end. He'd spent two weeks, at *least* two, maybe more, breathing in and out, counting his mistakes, recounting stories of FSB exploits to his companion in the dark. Without mentioning her name, he'd told Kazlov about Sarai, about her beautiful eyes, the way she could calm him, save his world with her smile. He'd even confessed his betrayal, and eventually, his faith. After all, he was already in the gulag. And Kazlov had listened. Mostly without comment.

Kazlov had been a Party man. Most politicians were, even in the new regime. But he believed in capitalism, and democracy. He believed in a future for Russia.

And, as the darkness pressed against them, the hours cold and piercing, Kazlov had voiced his own questions of faith for Roman.

Questions that drilled into Roman's brain as he walked through the prison and out into the snow.

"You say your God loves you. Then why are you here?" Kazlov's voice had sounded strained in the darkness.

Choices? Crimes? Man's sinful nature?

"Because God wants me here," Roman finally answered.

"But why? I don't understand why you'd follow a God who does bad things."

Roman saw his own wry smile in the darkness. "God doesn't do bad things. That's the paradox. We filter what God does through our understanding of the world, not His. There's a story of a man in the Bible named Joseph. He was sold into slavery, then spent seven years in prison. In the end he became head of Egypt, a hero to his people and saved them from destruction. He knew that what Satan meant for evil, God meant for good. He just had to trust God enough to follow him each step of the way. God has a bigger plan than all of this."

Kazlov fell silent, but Roman's own words had resonated with him. "I don't know, Governor, but what if God sent me here just to sit here in the dark with you? Maybe it's not about me, but about you."

Roman had leaned his head against the concrete. His wounds were healing. It no longer felt like liquid fire to breathe, which told him that maybe his ribs had only been bruised. And his face—well, the swelling had gone down around his eye and his mouth felt healed, if not still slightly sore. Most of all, the searing pain at his betrayal of Sarai had lessened to one long ache. He prayed every day that God would make something good out of the pieces of his life.

"I'm not a worthy man, Novik," Kazlov finally said. "Why would your God look in my direction, let alone send you to suffer with me?"

Roman saw himself fifteen years ago, young, baffled at the friendship of an American who might someday be his enemy. "Funny, I asked the same thing about Jesus. Why would he die in my place? I didn't deserve it. And the answer—because God loved me. A famous martyr—Jim Elliot—once said, 'He is no fool who gives us what he cannot keep to gain what he cannot lose.' That's why I can sit here in the dark with you and know with certainty that if I die tomorrow, I'll have no…or few—regrets. I can't lose what matters most—eternity.

"And maybe God wants you to know that."

Kazlov said nothing. But later, as Roman lay in the darkness, he heard something that sounded like sobs.

Roman had prayed for him, feeling something heavy unlock from his soul. He had the strangest feeling that perhaps he was cut out to be a missionary, just as Sarai claimed. Except in ways neither had imagined.

Now, he hoped those questions were haunting Kazlov, driving him to consider every step as they stumbled down the corridor. Roman steadied the governor as the guard opened the door to the outside yard. A layer of fresh snowfall licked into the hallway, across the top of his feet. Outside, the sun shone down, but the wind found his bare chest and the line of sweat between his shoulder blades, and froze it to a fine film.

"Outside," said the skinny guard.

Roman saw more guards. Two of them, standing with their backs to them. His throat dried and he forced his feet forward. "This is illegal," he said. "Even in Russia. You can't just shoot us without a trial."

"Tiha!"

Roman clenched his jaw, tightened his grip on Kazlov. The governor's face had turned white, his expression stony.

"Go back, son," the man said. "I'll not have your blood on my hands."

Roman glanced at Billy Club. Probably any announcements toward turning back would fall on mute ears. Besides, he'd sworn to protect and serve the government of Russia. The people of Russia. He wouldn't die like his father, a coward, alone in his disgrace. He'd stay the course.

Not only that, but deep in his soul, he knew God wanted him to stand up for righteousness beside Governor Kazlov. He just wished his last moments with Sarai hadn't been filled with his betrayal. He tried not to let her voice weaken his steps.

Glancing at the guards, he gauged the distance between them and the walls. "You could run for the gate," he whispered to Kazlov. "I could try and deflect them—"

"No. This is a crime against the freedom of Russia. I'll not run like a criminal."

The wind buzzed in Roman's ears, turning them to ice. He should have guessed they'd send them north, to the gulags of Siberia.

"Stop here," Billy Club said.

The younger guard stepped away, leaving Roman to stand in the middle of the yard. Roman moved in front of Kazlov, between him and the soldiers with the semiautomatic weapons. The sun shone down on them, and he heard the wind hum as it skimmed the trees beyond the prison walls. He could barely wrap his mind around the truth. He was about to die in the middle of Siberia, barefoot, a prisoner in the gulag. He felt like gagging.

And ye shall seek me, and find me, when ye shall search for me with all your heart.

Lord, how can I seek you in this? The thought seem ludicrous. *Still. I trust you, even in this death.*

Whomever loses his life for my sake will find it…

The executioners turned toward him, heads down, checking their weapons.

Roman's heart stopped.

They aimed.

Roman lifted his chin. "Be strong," he said to Kazlov and closed his eyes.

They fired.

Billy Club went down, screaming, a bullet through his leg. The other guard dropped to the snow, hands over his head. "Don't shoot!"

Kazlov's knees gave out and Roman fell into the snow beside him. He stared speechless as Genye ran toward him, an ill-fitting *shapka* crammed on his head. He scooped up Kazlov by the armpits. "Run, Roman!"

What—?

Roman glanced back at the guards. Billy Club still squirmed on the ground. The other guard, however, looked up at him, and nodded.

What—?

"Did you hear him, Russki?"

Roman looked up, and words left him as David Curtiss pulled him up. *"Begee!"*

How did— Only, he didn't ask because he was running, and fast toward the end of the yard. And then the humming made sense. A helicopter? A Russian Mi-24 Krokodil. Where had they pulled that out of the ancient arsenal?

It hovered just inches above ground, and Roman shoved

Kazlov into the bed. A hand reached out and Roman grabbed it. Vicktor pulled him aboard.

"Go, go!" David yelled as he followed Genye into the chopper.

Roman sat on the deck, shivering, as the ground dropped out. They soared over the prison gates just as guards streamed out of the building.

Across from him, David, dressed in the getup of a Russian prison guard, including a green woolen *shapka* and matching green uniform, grinned. "Found you."

Roman shook his head, trying to keep up. Beside him, Genye pulled off his jacket and tucked it over Kazlov. Vicktor, in the front, did the same with his and handed it to Roman.

Roman huddled under it, letting the whir of the blades fill his disbelief, his lack of words.

David, Vicktor and Genye had rescued him?

"How's our hero doing back there?" He heard a voice yelling over the din. An English-speaking voice. Mae? His pilot friend from Alaska? Oh, the National Guard would be happy with her.

He cut his gaze to David. "I don't get it!"

David smiled, and Roman recognized mischief in his eyes. "Ask Sarai. She's waiting for you."

Sarai? Waiting for him?

He hoped it wasn't with a right hook.

Sarai paced the military compound, her stomach roiling. Anya sat on the vinyl chair, wringing her hands, shaking her head.

The only one not stressed seemed to be Yanna, who had her ear pressed to a two-way radio. "They're out!" She ran over to the duo, her dark eyes shining. "They made it!"

"Not yet they haven't," said Major Malenkov.

Sarai gave him a dark look. He hadn't been thrilled with her plan, in fact she had a gut feeling that if he had his way, he'd ship Roman back to Khabarovsk territory and slap him in another gulag.

Only, that would be minus her testimony. And, Julia Bednov's, now in a safehouse in Khabarovsk. She could hardly believe she'd talked the woman into testifying against her husband.

Of course, she'd had to sober her up first. And when she did, just like she suspected, Sarai discovered a woman broken by loss, without hope. Yet Julia possessed enough anger and inside information to put Bednov away in his own gulag.

It helped that Moscow had squeezed the truth out of Bednov's accomplice and tax-evading partner, Gregori Khetrov, still sitting in Lubyanka.

Hopefully, Bednov was in custody by now. Julia had been right about Roman's life being in danger. She even knew the name of the gulag where he'd been taken—a private gulag near the Yakutia border they'd tracked down through Genye's ex-military connections.

Sarai had never been so thankful for her brother's Special Forces background. He flew into town and mustered forces like General Schwarzkopf. Even got his old friend, army pilot Mae Lund, to do some clandestine flying.

Thankfully, Roman's boss had been willing to break a few rules if it meant restoring glory to his department.

Roman still might do time, but hopefully it would be behind a desk. *Safely* behind a desk.

"ETA, twenty minutes," Yanna said. Sarai stared out the windows. Snow crusted the edges of the helicopter pad. Beyond that, old AN-2s and military vehicles rimmed the tarmac. The base, just inside Yakutia, was run by one of Genye's friends.

Obviously, she had a lot to learn about Anya and Genye.

In fact, they'd opened the clinic without her, and Anya had found two more cases of radiation poisoning—cases she'd sent on to Moscow for advanced care.

And, with the patients they had in-house, Genye started a Bible study.

Sarai's throat felt raw and thick. She'd been holding on so tightly, she hadn't seen God raising up her replacements.

She stuck her hands in the pockets of her parka, then took them out and clasped them in front.

Paced.

Breathed.

Wiped tears.

Stared out the window.

C'mon!

She sighed heavily as Anya came up to stand beside her. "He'll be okay, you know."

Yeah. Maybe physically, but she'd seen the look on Roman's face when she said she hated him, and well, he might walk right past her with a cold nod.

She deserved that. Because, frankly, that's what she'd done to him all those years ago.

I was shattered when you left.

Now she knew how that felt.

I'm sorry, Roman. So, so sorry.

Her eyes burned and she fought the tears. She didn't want to be crying when she saw him. Or at least, not right away.

She heard the hum of the chopper the same time as Anya. Anya beelined to the door. Sarai followed and they stood out on the tarmac, hands in their jackets as the wind tangled their hair and the roar of the engine buzzed their ears.

She saw Roman sitting in the back next to an elderly man. The chopper landed, and David climbed out first, helping the man out. Roman followed.

Sarai braced herself. Roman had his head down, his hair blowing in the stiff wind. He hunched over until he was clear of the whirring blades. She stayed still, watching.

Then, he looked up.

She wasn't prepared. Not for the bruises, the opened stitches over his eye, or the blood across his nose. Nor for the look in his eyes.

Longing. Sorrow.

Love.

"Sarai," he said, and his voice sounded wrecked.

She launched herself toward him, wrapped her arms around his neck, holding tight. She felt his arms embrace her, but she didn't let go, just buried her face in his neck and sobbed. "Roman, I'm so, so sorry. I didn't mean what I said. Not at all. I love you. I love you so much that all I do is hurt when you're not with me. I don't care that you're a cop. Just please, please forgive me. Please—"

"Sarai."

He pulled her arms from around his neck and her heart stopped cold. Her mouth felt tinny as dread pooled in the back. She let go and slid down to the ground, unable to look at him.

He couldn't forgive her.

She didn't blame him.

"Sarai." He tucked his hand under her chin. She refused to look at him.

So, he bent down, looking at her sideways. His eyes glistened. With tears? "I love you, too."

Her mouth opened. Nothing came. She just stared at him. Watched his beautiful smile, saw the truth in his incredible eyes.

"I love you, Sar. I always have. All I wanted was to be enough for you and for you to trust me—the real me. The guy who sometimes gets in trouble." His smile dimmed. "I'm sorry I failed you."

What? "Roman, you didn't fail me. You saved me from who knows what? And as for being enough…don't you know that you overwhelm me? You take my breath away every second I'm with you. That's why I ran. Because I couldn't control you and my love for you scared me." She swallowed, seeing suddenly the truth. "But I can't live in fear anymore. I trust God enough to let you be who He wants you to be. Who He wants us to be. I'm sick of trying to keep you—and me—out of trouble. I give up." She smiled and touched his face. "I just want to be with you."

She saw when her words settled into his heart. He smiled, and it was the most delicious smile she'd ever seen. One that had her stomach curling with delight. He cupped his hands around her face. "Be with me? Does that mean you trust me?" He raised one eyebrow.

She felt a blush heat her face. Swallowed. "Yeah. I trust you, Roman."

He kissed her. Sweetly. Gently. She felt him tremble and knew that there was passion behind his touch. She even saw it in his eyes as he pulled away and touched her forehead to his.

"This won't be easy," he said softly. "But I think we can trust God to work it out, right?"

She nodded, feeling her throat thicken, and looked down. And saw him standing in the snow in his…bare feet?

"Roman, get inside, right now!"

He grinned, tucked his arm around her and pulled her tight against him. "Anything you say, Doc."

They walked inside, where Vicktor and Genye were briefing Malenkov. Sarai sat Roman in a chair, opened his jacket. She tried not to wince, but he was covered in bruises. Foot-shaped bruises.

Why did she always break out in tears around him? She'd

probably have to get used to seeing bruises on him. She swallowed hard and began feeling for broken ribs.

Roman closed one eye now and again as she probed. "Who did you bring with you?" she asked. She pulled off his jacket, saw similar bruises on his back. He'd been beaten but good.

"Governor Kazlov."

Sarai stopped. Looked at Roman. "You're kidding. I thought he was dead."

"He nearly was. They were going to execute him."

"You *thought* they were going to execute him." Vicktor sat next to Roman. "You didn't recognize Artyom, Yanna's computer tech? He wanted some fieldwork, so we sent him in." He surveyed Roman's face. "You're looking sweet. Please tell me the other guy looks worse."

Roman grimaced. "There were a lot of them. But I got a few licks in."

He glanced at Yanna. "Is Artyom okay?"

Yanna smiled. "He called right after you took off. He's on his way." She glanced at Kazlov, now using Malenkov's cell phone. "We didn't expect the grand prize. Artyom was supposed to find your cell, and we were going to stage a breakout. He called us early this morning, when he heard about the execution orders for Kazlov. We were all counting on your hero tendencies to jump in and try and save Kazlov's skin. And, if you didn't, Artyom was going to make sure you did. Good thing you always have to be a hero."

"I think God is the hero here," Roman said.

David joined them, crouched beside Sarai and put his arm around her. "Anyone ready to go home?"

Their getaway pilot, Mae Lund, strutted into the building. Although still wearing her flight suit, she held her helmet under her arm. Her red hair had grown since Sarai had seen her last. Normally pinned up, it spilled out of the bun at the base of her neck.

"Mae!" Roman shook his head as if in disbelief as Sarai sprang to her feet and clenched her old friend in a grateful hug.

Mae glanced at Roman. "Are you ready to go home?"

David held out his hand to Roman, helping him up. "I can't tell you how grateful for what you did for Sarai."

Sarai thought she saw her brother's eyes glisten.

"Thanks. It was worth it." Roman's gaze met Sarai's.

Everyone went quiet and Sarai searched Roman's handsome, bruised face. She was worth it?

Roman had to have seen the question on her face, because he leaned close. "Yeah, Sarai, you're worth it." His voice turned rough-edged, full of emotion. "Don't you know I'd die for you?"

Sarai closed her eyes and pulled him into her arms, not caring that David and Vicktor and even Mae watched them. She laid her head on his chest, hearing his heart beat, so very thankful for his heartbeat, his arms around her solid, and protective. Reaching past her facade to the truth.

She'd been so painfully stubborn that God had to yank

her into her darkest fears, and shake her free of her hold on her dreams to get her to realize she *did* need a hero.

God. Who loved her enough to send his agent Roman Novik into her life to prove that when she surrendered one life…she found another.

Right here, in Roman's embrace.

"I love you, Roman Novik," she said softly. "You're my hero."

QUESTIONS FOR DISCUSSION

1. Sarai believes that she's been called to be a doctor, and because of that, she sacrificed her relationship with Roman, who she believed didn't share that goal. What sacrifices have you made for something you've felt "called" to do?

2. Roman is asked to put his career on the line when David Curtiss, his best friend, calls him. Why does he make the decision he does? How do you feel about that decision? What choices have you made that could have compromised or did compromise your future for the sake of friendship?

3. Roman and Sarai had a summer romance, and while they haven't seen each other for ten years, they still hold on to that romance. Have you ever had a summer romance and how did it affect your life? How does that affect you today?

4. Roman and Sarai both notice that the other has changed. Still, the old flame quickly reignites. Why? Why is the timing better or worse now than years earlier, when they were both building their careers?

5. At the beginning of the book, Sarai is trapped due to world events. How have world events shaped your life?

6. Roman, after chasing Sarai to dacha, confronts her with a question about trust. What is it? How does Sarai see herself in relationship to her work? How does Sarai show that she does or does not trust God?

7. Roman's father died an alcoholic, similar to many Party men after the fall of Communism in Russia. Why do you think he felt so disillusioned?

8. When Roman breaks into the nuclear plant and then falls through the ice, Sarai makes a decision in order to save his skin. What is it? How does this event confirm in her heart everything she believes about Roman? How does it change her feelings toward him and their future?

9. Roman struggles with two goals: saving Sarai and arresting Governor Bednov. Why does this struggle lead to his arrest later? Why, when Vicktor shows up at the medical clinic, does Sarai feel deceived by Roman?

10. How do Roman's worst fears come true? What regrets does he have? How does he, while sitting in his prison cell, see God at work in his life? How have you hung on in your own dark times in life?

11. Sarai is able to save Roman, and in a way help Julia Bednov heal. How? What decisions has she made about her life and her relationship with Roman? What has happened to the Savior's Hands Medical Clinic?

12. Sarai and Roman both take a look at what it means to give up their lives for Christ. What definitions of *life* did they have, and how did those change? How did Sarai and Roman both find "life" in the end? What do you think Christ means when He says, "Whoever loses his life for me will find it?"

It's beginning to look a lot like chaos...

Baking cookies, sitting by the fire, caroling...not! For these stay-at-home moms, the weeks before Christmas are anything but quiet. With a little help from each other, though, the SAHMs just might be able to keep the season jolly!

On sale November 2006.
Visit your local bookseller.

Steeple Hill®
www.SteepleHill.com

SHME570TR

Two inspirational holiday novellas from bestselling authors

CATHERINE PALMER

and

JILLIAN HART

On sale November 2006.

www.SteepleHill.com

SHCP571TR

On sale now.

Gracie Benson is running for her life—and maybe for the lives of millions of others. With the help of FSB agent Vicktor Shubnikov, Gracie must escape Russia and the culprits who are after her, for the top secret that she unknowingly has in her possession. Can Gracie outwit her enemies before they outwit her?

Visit your local bookseller..

www.SteepleHill.com

SHSMW544TRR

Look Out, World...

Everything's Coming Up Josey

On sale now

When things weren't going Josey's way, she decided to skip town—to Russia! True, life as a missionary in Russia has taken some getting used to, but it's getting her life to thaw that's the real challenge!

Visit your local bookseller.

www.SteepleHill.com

SHSMW561TRR